Far From the Trees

The Troubled Sons of an American Neighborhood

Far From the Trees
The Troubled Sons of an American Neighborhood

Outskirts Press, Inc.
http://www.outskirtspress.com

ISBN: 978-1-4327-3739-9

Outskirts Press and the "OP" logo are trademarks belonging to Outskirts Press, Inc.

PRINTED IN THE UNITED STATES OF AMERICA

For the five I came to live with and
the four who came to live with me…

"They are like trees planted by streams of water, bearing fruit in due season, with leaves that do not wither; everything they do shall prosper."

[Psalm 1; verse 3]

One
The Settlement...

Kingman Boulevard was no mean street. It ran right through the soft, chewy center of the candied neighborhood we moved to in the summer of 1955 when I was not yet two years old.

Lawns stuck out of the homes like green welcome mats. In ours a small, misshapen mulberry tree bubbled from the grass between the gravel driveway and the stone path that wound from the sidewalk to the front steps. The two-story frame house where the six of us lived stood subordinately in the shade of the biggest maple tree I've ever seen; one that was surely home to whole villages of birds and squirrels.

I don't recall much prior to my stint in kindergarten, and not a great deal even of that. It's fair to say that I learned something short of all that I would really need to know. Three things stand out: I established my first friendship – Billy, a kid from across the street; I was caught in the act of peeing outdoors by an older girl who lived nearby; and most notably, I broke my leg coming down from that grand maple.

The broken leg was a seminal event in my life because I regard it now as the template for my relationship with my brother Mark. Mark is five years my senior, so he was ten that day in the fall of '59 when he coaxed and boosted me onto the lowest of the tree's muscular limbs during an after-school round of hide-and-seek.

Witnesses were divided as to whether I fell or jumped from my perch, and I myself cannot be sure. What I am certain of is that Mark put me in that tree and when I got out my leg was busted.

I came home from the hospital a couple of days later sporting crutches and a cast that ran the length of my right leg, and Mark was lying in wait to salt my wound. He insisted I demonstrate the crutches, so I scooted nimbly across the living room. When I pivoted in the front hall I spun out on a throw rug and went down in a painful heap. That was it for the crutches. By the time my cast came off, I'd worn a hole in it near the ankle by dragging it around for six weeks.

And so it went with Mark and me. I was his in-house guinea pig, punching bag, masseur, crash-test/ventriloquist dummy, all-purpose little brother.

I was known as commonly in those days as, "Little Wellman" as by any other moniker. Mark was Mission Control and I was the lunar rover. The light bulb over his head would flash and off I'd go, wandering into our parents' bridge party wearing one of mom's bras loaded with grapefruit; up to some innocent stranger's home to thieve their morning paper and fling it on the roof in retaliation against a rival paperboy; to a neighbor's porch to ring the doorbell and run for my life while Mark and his cronies giggled in safe seclusion; up on the small balcony that jutted from the back of our house inhaling cigarettes with Mark et al. laughing while smoke backfired out my orifices like exhaust belching from a jalopy.

Little wonder that I once revolted by snatching a wad of paperboy cash from his dresser drawer and tearing it into green confetti while he looked on in horror. But my rebellions were infrequent and quickly put down.

He would punch me in the arm and ask the unanswerable question: "Did that hurt?" If I said, "yes," he'd say, "Good, I think I'll do it again." If I said, "no," he'd say, "Guess I didn't do it hard enough," and drum me with renewed vigor.

When we shared a bedroom I was required to tickle his back for three more songs before I could turn off the radio and go to sleep. Taking the chance that he was asleep before three songs were up was like asking myself the unanswerable question.

Once we had our own fraternal tomatina, slugging it out with a crate of tomatoes at point blank range, a spontaneous and rather abstract rouging of the kitchen walls and floor. Most of our later messes were made separately.

Mark's self-appointed duty was to toughen me and he relished it. He was a bastard in the finest tradition of big brothers everywhere, and it was not until the arrival next door of the Dean family in 1960 that my emancipation began.

* * *

The coming of the Deans was a linchpin to the settlement of the neighborhood in a couple of ways. The family included three boys, and would later add a fourth. Wayne was seven, just a year older than me, Stu was five, and Craig was three when they arrived. Not only did their company reduce my exposure to Mark and his big brotherly machinations, their backyard ran as deep as a football field, that being only one of the many uses we made of it. The opening of the Dean property was the Louisiana Purchase of my youth. Besides football, the Great Plain next door was the site for baseball, basketball, golf, excavation, cherry-picking, walnut and dirt-clod wars, kite flying and garage-roof jumping by day. After sundown we moved on to nocturnal antics like Ghost Comes Out at Midnight, which amounted to hide-and-seek by a more blood-curdling name, and Peeball. Peeball was an earthy, primitive variation of soccer in which all of the players simultaneously urinated on the ball before the game began. The game then consisted of the players, each a team of one, kicking the piss-marinated ball at one another. If the ball hit you, you were out. Depending on the number, elusive-ness and bladders of players, there were occasional intermissions for re-anointment of the ball.

The Dean boys bragged a lot about their dad, not without cause as we shall later see. But their mom was gorgeous beyond the bounds of mother-hood, and perhaps the first of many things next door that inspired me to lust, envy and covet.

The Deans were free-spending frontrunners who got more allowance and rooted for the Yankees. They had a dog named after Mickey Mantle. I had to let my mom cut my hair to scrounge fifty cents together, and my dad afflicted me with the Cubs. The Deans had twice as many cars [two] as we did, both of them with automatic transmissions - and one of them was a convertible! They took their take-out at the trendy new joint with the golden arches while we went down with the ship of Henry's Hamburg-ers, forever home of the best two-bit burgers I ever ate – about the size of a quarter and priced accord-ingly. The lucky Deans even had a color television. Yes, they seemingly had it all, but fortunately for the rest of us, their backyard was so big they couldn't control their borders and we got in.

* * *

Just a year or so after the Deans moved in the Leonard family bought the property adjacent to their southern boundary. Three more boys who, like the Dean kids, ranged from slightly older to slightly younger than me; Stephen, Marcus and Phil. Marcus was my age. They also had a girl, Carrie, who was their youngest, and would eventually have a younger sister of her own.

Just as acquisition of the Dean territory stretched our physical boundaries, Stephen Leonard would broaden the group's consciousness beyond the horizon of sandlot sports.

On the day the Leonards pulled into their new driveway there was, as usual, a whiffleball game in progress on the Dean grounds. We paused, not so much to welcome the newcomers as to check them out. There was wariness and curiosity all around, not unlike the dynamic when dogs first meet and sniff out the essence of one another.

It wasn't long before we were teasing Phil about his wingtip shoes which he removed and threw at us. The Leonard boys were then quickly absorbed into the game, but in due course Stephen, the renaissance kid, would divert our interests as widely as butterfly, coin and stamp collecting. He even facilitated a group study of astronomy for a time which was further encouraged by the proximity of an observatory on the grounds of Waveland, the nearby municipal golf course. The Friday night stargazings at the observatory held under the auspices of Drake University were thusly added to a long list of recreations staged on what was primarily, but by no means exclusively a golf course. Waveland was like the Deans' yard plus hills and minus parents at the window. As our thirsts and curiosities grew, so would the assortment of private uses for a public golf course under the cover of a starry night.

Like our family's, the Leonards' path to this promising place and time twisted and turned over the course of generations through Norway and Minnesota. That might have meant something to our parents upon their meeting and discovery of shared heritage. Maybe Mildred and Jean got together for coffee and a couple of "uff da's" once in a while. But their kids were oblivious to whatever we had in common beyond our stomping grounds. We were All-American urchins, roaming widely through childhood, ignorant of the past and impatient for a future that was coming faster than we knew.

The Dean yard was our jumping off point, but the Leonard home was an occasional headquarters because of Stephen, who was becoming a leader in the emerging hierarchy. He was the eldest of the core group, and also perhaps the strongest personality. Besides the more refined diversions he brought to our agenda, he also led us into battle with the barbarians from a neighboring district who favored military play. If someone from our block's out-manned band of guerillas was captured, they were imprisoned under guard in a backyard tool shed on 45th Street that doubled as a prison camp. Lacking equivalent facilities and the manpower to staff them, we practiced catch and release. When we grabbed up someone from the enemy ranks, he'd face a firing squad of green apples or snowballs, depending on the season, against the back wall of the Leonard garage before being let go.

I've forgotten if we had any awareness that real soldiers were soldiering in Southeast Asia while we played army on and around Kingman Boulevard in Des Moines, Iowa.

* * *

Early in 1964 the Donald family moved in three houses around the bend from the Leonards. Three more kids joined our swelling ranks - the neighborhood demographics were rapidly changing. Fred was in the same grade as my brother [though a year younger], Lynnette was a year ahead of me, and Laura a year behind.

A grassy, bell-shaped plot lay between the Leonard and Donald homes. We called it simply, "the island" because it was surrounded on all sides by the tines of pavement it forked into the road. The island had utility as a secondary baseball field. 43rd Street running along its eastern edge served as the equivalent of the warning track in big league ball-parks [warning tracks are swaths of finely crushed rock between the outfield grass and the wall designed to alert outfielders in concentrated pursuit of deep fly balls that they're about to run into something]. Anything hit across 43rd Street on the fly was a home run.

Our lives were more gently curved than sharp cornered, and we patrolled our jurisdiction like steeplechasers via shortcuts through bushes and over fences. Euclidean hunches as to distance saved by straight lines traversed on foot were always weighed against the impulse to mount bikes and race over less direct routes. For a while we were entitled to believe we knew what lay around every bend.

The immediate impact of the Donald threesome on our burgeoning band of scallywags was muted for two reasons: Girls were decidedly outnumbered in the area and regarded in a range from benign neglect to utter disdain by us boys. Also, Fred didn't transfer schools when his family moved, so he and my brother Mark wouldn't become classmates until later at [Theodore] Roosevelt High School, where Fred's dad happened to be the football coach.

Roosevelt was just south of us, barely a dirt clod's throw from the island. Just south of Roosevelt the MacVicar Freeway was under construction, a local spur of the interstate highway system and a harbinger of gathering speed in the American ways of life.

Roosevelt was the place where we'd line up and march through to get our sugar-cubed polio vaccine early in the '60's. The scourge of polio became suddenly the least and briefly the last of worries for the biggest generation in American history.

* * *

By the time the Beatles made their watershed appearance on, *The Ed Sullivan Show* one Sunday night in February of 1964, our neighborhood as I have ever since remembered it was settled.

Other offspring of the four families whose lives and backyards now bumped against one another included my sisters Martha and Mary. Martha is the eldest of us four siblings, two years beyond Mark, and Mary the youngest, two years shy of me. They were chronologically positioned to put the clamps on their brothers, but otherwise not equal to the task. I cannot account for the M that begins each of our given names. It has always been my understanding that my older brother and sister were in the thrall of the Peter Pan story when our mother unleashed me into the world, and that it was in acquiescence to them that I was named Michael after the youngest in the Darling brood. As for the sisters with the same names as the biblical duo, well, there are some parallels, though I can't say that was what our parents had in mind.

Danny Dean was born in 1961 after his family settled on Kingman, and Marie Leonard would arrive in 1967, the sixteenth and last of our generation spread amongst four homes and families; ten boys and six girls sprinkled over the score of years spanning the late 40's to the late '60's.

Scattered elsewhere around the block were still more kids, although my pal Billy was gone before first grade. Straight across Kingman from us, separated by block-long capsules of greenery that bisected the boulevard and anchored lamp posts, were the consecutive homes of the big girl, the quiet boy, the imp and the blonde kids. Next to us, on the side opposite the Deans lived a grim Open Bible family. Like us, they were a family of four children – two boys, two girls - whose first names not only began with the same letter [J], but whose middle names rhymed! They had us there.

It was not Des Moines' most affluent sector, but it was nicely upholstered - pillowy and shaded - and populated by an array of the town's most distinguished citizens and notable sons and daughters.

Just across the street from the Leonards lived Robert D. Ray, who would be elected Governor in 1969 and hold the office until 1983. Later he would serve shorter terms as mayor of Des Moines and president of Drake.

Next door to the Rays was the childhood home of Cloris Leachman, a name that became widely recognizable after she won an Oscar in 1971 for her role in *The Last Picture Show*. Later she would add a Golden Globe and nine Emmys to her trophy case.

One of the Donalds' next door neighbors on 43rd Street was Jolene Wolf who was named Miss Iowa and represented the state in the Miss America Pageant in 1962.

Within a one-mile radius of the big maple on Kingman Boulevard were a branch of the public library, a city park that included a swimming pool, an art museum, municipal tennis courts, a municipal golf course [another authorized use for which was sledding in the winter], a drugstore complete with a soda fountain, a church, a synagogue, two public schools, a community playhouse, two mom-and-popsy shopping centers and three one-screen, free-standing movie houses.

No, Kingman "Backyard," as I referred to it in little kid dialect before I was capable of pronouncing the word boulevard, was no mean street. It was a good place at a good time and we were good kids with good parents.

We were the first people I ever knew.

Two
The Trees...

Ward Wellman was a chivalrous man who took others more seriously than he took himself. Think Sir Bozo. He so enjoyed the sound of his children's laughter that he was only too happy to play the fool that he might hear more of it around the house. He was utterly without pretension and also the truest gentleman who's yet appeared in my life.

Shortly after his death in 1993 Martha, while sifting through his material remains, found a laminated card he carried in his wallet. This is what it had to say:

THE TRUE GENTLEMAN – The true gentleman is a man whose conduct proceeds from good will and an acute sense of propriety, and whose self-control is equal to all emergencies; who does not make the poor man conscious of his poverty, the obscure man of his obscurity, or any man of his inferiority or deformity; who is himself humbled if necessity compels him to humble another; who does not flatter wealth, cringe before power, or boast of his own possessions or achievements; who speaks with frankness but always sincerity and sympathy; whose deed follows his word; who thinks of the rights and feelings of others, rather than his own; and who appears well in any company, a man with whom honor is sacred and virtue safe.

John Walter Wayland

Wayland was a history teacher from Virginia who apparently submitted his notion of a gentleman to *The Baltimore Sun* when that newspaper solicited readers' thoughts on the subject for a contest in the 1930's. His winning entry was later incorporated by Sigma Alpha Epsilon as part of their membership creed.

My father must have adopted it as a personal standard when he pledged SAE at the University of Iowa where he would graduate in 1940. I have difficulty imagining him a frat boy, but Wayland's description fit him well.

It's interesting that Wayland's gentlemanly specs also appeared in manuals at the Naval Academy in Annapolis because the other laminated card our father carried in his wallet was a copy of The

Cadet Prayer from West Point where he was a plebe in 1936 before bad grades and bad eyes sent him home two years later.

His cadet service record measured him variously as 5'8", 137 lbs.; 20/80 vision in his right eye, 20/100 in his left; and a total of 33 demerits out of an allowable 115 [five –his worst offense- for being three minutes late to formation; four for an improper haircut; two for not sleeping in pajamas; one for drying a sock on the radiator]. He received a "favorable" rating [equivalent to a grade of B] from the Commandant of Cadets in December of 1937, and his tactical officer noted then that, "this cadet is very good officer material." Three weeks later he was discharged when he received D's in physics and math to go with his poor scores on the vision exam.

Still, the place marked him indelibly. There was always a soldier's sense of duty and discipline about the way he conducted his affairs, and even a military precision in the way he wielded his knife and fork at dinner or shifted gears when driving a car. Not only was he never late for anything, he tended to arrive with extreme prematurity.

He had a way of introducing his family to others that made us feel special and his children assigned him no demerits as a father. If others ever levied against him in that role based on the misbehaviors of his two sons, I cannot say.

Dad was the youngest of three boys, so he knew that rank had its privileges long before his time at

West Point or his service in the Army during World War II. He helped me to see Mark's hazings in their broader anthropologic context by telling me stories of commiseration. Like the times his *two* older brothers, Russell and West, were getting ready to go fishing. They practiced by casting their lines out into the yard. When they reeled in and their hooks were gone, they dispatched their barefoot little brother into the grass to walk about until he "found" them.

Our father was less inclined than our mother to tell stories and resorted more to physical comedy to entertain us. He had a peculiar outfit that he donned for yard work: an old pair of suit pants, rolled up to Capri length, no shirt, dark socks, a dilapidated pair of old wingtips and a handkerchief tied around his head for a sweatband.

He'd come inside from mowing with sweat-fogged glasses, grab a beer, down a gulp, and then let out a guttural belch followed by the suffix "ski," or "ovich," or sometimes both, as though he were announcing someone's surname upon their arrival at a royal ball. Then he'd light up a Chesterfield and spew smoke rings like they were soap bubbles on command from his adoring children who regarded him as some sort of half-wizard, half-jester. He made up funny names for the self-important like Homer Bedpan and Big Chief Squat-and-drop-it, and his language for indelicate subjects was quite lush. For instance, I was approximately a young adult by the time I knew there was a Holland Tunnel in New York besides the one that formed the home stretch of the human intestinal tract.

Dad was perfectly willing to suffer our clumsy pranks for the sake of a family chuckle. Mark might offer to bring him a cup of coffee, a dead giveaway that something was up. But dad would play along, grimacing right on cue upon tasting the salt that had been substituted for sugar while we roared with delight at having "tricked" him. Then of course he would drink the rest of the coffee, because to pour it out would have been wasteful, and waste was the cardinal sin for the generation reared during The Great Depression. That's why he was the concoctor of some of the most repugnant sandwiches imaginable, fashioned from whatever lurked festering in the nethermost regions of the kitchen. How does a hard crust of rye with braunschweiger, horseradish, wilted brown lettuce, the wrinkled butt of a green pepper and sliced beets, precariously topped off by a heel of white bread sound?

If this seems more the portrait of a clown than a knight, be assured that his public sense of decorum was even more acute than his private and self-deprecating irreverence. My father's greatest attribute was his humility. He was a lay reader at St. Luke's, the small Episcopal parish which was probably the single most significant discipline from his own life that he imposed upon his kids. But I wasn't convinced of my father's faith because he preached it at us. He demonstrated it in many ways, like when I'd hear him off by himself in a corner of the house on Saturday afternoon, practicing his readings for the following day. And when I saw him kneeling in church or bowing his head at our dinner table, it was obvious that there was something going on inside of him. He was a good work, not a sermon.

On Sunday mornings he'd squat, facing me, to knot my tie, toothpasty gusts wafting over me like the breath of God. He tied good knots. I believed in him.

Vocationally, he didn't accomplish very much. His career consisted of a series of middle management positions in companies like Solar Aircraft, Brady Motor Freight, Buster Nut Co. and Pittsburgh-Des Moines Steel. His job titles included Dispatcher and Traffic Manager.

We lacked material trappings, a fact that confused me as a child because I thought my father's considerable merits were obvious and should produce wealth as surely as plants grew from the soil. His wallet was usually light of cash, but he was literally a card-carrying gentleman, especially where a particular lady was concerned.

Mildred Hillestad must have been an easy mark for dad's charms, packaged as they were in his smartly pressed Army uniform.

They'd both grown up in Des Moines, dad graduating from Roosevelt at sixteen, and mom from East High across the river where she was raised on an especially arboreal block of Thompson Avenue.

Their wedding pictures show a uniformed officer and devout gentleman standing at the attention of a striking, vivacious chorister from St. Olaf College. I wonder if she ever sang to dad when they were courting. If she was a sucker for the way he carried himself and treated her, I can imagine him spellbound by the Lutheran maiden purring aphrodisiac rhapsodies from the hymnal.

They married in 1943 at Central Lutheran Church in Des Moines before dad went overseas and served in a non-combat capacity in London. Eventually he rose to the rank of Lieutenant Colonel in the Army Reserves.

From the time Martha was born in 1947 they devoted themselves to parenting.

Mom never made it back to graduate from St. Olaf, the college on the hill in Northfield, Minnesota where her life was set to music and she sang under the direction of famed choirmaster F. Melius Christiansen. The hints she dropped around the house nudging her four children toward the arts fell on tone deaf ears, so she soothed herself with soft hummings of "Beautiful Savior" while methodically stirring white sauces for creamed tuna, chipped beef and peas, all of which I left home supposing were widely regarded as the delicacies I knew them to be.

Besides her family and vocal music, mom's great love was reading. She did it as habitually as she smoked, probably a carton and [at least] a book per week. Unlike dad, she did not blow smoke rings for our amusement. Instead she softened our lives in lots of subtle ways. We were always awakened on school days with cheerfully crooned orders to, "cast a smile upon the day," or, "let us now be up and doing."

While I ate poached eggs on toast and blackened my elbows on the sports page newsprint, she'd give my jeans a "lick and a promise" on the ironing board. They were still warm when I slipped them on and felt like more than just a pair of pants.

To this day I prefer buttered bread in my sandwiches and peeled tomatoes, thanks to her spoiling. And with all due respect to my wife's devotion, money back guarantees and the various assurances recorded in scripture, I have known no greater comfort than the feeling of my mother's arms, one wrapped around my belly, the other across my forehead, while I threw up in the middle of the night.

When it became necessary for her to work at a time when two-income households were unusual, there was at least the consolation that she got jobs as the librarian at various public schools in Des Moines. All of her considerable labors, in and out of the house, were ones of love. Still, she was occasionally heard privately weeping, off by herself like dad practicing his readings or Christ at Gethsemane. Maybe her tears were confessional. Her mind wandered sometimes while she stirred those sauces to places she might have gone if she'd kept singing and finished college or to places she visited in books. Perhaps she was ashamed and guilt-ridden about long-harbored, unrealized daydreams, but I feared her tears were ones of unhappiness.

Children are as worried by a mother's tears as they are comforted by a mother's embrace.

The laminated card she carried in *her* pocketbook quoted George Bernard Shaw: "This is the true joy in life, the being used for a purpose recognized by yourself as a mighty one; the being thoroughly worn out before you are thrown on the scrap heap; the being a force of Nature instead of a...selfish little clod of ailments and grievances complaining that the world will not devote itself to making you happy."

When I cast my crutches aside and dragged my cast through kindergarten it was my mother who carried me up and down the stairs to and from my classroom at Hubbell Elementary School. Little did either of us know.

* * *

Ed Leonard and Jean Nester were not attention-getters.

He had thick dark hair, ears that looked tugged upon and a soft voice that lent itself well to his practice of pediatrics. His gentle tones offset the abrupt, unavoidable stings and jabs that his healings sometimes required.

She was a short, sturdy, Nordic brunette with her volume set on murmur and a reassuring smile that punctuated most of whatever she had to say.

They grew up in the cold of the northern plains

and hard times. Ed went to work in the town drug-store after his father died when he was young. His role as the older brother became more breadwinner than bully in his father's absence and he helped pull ends together for himself, his younger brother and their hardened, widowed mother.

He was first attracted to Jean's more flamboyant older sister Mary Lou who would ironically be the one to contrive the couple's first date. Depression induced frugality marked their unvarnished court-ship at a time when romance didn't have much of a jingle in its pocket. What they saw was what they got.

Ed enlisted in the Navy near the end of WWII after graduating from the University of Minnesota with a degree in Pharmacy to go with his bachelor's degree from the University of North Dakota where he'd first met Jean. He knew his student deferment from the draft wouldn't last so he picked the branch of service that seemed least objectionable and most survivable.

Marcus says their father never talked much about the past, preferring to emphasize what lay ahead, but when prodded by his curious children he did share one vivid combat experience: The ship he served on had been attacked by Japanese kamikaze pilots and there were many casualties on board. One of them was a black sailor who worked in the ship's galley. His wounds shouldn't have been life threat-ening, but were serious enough to prioritize him un-der combat triage procedures. Instead he was ignored by Southern doctors who treated whites less seriously injured and he died in the arms of a medically untrained pharmacist's mate, taking whatever remained of Ed's innocence and North Dakota naivete with him.

With his eyes now wide open, Ed rode the GI Bill to medical school after the war, and he and Jean were married in 1950 while he finished at the University of Chicago.

He'd always wanted to be a doctor, perhaps because growing up in the midst of widespread hardship steered him in ways that would alleviate suffering, particularly during childhood which he was determined to make more pleasant than his own had been for as many kids as possible. Watching helplessly while a comrade who might have been saved instead died in Ed's arms during the war just deepened his long-standing ambition to become a healer.

Dr. Leonard even made house calls! He came to our house late one night when Mark and his wife Marcia were living upstairs with their baby, my nephew Christopher, who was sick. Both Christopher, in 1967, and Dr. Leonard, in 1922, were born less than a full gestation after hastily arranged weddings.

Ed and Jean were private and stoic. But they shared a fervent if not demonstrative faith that each child was a miraculous droplet of life. It was in that light that they lost and then regained their footing when two of their own five miracles were revoked.

After his medical practice was established and thriving, Ed purchased a small farm not far from Des Moines where his kids could taste his rural upbringing and he himself could keep it physically as well as emotionally close. Once on a weekend visit there he upset a beehive and suffered the consequences. One of the small girls from our neighborhood who was along on the outing remembers being surprised to realize that Dr. Leonard was not impervious to pain.

Christ may have said, "Let the little children come to me...," but sometimes it made more immediate sense to send them to Dr. Leonard.

Minnesota estimates itself to be "The Land of 10,000 Lakes." Add a couple more zeroes and you could just as well be talking Lutherans. The Leonard newlyweds were just a couple more hardy Lutherans, descendants of Rolvaag's, *Giants in the Earth,* who wandered circuitously into Iowa.

When they moved into our neighborhood they continued their membership at St. Mark's in West Des Moines. Ironically, this was to be the place where an unconvincing and insensitive pastor trumped Ed's deep feelings about the natures and meanings of life and stunted Marcus Leonard's faith.

The Leonards had come a long way by the time they arrived at their stately red brick colonial in our neighborhood. All the way from hardscrabble, Depression-era North Dakota by way of Minnesota, Chicago and naval service somewhere in the Pacific; all the way from sixty-bucks-a-month living quarters on sixty-bucks-a-month intern's wages. Their new address was an easy one to get used to, especially in the decade of "space race" countdowns: 4321. The Leonards were on the launch pad.

* * *

When Carl Dean graduated from Roosevelt in 1950 he was the first to leave with nine letters, earning four apiece in football and basketball and one in baseball just for the hell of it. Besides sports, his other great distinction at Roosevelt was Marsha Hallett. On one of their first dates he announced to her that they would marry one day – more a prediction than a proposal – and so they did in 1952 while both were at Iowa State University, thirty miles north of Des Moines in Ames. Carl had originally headed to Oklahoma A&M, now Oklahoma State, on a basketball scholarship. Marsha, her life by then in lockstep with Carl's, came too, and became the school's homecoming queen. There could not have been a more quintessential American couple in the early 50's than these two; King Jock and Her Majesty. But they abdicated their Oklahoma thrones when Carl decided to transfer to Iowa State in the wake of, "The Johnny Bright Incident."

Bright was a black football player for Drake, good enough that he was being touted as a Heisman Trophy candidate when the Bulldogs came to Stillwater, Oklahoma for a game in October, 1951. Carl

Dean, who was also playing football in college, was so appalled when a teammate, Wilbanks Smith, deliberately broke Bright's jaw that he left the school and didn't look back. The Des Moines Register's photo sequence of Smith's vicious blow, like looking through a microscope at a virulent strain of bigotry, would eventually win a Pulitzer Prize in 1952.

Once settled in Ames the charmed couple stepped off the wedding cake and got down to business. Carl played basketball en route to his graduation in 1955 and Marsha dropped out of school to bring forth first Wayne, in 1953, and then Stu, in 1955.

His name was just as cut-to-the-chase as he was. Carl Dean. Two syllables, eight letters, a one-two punch of a guy who worked hard and succeeded as routinely as he awakened each morning. Not yet thirty, he was already prospering in the paper business by the time he moved his family next to ours on his way up the American ladder. Several years later he forged from a potion of his own sweat and vision a corporation that still thrives as a wholesaler of industrial and commercial papers.

The lives of the high school sweethearts were coming full circle. Carl had grown up maybe a mile north of Kingman on 41st Street. Marsha lived on Cottage Grove, another nearby street, as a little girl before moving to sycamore-lined Polk Boulevard. Polk, like Kingman, was notable for the grassy zipper that ran its length separating the lanes of traffic. On Polk, Marsha lived within sight of Roosevelt where she met the biggest man on campus, the un-stoppable Carl Dean.

That house would later crumble in the path of the MacVicar Freeway. The changing times too were unstoppable.

There was enough truth to Carl's story to form the basis of his sons' backyard tall tales about their father slaying Sam Snead on the golf course and kicking footballs through the clouds. His resume lacked only military service.

Carl and Marsha were younger than my folks and the Leonards, graduating from high school about the time their eventual neighbors were set-tling down and starting their families. When I first realized the parental age range I remember thinking that it explained Mr. Dean's virility and Mrs. Dean's prettiness. Her appearance seemed to matter more to her than the other mothers' did to them. She was made up on a daily basis. In our house and the Leonards' too I suspect it was enough if the beds got that sort of regular attention.

Marsha Dean actually was a pretty fair facsimile of June Cleaver from the old *Leave it to Beaver* TV series, right down to the dresses, earrings, lipstick, pearls and male offspring. But it was the Wellman boys that drew the comparisons to Wally and Bea-ver since we had the dad named Ward.

It's hard to know what to believe when you're in the hyperbolic chamber of childhood swapping baseball cards and bullshit with your pals. Kiddie cocktail parties of sorts, these casual duels of braggadocio eventually sophisticate into boastings at the country club or competitive philanthropy at black tie fundraisers. As apprentice manure spreaders, we trained hard to strike the right balance of trivia and folklore while jockeying for status within the growing pack - "I'm part Norwegian; my great, great uncle was 'The Devil of the North Sea'" – based on exploits, real and embellished, of our parents and ancestors before them.

Carl Dean was tough to top, in fact *and* fiction. The man was a natural born scorer.

* * *

Lon and Ella Donald also grew up in Des Moines and both graduated from North High School. He was older than she and came back to finish school after his military service. They married while both were enrolled at the old Iowa State Teachers' College, now the University of Northern Iowa, and their son Fred was born before they graduated. He was their first of many thousands of students.

Lon was a good athlete who had the choice of scholarships in football and baseball or the GI Bill to subsidize his college education. His athletic prowess and training as a teacher merged into a career as a high school football coach, and by 1957 he had wound his way through Earlham and Iowa Falls back to Des Moines. He became the head coach at Roosevelt, not far from the neighborhood where he'd grown up. In 1958 his team went undefeated and won the mythical state championship, shutting out six opponents and allowing only twenty-one total points in eight games.

[One of the members of that team was my cousin, John Wellman. The next year, when John was a senior, he was blinded by his best friend in a hunting accident. John endured many surgeries, first to save his life and later to build a new face where a handsome one had been before it was literally blown off in the accident. When John went to law school at Drake my father, whose brother West was John's dad, and many others from St. Luke's read his textbooks onto reel to reel tape recorders so he could study for exams. He earned a post-graduate fellowship at Yale Law School before embarking on a long and distinguished career directing the Public Defender's Office in Polk County, Iowa. When I broke my leg tumbling out of our maple tree a small article in *The Des Moines Register* identified me as the cousin of John Wellman, the recently blinded teenager. It would become a flattering association for me.]

Ella Donald was the one who rose through the ranks of the public schools and became the principal at East High while Lon settled in teaching history and coaching football at Roosevelt. He was the face of the school in many ways during a period of athletic prosperity in the 50's and '60's, and ringleader of the coaches who ruled the campus at an innocent time before there was any need for liaison between police and the high schools in Des Moines as is now customary.

Like Carl and Marsha Dean, Lon and Ella Donald were hard not to notice. They too made an attractive pair, both with dark hair which would sprout anew in each of their children.

Lon supplemented his teaching and coaching salary by selling Chevrolets. He always had a new ride, barely acknowledging the stop signs in the neighborhood that slowed his route to the main streets where he could drive his cars the way he drove his football teams. He had a commanding presence, confident and funny, the kind of man who used profanity as an expression of humor as well as anger or frustration. "Hell's bells!" was a favorite idiom of his, and I would often hear them ringing when I played football for him some years after we first became neighbors.

* * *

The eight parents whose children romped about our neighborhood in the wild were a formidable bunch. The fathers were gentlemen, doctors, soldiers, churchmen, athletes, coaches and entrepreneurs. Separately and together they were a good example. The mothers were primarily homemakers when that role was still lustrous, but they were also teachers and librarians. They sometimes played bridge together, but the fathers rarely if ever socialized with one another. It was the children that bound us all together.

There was no divorce, no scandal, no abuse of substance or person swept under the group's rugs that has ever come to my notice. Us kids walked both ways to school and rode our bikes like barefoot, ball capped cowboys in the summertime. We were beckoned home for hot home-cooked suppers by parents hollering out back doors over a comforting ambience of birdsong and the occasional bark of pet dogs that were as unfettered in that place and time as were their child masters.

Parenting that would be negligent and reckless by today's standards was actually quite affectionate in ways that were easier to feel than they are to explain. We were left to ourselves to contrive and oversee our own recreations, which we managed to do quite nicely, and most of whatever competition sprang up amongst us was neither arranged nor witnessed by our folks. Very little of our constant activity was ever photographed or documented in any fashion. Our uniforms consisted usually of blue jeans, white t-shirts and black sneakers.

Given all that we had in common it seems remarkable now that the first occasion which brought all two dozen members of the four contiguous families to the same place at the same time may have been a funeral. We didn't barbecue, worship or vacation together. But we did live and learn together in ways that people don't as much anymore.

Our parents threw us together instead of pitting us vis-a-vis one another. They were providers more than they were orchestrators; ultimately they would become naive enablers. Maybe they left too much to chance. But that doesn't excuse parents nowadays who put their kids in sports programs before they're even in school and can't wait to find out who's better than who at what. Our parents just couldn't wait to be parents.

The way they went about raising their families used to be part of the amorphous, laissez faire lifestyle known as The American Way, which held that cream rises inexorably to the top. It was more or less equal parts theology and science because it demonstrated faith in what they supposed were divine principles of a natural order.

The new paradigm is a variation of the old Eastern European Olympic model of identifying, segregating and developing potential from early ages. It strikes me as a rather vain and vicarious approach masquerading as good parenting.

Forget perfect, even in a world that just deserved an A minus, our parents' methods would be vindicated before we're through here. But if Norman Rockwell could have illustrated our years together, he could not have depicted all that happened after we parted ways.

Three
The Days…

From the start Wayne Dean was a sophisticate. He was seven and I was six when we met, and in no time he whisked me off to the magic land of baseball cards. I remember the first thing he ever taught me.

"Do you know what a team is?" he asked while fanning swiftly through a shoebox full of cards. I thought I did since Mark by then was playing for the Raccoon Valley Cubs.

"*This* is a team!" he declared, handing me a card with a picture of the Cincinnati Reds on the front and a listing of their statistical leaders from the previous season on the back.

I quickly caught on to the idea that when a pack

included a team card, it was like getting twenty-five players in one. If you didn't yet have a Mickey Mantle card, but you had a Yankee team card, you could point to one of the indistinguishable faces on it when somebody was celebrating a Mantle acquisition and say you already had him. Team cards were prized. Typically they were placed atop a stack made up of individual player cards from that team. Each team stack was then rubber banded together. This was how we organized our collections. I peaked at a young age in organizational skills.

You couldn't play little league until the age of nine back then, and girls of course couldn't play at all. The first year all you got for a uniform was a t-shirt with the little league emblem on the chest. The protective headgear for batters was a flimsy wrap-around device, sort of like what wrestlers wear to protect against cauliflower ears. My brother Mark called them "ear brassieres."

While we waited impatiently for little league eligibility, we played sandlot ball as often as possible. Everybody tallied their home runs over the course of a season, and every year Wayne was first and I was second. We started out with whiffleballs and bats. Then we started hanging around the Rexall Drugstore in the Uptown Shopping Center where we could get performance enhancers for a dime – rubber balls.

We were getting bigger every year, using wooden bats and the juiced balls, and the homer totals inflated exponentially, from modest double digits in the first summer to several hundred per kid per year by the time we outgrew our playgrounds.

Since Wayne was a year older I could only watch his first year of organized baseball. His father coached their team and one day entrusted to Wayne an 18-0 lead when he brought him in from the bull-pen to pitch with the bases already loaded. In the big leagues such an assignment would be considered "mopping up." But handing an eighteen run lead to a nine-year old pitcher can be like handing him a lit match. When Wayne turned his hose on this one, gasoline sprayed from it. He walked nineteen straight.

Wayne was wild. His dad was patient. The die was cast.

I looked up to Wayne in many ways. From my vantage point a grade beneath him at school I could see that he was accorded great social status. He was clearly one of the snappiest dressers at Hubbell, a regular customer at Reichardt's, the men's clothier in the other nearby marketplace known as The Roosevelt Shopping Center.

Reichardt's was owned by Bill Reichardt, a former football star at the University of Iowa who was named the Most Valuable Player in the Big Ten by The Chicago Tribune in 1951. His shop was a bastion of traditional men's dress, priding itself on its resistance to trendiness in the fashion world, and it was also the hot spot for young swells on our side of town to outfit themselves. "Burnt Ivory" penny loafers were a status symbol I never achieved, their

$20 price tag being beyond our means, but Wayne had a pair. He also had bottle-green, v-neck Alan Paine sweaters, a London Fog jacket, an assortment of button-down Gant shirts and a drawer full of "Roosevelt socks."

Reichardt's carried a line of white sweat socks by Wigwam that were topped by a double-stripe of navy blue. The Roosevelt school colors were navy blue and white, and the fashion of the time was for local schoolboys to wear jeans that ran a little short. To be decked in burnt ivories stuffed with Roosevelt socks topping out just beneath the hem of a pair of Levi's "wheat jeans" was cool. Wayne was cool. He had a precocious facility with girls that wasn't so easily taught as his lessons in baseball cards. But in this area too, pictures were instructive.

We weren't actually interested in girls so much as we were in women – naked women. Our interest was inflamed by an elaborate means we devised for expanding our inventory of periodicals to include – shhhhhh – Playboy!

Mad Magazine was a favorite; comic books of course; monster mags were really big back then, full of pictorials of The Wolfman, Frankenstein, Dracula and The Mummy [the effect of which on adolescent boys was the inverse of Playboy's]. Copies of all of those were strewn about in the treehouse that stood in the backyard of the Ahrolds on 43rd Street across from the island. Billy Ahrold was one of my brother's sidekicks, and his treehouse was a place where the whole neighborhood had visitation privileges. It wasn't really a treehouse; it was a clubhouse on stilts that you entered through a door in the bottom after climbing the built-in ladder, but everyone called it a treehouse. There were sleeping bags carpeting the floor and the walls were screened in and we used the place to play teenagers or sometimes even adults with everything from Swisher Sweet cigars to – shhhhh – Playboy! Playboys were *not* strewn about our communal reading room; they were contraband, forbidden fruit, after all. Since our possession of them was the illicit culmination of an intricate conspiracy, a mission if you will, they were destroyed following our frenzied perusals, just as Mr. Phelps' tapes were after he listened to recordings of his orders on *Mission Impossible*, a TV series that came into production about the same time as our hormones.

This is how we subscribed to – shhhhh – Playboy: a group of us would nonchalantly stroll into the Rexall, the same place where we got our juiced balls for the sandlot. There was a recent graduate of the Drake pharmacy school named Chuck who had to be on duty or we would abort. It's clear now that Chuck was complicit in our capers without ever telling us so. Agent #1 would approach the counter and buy some penny candy and a couple of comic books from Chuck while Agent #2 casually leafed through magazines on the rack below the front window and Agent #3 created a diversion at the soda machine in the middle of the store. When Chuck went to investigate #3's soda malfunction, #1 sidled up to #2 at the magazine rack who slyly slipped a – shhhhh – Playboy into the comic book sack before heading back to join the confusion at the soda machine and further distract Chuck. Then #1 walked briskly out the front door and jumped on with Agent #4 waiting outside on the getaway Stingray. #4 raced off with an adrenaline and testosterone martini thumping through him to the beat of the *Mission Impossible* theme music. Within minutes the team rendez-voused at the Ahrold treehouse to fight over the spoils. Eventually the photographic evidence was incinerated, but not until the exquisitely naked forms of Ursula Andress and others had set our adolescent blood to boiling and redistributed a good portion of it. You can bet that none of us ever consulted Dr. Leonard about the duration of arousals which routinely persisted in excess of four hours.

Shall I apologize because recollection of our larcenous, lustful adventures conjures more nostalgia than shame? I'll save that for other dates and deeds. As for – shhhhh – Playboy, we were lucky that it took such elaborate measures to quench our natural curiosities about female contours. Nowadays kids come home from school, sit down at the computer and, within a few keystrokes, they can see parts of the human body in live action that we literally had to steal furtive peeks at between games of sandlot doubleheaders. There is nothing left anymore to kids' imaginations. They've been rendered as superfluous as an appendix or tonsils.

There was a dynamic at work between Wayne

and his brothers that was not part of my relationship with Mark. There were three of them bunched within four years of one another when they first came to Kingman. So even though Wayne was the eldest, their pecking order was clogged and there was more jostling for status than there was between Mark and me, separated as we were by some five years.

If Wayne came home from a shopping trip with new clothes, Stu and Craig would get the receipts out of the bags and demand equal cash compensation from their mother.

Meanwhile, next door, I knew my place. I was quite willing, honored even at times, to toddle along in Mark's considerable shadow. When he and I were twelve and seven, I landed a spot on those Raccoon Valley Cubs as batboy, a post that came with a full uniform! Mark was one of the stalwarts on a great team that steamrolled through the league undefeated before advancing to the county tournament.

The tournament pageantry included pre-game introductions and the pre-game introductions included batboys! When my name was called I trotted out to join the line of Cubs, consciously trying to look and move like my big brother. This reward was worth playing catch with him, another ritual that featured an unanswerable question: "Am I throwing too hard?"

The Cubs won the county tournament and we threw in with a celebratory motorcade around town in our old Plymouth, sarcastically known as, "The Blue Arrow." Somewhere far from Kingman Boulevard the horn of the Arrow got stuck. I can hear it still, trumpeting the triumph of the best Cub team of my lifetime.

In those days I enjoyed being "Little Wellman." It would be some time before I tired of looking and acting like Mark.

Eventually Wayne Dean and I became teammates, putting our backyard rivalry aside to join forces on the Raccoon Valley Orioles for two seasons. Neither edition of that team amounted to much, certainly not on the scale of the 1961 RV Cubs. We lost roughly as many games as we won, but established some enduring relationships along the way.

We played our games at a site where high-rise condos now stand. There were two diamonds, one of them slightly elevated atop a small hill. On the back of the concession stand were painted Grantland Rice's famous words:

"For when the one great scorer goes to mark against your name

He marks not whether you won or lost, but how you played the game."

Grantland Rice was the pre-eminent American sportswriter of his time. He saw the poetry in sports and wrote it. He died the same year I was born.

We used to stand against that wall, blotting out Rice's assertion, when we lined up to pose for team photos. There in the front row is our best pitcher, the guy who sold the best pot and hash at Roosevelt a few years later; next to him is our shortstop, heir to the state's largest beer distributorship and a budding neo-con; in the back row are Wayne and me, smiling on cue, yellow caps pushed back just enough to expose his blonde bangs and hint at my homemade butch.

No pictures were taken of individual players at that time – just teams. Great pictures of great American pals, offspring of the children of The Great Depression, paused and posed for a moment on their way to The Great Explosion.

I think I was in third grade and Wayne in fourth the first time I got to spend the night at his house. I know for sure that the centerpiece of the evening's agenda was the late movie on TV that followed the ten o'clock news. I'm not sure if it featured The Mummy, The Wolfman, Frankenstein or all of the above, as lots of the films from that genre somehow managed to do, but I know that I was scared witless and couldn't have been more pleased. This was also about the time in my life that Wayne introduced me to an exotic treat known as pizza. I was thoroughly his protégé and loving it.

On schooldays we had our jeans grass stained playing ball in the Deans' yard before we even left for school. In the summertime, just when you'd think life could get no better, someone would report hearing a faint, far away tinkling. We'd all silence ourselves and listen together. Then, sure enough, we'd hear them, like the first sounding of a ship's fog horn as it nears a port of call or a train as it whistles along the outskirts of town; herald bells jingling in July.

"ICE CREAM MAN!" everybody screamed together before scattering to their respective homes to scrounge dimes. Like something straight out of the board game *Candyland* a man would appear riding what amounted to a big tricycle equipped with an ice chest full of frozen confections – popsicles, bomb pops, drumsticks, ice cream sandwiches. It was like outdoor room service for kids. When I first saw the Mel Brooks movie *Blazing Saddles* in 1974, I thought of the ice cream man when Slim Pickens and the posse rode up to the toll gate in the desert and Pickens hollered, "somebody's gonna have to go back and get a shitload o' dimes!"

A ten cent popsicle delivered curbside was the perfect capstone to a day spent snitching crushed ice from the milkman's truck, following the street cleaner on bikes to pluck golf balls and other treasures buried in its sweepings, flinging grapes all the way from produce to frozen foods at Safeway and lighting farts with stick matches we struck on the concrete basketball court in back of the Deans' garage.

After handing down the combustibility of flatus, Wayne moved on to other fireworks. The first time I lit the fuse on a Black Cat firecracker, I got no further in my throwing motion than right next to my ear before it blew up, giving my fingertips a sooty cast and inducing a brief deafness on my right side.

After that I was strictly a spectator at detonations. As for rectal flame-throwing, the whole gang retired after hearing an unsubstantiated report of a kid somewhere who sustained a scorched Holland Tunnel resulting from a backdraft.

Wayne Dean, like the times that were a changin' and my big brother, was exciting and dangerous.

The Leonard boys were the neighborhood naturalists. Stephen and Marcus applied outdoorsy principles gleaned from Boy Scouts to our day-to-day mischief. Marcus was a tree climber, undaunted by things I feared, like heights. He'd grin at me on the roof of the Dean garage while we lined up like paratroopers in the belly of a plane before jumping and free-falling to the ground, maybe ten feet below. Marcus was usually barefoot and bored. I was shod and terrified, but so powerful was the peer pressure to get my roof-jumper neighborhood merit badge that I'd swallow hard and leap. I always liked the feeling of the ground beneath my feet. There just seemed a greater margin for error on terra firma that I suppose was more important to me after the broken leg.

Patrols with the Dean boys found their way inexorably to the nearby shopping centers for soda pop and candy, but exploring with the Leonards was more like swinging vine to vine and foraging for snacks such as cherries or mulberries picked fresh from the tree. In season, the ground surrounding our mulberry was a blotter of deep reds and purples and bare feet were inked there beyond washing. I was a tenderfoot, owing mainly to the gravel in our driveway which was difficult to cross without shoes. But the rest of the herd, particularly Craig Dean and Marcus Leonard, scampered nimbly far and wide with nothing on their feet except callouses and a thick coat of mulberry primer.

Sometimes I'd sit beneath the apple tree in our backyard, leaning on its trunk with a salt shaker in hand and gnaw through several greenies. My mother would warn me through the window that I could expect a case of the "cobbywobbles," her homespun term for self-inflicted diarrhea. This was a variant of her usual term for number two, "bobo," which she used except in cases of innocently contracted illness, when the more clinical "BM" was invoked, to wit:

"Cast a smile upon the day. Let us now be up and doing!"

"[Moan] Mom, I don't think I can go to school. My stomach hurts [groan]."

"Oh, dear heart…maybe you just need to have a BM."

Truth was I had a hard time managing my BM's. We were so much outdoors that when one came on me I'd sometimes try to pinch it back by braiding my legs and clenching my cheeks. That didn't always work. Sometimes I came home with more than skid marks in my undies. I used to wonder what Superman did about BM's, eventually surmising that they were Clark Kent's responsibility. There may be no better measure of the free-flowing joy and freedom of our neighborhood than my occasionally opting for scat in the pants instead of a bobo break during pursuit of Tiger Swallowtails on a butterfly hunt.

Once we discovered a small bird dying slowly near the Leonards' swing set. Apparently it had fallen from a nest in the tall pine that towered in their backyard. We decided euthanasia was in order, but how? Marcus contrived a gallows using a brick, some twine and a crossbar on the swing set and the bird was quickly decapitated out of its misery, much to our fascination. This incident was in stark moral contrast to the time I casually fired a baseball toward a cardinal perched on a branch in our apple tree. My intention was to frighten the bird into flight, but I caught it flush in the breast and it fell dead to the ground. I was alone and I quickly buried the physical remains of what I'd done, but I had a harder time burying the fact that I was a killer of songbirds.

The general pleasantry of our little patch of paradise was increasingly against a national backdrop of historic and unprecedented goings-on. Astronauts were rocketing into space on a regular basis and being fished from the sea upon their televised returns home which were splashy in more ways than one. I was fascinated by America's adventures in outer space and riveted by Walter Cronkite's narration of them. When John Glenn blasted off in 1962 I was in second grade and very proud to note that history was being made within mere days of my birthday. I turned eight on February 24; just four days after Glenn became the first American to orbit the earth. I already linked my birthday to those of Abraham Lincoln on February 12, and George Washington on February 22. Now I was starting to feel downright destined for American heroism. But the beginning of the end of my days as an American boy came when I was in fourth grade.

Where were you? I was in Mrs. McIntyre's classroom at Hubbell when the news came that America's president was dying in Dallas; that he'd been shot in the head by a sniper. I remember where I was, but not much about what I felt or how people around me were acting. For sure, I was selfishly, childishly annoyed by the time round the clock; wall to wall television coverage of the assassination, the assassination of the assassin, and John Kennedy's funeral finally began to wind down days later.

The term "breaking news" was not then in vogue, but *Breaking News* could have been a TV series that premiered in 1961 when Alan Shepard took America into outer space for the first time and enjoyed a nice run up through Richard Nixon's impeachment and resignation in 1974. There wouldn't have been too many re-runs either, though certain themes, like political assassination, manned space flight, political protest and race riots would have been recurring ones.

News of Kennedy's death was like "FIRE!" screamed in the American theatre. Hell's bells started drowning out the ice cream man's.

Later in my fourth grade year I was taken out of class to meet with a woman who asked me lots of questions. Sometime after that I was informed by my parents that I was one of a group of Hubbell students that would have the opportunity to go to Windsor Elementary the next year to be in an "academically talented" class. When the deadline came for a decision I was encouraged by my folks to take the chance, but I think it was ultimately my call. Surprisingly, I went for it, partly because I thought some other Hubbell kids would too. None did.

Windsor was a couple miles west of Kingman, and to get there each day I had to walk the beautiful block up 44th Street to University Ave. to catch a city bus. At first my new routine was unnerving. Instead of walking a few blocks with some combination of Deans and Leonards, I walked alone to catch a bus and ride with mostly adults on their ways to work. But my short stroll was scenic, lined with elm trees that hadn't yet fallen in the epidemic of Dutch elm disease that would take a quarter million of Des Moines' trees by the end of the decade. They naturally canopied the long straight block of large homes with widely grinning front porches and deep back lots. It's still a stretch where homes sell without a sign ever posting in the yard.

At 44th & University I'd catch the bus and settle in for a ride up and down the biceps that flexed into the street dividing Waveland Golf Course from Glendale Cemetery. I liked the sound of the coins clacking through the counter as new riders came aboard and felt powerful knowing that I could bring the bus to a stop with one tug on the buzz cord.

My absorption into Windsor's mainstream was made quick and easy by one person: Tim Gebhart. Tim too had gone to Hubbell. In fact, we'd been in Kindergarten together there, though we hadn't really become close buddies by the time his family moved practically next door to Windsor's playground. When I stepped off the bus for fifth grade Tim was ruling the roost at my new school. For the next few years he would be the closest friend I've ever had. We alternated weekend sleepovers at each other's homes. When I was hosting, Tim was freely accepted into our neighborhood activities. He was quick on the giggle, almost impossible to keep from laughing, which was sometimes a problem if we were perpetrating mischief that required stealth. Tim's father was a colleague of Lon Donald's at Roosevelt. He taught economics and was also the school's athletic director. He had been an assistant coach on the 1958 mythical state championship football team. Tim also had an older sister, Pegg, who was a beautiful blonde cheerleader at Roosevelt. It was an unrealized fantasy of mine to catch a glimpse of her in some state of undress whenever I spent the night at the Gebharts'. The Gebhart connection, even though they lived outside the bounds of our neighborhood, nevertheless helped pave the way for assimilation of the Donalds. Fred Donald was a classmate of Pegg Gebhart and their dads worked and socialized together. Once in a while Fred put me and Tim in our place on the basketball court. He had short-cropped hair as black as his horn rims and he'd slip off his loafers and whip us at H-O-R-S-E in his stocking feet. I can't remember a specific thing he ever said to me but I distinctly recall that he was real smart and nicer to me than my older brother was. Mark, by the way, also changed schools the year I transferred to Windsor.

He was a promising athlete and troublemaker by the time he finished ninth grade at Merrill Junior High. Whereas my sister Martha attended Roosevelt for six years, grades 7-12, before graduating in 1965, Mark's class opened the brand new Merrill building in the fall of 1961. Mark broke the place in like a new pair of jeans or shoes – he was rough on it. He was on track to head to Roosevelt where his sophomore year would have coincided with Martha's senior, but instead our parents diverted him to Shattuck, an Episcopal military prep school in Faribault, Minnesota. His attendance there rippled throughout our family when he was home for breaks. For instance, our younger sister Mary and I would be conscripted into close order drill, armed with brooms or mops, so Mark could demonstrate the intricate maneuvers of Shattuck's "Crack Squad," the school's renowned drill team. Failure to follow his orders risked a resounding bop on the head with his school ring. Coming home from Shattuck where he was at the bottom of the food chain, Mark took full advantage of those he outranked –

namely Mary and me. He also brought home the best school cheer I've ever heard: "Shattuck, Shattuck, you are it! – S-H for Shattuck, I-T for it…"

About now I began to suspect that something was amiss on Kingman Boulevard. Sometimes I'd overhear Mark on the telephone recounting shenanigans from Minnesota; tales of our older cousin Ann sneaking from nearby Northfield down to Faribault with friends to rendezvous with Mark and his Shattuck comrades for walks on the wild side – drinking, smoking and, I speculated, the lowering of inhibitions and underwear.

Whatever fear I'd had of Mark previously was visceral. I did not enjoy being pummeled, tied in knots or floated as a trial balloon. But now my apprehensions concerning him took on a new, vaguer dimension. I was afraid for him in ways I couldn't exactly understand. I was privy to secrets that were of no use to me. There was no one to share them with. Telling our parents would be tattling and lead to reprisal. Telling my sisters invited the risk that they would tell our parents. Telling my friends wasn't an option because I didn't want them to know what I knew. Confiding that my big brother got caught smoking at military school and had to puff cigarettes under a wastebasket until he passed out [served him right for lighting me up on the balcony] wasn't the same as bragging about his undefeated little league team.

Mark's time at Shattuck did not change him the ways that West Point had changed our father. He simply took the place off when he removed his uniform and came home for his junior year at Roosevelt.

Meanwhile I joined Tim at Windsor's center stage. The principal there was the aptly named Dr. Wise, a truly good man who remains my friend to this day despite the fact that he hired my mother to be the school librarian during my sixth grade year. This made his job easier by re-routing my office referrals for things like throwing Billy Kreamer's watch in the urinal – not where I was aiming – to the library. But it made my job harder, even though I now had a ride to school every day. Besides the additional stress of getting sent to my mother instead of the principal, my first steps out of closeted heterosexuality were made more tentative and clumsy by mom's presence in the laboratory where I was trying out my moves. How could I tackle the objects of my affections in a lunchtime game of kickball with my mother standing sentry on the playground? While my love life stumbled out of the starting blocks, I flourished artistically, producing a ceramic ashtray for my parents and a set of wooden wind chimes that hung on display in Dr. Wise's office for a time. Today the ashtray holds an amalgam of buttons, rubber bands and paper clips and the wind chimes hang silently on the back wall of our garage where no breezes ever go.

Thanks to Tim, the move from Hubbell to Windsor was as seamless as a new kid in school could hope for. But not even the friendship of a popular student kept me from missing Mr. McGuire.

P.E. is always a preferred class in elementary school, but sometimes that's despite, not because of the teacher. Mr. McGuire was everybody's favorite at Hubbell. Before school in the fall and spring he was outside on the field the school shared with Roosevelt, its next door neighbor, throwing passes to hordes of kids who showed up early to play with him. On Fridays during the outdoor seasons the game we played in his class was called, "Russian Spy." It combined the red hot Cold War with the ascending popularity of James Bond espionage as agents in blue jeans tried to infiltrate the other side and make it safely back to freedom with secrets disguised as four-square balls. The risk of imprisonment for a few minutes in the custody of enemy girls was a negligible price in exchange for the privilege of playing in America.

After The Beatles landed in the winter of fourth grade, just a few months after Kennedy's assassination, Hubbell's hair started to grow. Beatles cards competed with baseball cards for shelf space at The Roosevelt Pharmacy and Matulef's, the small grocery across from Hubbell in The Roosevelt Shopping Center. Boys' shirts came untucked, and from my academic exile at Windsor I'd hear reports from the Deans and Leonards about Mr. McGuire wielding a pair of scissors at school, the better to trim Beatles haircuts and shirttails with. Surely Mr. McGuire's attempts to prune back the rebellions sprouting in his small plot of the American landscape were at least tacitly endorsed by Hubbell's administration and parents. Alas, his scissors couldn't stop a generation.

Probably the single most unsettling event to occur in our little terrarium happened in the fall of 1964, not long after I switched schools.

Phil Leonard was then in third grade at Hubbell, along with my sister Mary. Phil was something of a misfit right from that very first day when we teased him about his shoes and he took them off and hurled them at us. He was socially awkward in ways that neither of his older brothers was, given to communicating by grunts and mumbles and prone to tantrums. One day after school some bunch of us was zipping through the neighborhood, including Phil astride the bike belonging to his younger sister Carrie. Riding in the street, which was commonplace for us all, he veered toward the Dean driveway without looking back and was hit by a car. There was a close-up that night on the local news of the bell on Carrie's handlebars – a four-leaf clover. Phil's injuries were serious enough that he spent much of that school year convalescing at home. We were all shaken by Phil's accident. It was the first suggestion to us that our world was not impregnable. But in due course we resumed acting as though it was. Phil would never fully recover.

The growing society of peers within a backyard or two of one another had economic as well as social implications.

Before I had so many cohorts within shouting

distance I'd often go to the public library branch that was just a few storefronts down from the Rexall and scour the sports biographies section. I read the life stories of Richie Ashburn, Roy Campanella, Johnny Unitas, Yogi Berra and many other athletes. Such books always had a section in the middle, like an intermission, of black and white photos; highlights from the protagonist's life. Usually there'd be a wedding shot, a locker room scene with teammates pouring champagne on each other in celebration of a championship, a contract signing ceremony. A notable exception to the general mood of the photo collages that I remember was the picture in the Campanella story of a crumpled car, the one he crashed on a rainy night, resulting in paralysis and the end of his baseball career.

But I traded free books for nickel-a-pack baseball cards. I traded life stories and whole sections of pictures for cardboard photos with thumbnail stat sketches on the back and a stick of bubblegum to chew on while memorizing the stats. Instead of learning, for instance, that a certain big leaguer grew up in a home where only Italian was spoken and had older brothers who were forbidden to play pro ball by their father, I'd settle for where and when that big leaguer was born, which side of the plate he hit from and which arm he threw with – that and a stick of gum.

The problem became how to finance my cravings for cards and gum and keep up with the Deans.

I resorted to petty theft. Actually, in retrospect

maybe it wasn't so petty after all. I'd swipe change from my mom's billfold and head for the Roosevelt Pharmacy to buy a few packs of baseball cards. Then I'd sit at the soda fountain sipping a mug of root beer like I was Marshall Matt Dillon from the TV series *Gunsmoke,* dropping by the Long Branch for a cold one and a gander at Miss Kitty's cleavage. The trouble with that fantasy was that Nellie, the plain matron of the soda fountain, hardly approximated Miss Kitty [though she did fry up a tasty "Nellie Burger"]. *Gunsmoke* was my dad's favorite show. The thing I always noticed about Marshall Dillon's complimentary beers at the Long Branch was that he *never* finished one! I never understood that. I always drained my root beers.

One time I snatched two bucks from mom's purse, a brazen escalation into paper currency, and went straight to Matulef's where I bought an entire box of baseball cards – forty packs! – in one fell swoop. I took them across the street and went through every pack while watching a Roosevelt baseball game. I was drunk on bubblegum, publicly flaunting my wad of cards with no plausible explanation for how I'd come by the cash to buy them. I'm certain I was caught because of the flagrancy of my crime, but I don't recall the consequences.

In the wintertime I sometimes earned honest money by going door-to-door looking for snow-shoveling jobs. We'd clear an entire driveway and throw in the sidewalk and front steps for five bucks. But during baseball season I wasn't about to mow lawns for extra money because we didn't have a power mower.

I'd watch in amazement when dad mowed our grass. He'd have those blades that were shaped and aligned like DNA helixes spinning so fast that they would actually generate their own manpowered, high-pitched whir. Mark was able to manage the primitive machine enough to get the job done. But in my hands it was damn near an immovable object. Seeing the Dean boys fighting next door for turns on their riding mower only added to the dread when I was assigned mowing duty on our grounds. Besides, we didn't get paid for pitching in around our house. Our parents weren't only a little challenged in terms of cash flow; they were also of the old fashioned mind that the four of us kids should help out now and then in exchange for our free room and board.

One occasion that sticks out as an exception to their generally tight-fisted fiscal policies was the year our band laid siege to the Iowa State Fair. I was eleven and my parents staked me to the tune of four dollars, the largest sum ever in my possession to that point. Somehow I spun it into the gold of a twelve-hour adventure.

A carload of us was dropped at the main gate of the fair around nine in the morning. We ranged in age from probably ten to twelve. The only role in the outing played by an adult was chauffeur. Once inside the grounds and loose on the midway I won two large stuffed animals right out of the chute. After lugging them around all day I ended up selling them around suppertime for a buck apiece to a lady with two crybabies in tow. By then I was tired and hungry, I was broke, and the corn dog and soda I bought with my proceeds sustained me until mom picked us up at dusk.

The ride home in our Chevy station wagon was a long one from the eastside back across the river to our territory. The passengers snoozed fitfully in the overloaded car, semi-anesthetized by exhaustion and the pungent mixture of deep fried kid sweat, cotton candy farts, root beer burps and mom's cigarette smoke. We lurched back and forth en masse with every depression of the clutch and shift of gears. Rain splatted on the windshield and made it look like the pock-marked surface of the moon. The only child restraint in the vehicle was mom's right arm which thrust out straight across the front seat whenever sudden stops were necessary.

I never again won any games on the midway. Selling those two stuffed animals for food was like pawning medals, but as mom often said in defense of me when my appetite came up for discussion, I was, "a growing boy."

The best legitimate source of funds I landed as a kid was at the Prouty house. The Prouty sisters were two old spinsters who lived about halfway up the Eden-like block of 44th Street between Kingman and University. One Sunday after church one of them fell and broke her hip getting out of their car and eventually her rehabilitation progressed to the point of a daily stroll aided by a walker. My assignment was to help her in and out of bed and walk behind her to catch her in case she fell. In exchange for tolerance of a geriatric ambience and the glacial pace of the pedestrian laps around the house I was paid two bucks per day, every day. Sadly, within weeks the fallen Prouty sister was ambulatory again and my brief internship as a physical therapist ended.

However burdensome mowing the lawn and shoveling snow could be, leaf gathering in the fall was downright recreational. The one state-of-the-art labor-saving device our father ever purchased was a leaf sweeper. It was maybe four feet wide, a walk-behind canvas tarp on a metal frame that caught the leaves swept into it by a rotary brush running the length of the axle between the front wheels. Compared to our lawnmower this contraption was a Ferrari; we fought for turns on it like the Deans jockeyed for control of their lawn tractor.

Best of all though was the fact that once the sweeper was full we simply dumped its contents onto the driveway approach and put a match to them! Leaf burning here in Des Moines is long gone, like paperboys, milkmen, and pedestrian school children. I have a hard time reconciling the fact that it pollutes the air, but even so, shouldn't it be exempted from classification with bus exhaust and factory emissions? Tending a smoldering pile of leaves as a setting autumnal sun gave way to a swollen harvest moon was not a bad thing. The smoky aroma of burning maple leaves ranks right alongside bacon on the stove and bread in the oven if you ask me and is good for any community's morale. Every year I contemplate setting my yard ablaze as an act of civil disobedience but I lack courage to go with my conviction that leaves are better [and easier] burned than bagged.

Once the leaves had all been swept, piled and burned it was time to brace for winter. There was more to the bleak season than shoveling snow. Forts were fashioned out of the stuff on the Deans' back tundra and we hurled snowballs at one another by the hundreds. When we tired of warring, whether intramurally or versus the Payne army bivouacked on 45th Street, we'd repair to Waveland for some alpine fun. The ninth fairway was long and steep, as blindingly white by winter as it was verdant green by spring. The laborious trudge to the summit at first seemed worth the exhilarating plunge down our modest mountain, but it was never long until the ratio of labor to play seemed out of whack; along the lines of working all year for a week or two of vacation. Still, the Christmas that featured my *Flexible Flyer* sled to go with a new baseball glove and a new basketball was the best haul I ever made.

The other venue in our biathlon was the corner of 44th and University which presented a prime vantage point for throwing snowballs at buses. This was more exciting than aiming at each other. A bus was a great big moving target, and there was a satisfaction when you broadsided one with a well-

packed icy baseball that was primal, like bringing
down a mastodon with rocks. Plus, there wasn't
nearly the risk that a bus driver would pull over and
chase us on foot that there was when we threw at
cars.

There was a rivalry then between children and
adults that was healthy and born of mutual respect.
Yes, we ventured out of bounds now and then with
things like water balloons and snowballs. Hell, we
only had three TV channels to keep us indoors and
tranquilized. But if we got caught making mischief,
we took what we had coming to us. So what if we
used fake names when some enraged motorist managed to catch one of us for snowballing his car? At
least we showed him the respect of putting our tail
between our legs instead of getting in his face and
daring him to mete out some discipline.

Mr. McGuire wondered aloud about changing
dynamics at his retirement party years ago when he
told Jean Leonard that kids weren't the same as they
used to be. I guess getting them to yank up their
pants was tougher than getting them to tuck in their
shirts. I wonder if he ever tried replacing "Russian
Spy" with a game called "Islamic Terrorist." I wonder if it could be parents who've changed.

During the 1960's Des Moines still had two
daily newspapers, both of which were published by
the Cowles family. In the morning, *The Des Moines
Register* was delivered by an army of children that
included my brother Mark. The *Register* was highly
regarded; a paper that won Pulitzers on the news

side as well as the one that was awarded for the photo sequence of "The Johnny Bright Incident."

The *Register's* sports pages were staffed by a core of reporters that stayed at the paper for many years and gave it a continuity and familiarity that many Iowans of my vintage still miss. Maury White, Buck Turnbull, Bill Bryson and Ron Maly supplied the stories and numbers that I devoured every day right down to the last morsel of agate type [Turnbull's son Gary was a classmate of mine who shall resurface later]. There were also syndicated features like the columns of Jim Murray from *The Los Angeles Times* and "You Be the Quarterback," a multiple choice quiz published under the auspices of Duffy Daugherty, the football coach at Michigan State. A game scenario would be described and the reader would then try to select the right play call from the four options provided. It gave us something to argue about on the way to Hubbell in the mornings and helped set the mood for tossing the football around with Mr. McGuire before school.

On Sunday mornings in the fall there was nothing like a plump, juicy "Big Peach" for breakfast. "The Big Peach" was the name given to the Sunday sports section because of the tinted newsprint it ran on. The *Register* became famous after the Bright incident for the aerial sequence photography that decorated its sports pages during the football season. Directional arrows were superimposed on the black and white shots that showed how key plays developed from start to finish. The technique was a bit like primitive motion pictures and thawed back to life moments frozen in time by still photography.

The afternoon paper was *The Des Moines Tribune*. The thing I best remember about the *Tribune*, defunct since 1982, is Gordon Gammack, who wrote a popular column. I always thought the unflattering headshot of Gammack that adorned his space resembled the Martians that appeared in one of my favorite episodes of *Superman* on TV.

The only kid on our block who had a *Tribune* route was Stu Dean. *Tribune* carriers had to deliver Monday through Friday after school. They got Saturdays off to rest up before making their rounds with the obese Sunday *Register* which even then seemed overstuffed with advertising.

Any paperboy would tell you that the worst part of the job was collecting. Delivery was more physically taxing, but required no people skills and could be accomplished whether or not a subscriber was home. Collecting subscription fees had to be done at night and involved actually approaching a house and ringing the doorbell to talk to someone instead of simply tossing a paper on the porch and moving on. Many of the customers you caught at home would make excuses why they couldn't pay for the last week's deliveries. Perhaps they didn't feel obliged to pay because their paper somehow ended up on the roof once in a while.

For all of his guerilla tactics in the ongoing skirmish with the carriers on the adjacent route,

Mark was a helluva paperboy. He had a way of folding the *Register* into a tight square that made it aerodynamic. The range and accuracy of his flings were inspiring, whether his target was a customer's stoop or the rooftop of a competitor's client.

In 1982 a twelve year old boy named Johnny Gosch disappeared while delivering the Sunday *Register* in West Des Moines. Two years later Eugene Martin vanished doing his route on the south side of town. Neither case was ever solved. Now all the paperboys are gone.

Mark made his newspaper rounds on a red Schwinn Tiger. If he forced me along he had to "buck" me; that is, give me a ride on his handlebars. That probably accounts for my aversion to riding on motorcycles. Stu Dean, to his credit, earned the money to buy himself a ten-speed bike through his paper route. His brothers had Stingrays. The Leonards all had bikes. My sisters had bikes. Sometimes I rode Mary's little blue Schwinn Tornado. It handled well and was sporty despite being a girl's model [it didn't have an emasculator running from the seat stem to the handlebars], but it wasn't mine. I had no bike of my own. Then one day dad returned from visiting his brother West and his family across town and announced that he had a bike for me. Well, sort of. He yanked something out of the back of the station wagon that was a bicycle only in the sense that it had two wheels, and even they looked odd; very pudgy. The thing had no fenders. The seat was quite ample; big enough to handle my whole butt and then some. All in all, my "new" bike looked like something a circus clown would ride. All it needed was a Harpo Marx horn to honk. I was the laughingstock of the block, but at least I was on the road – until one day when a pack of us took off on an aimless ride.

We headed up Kingman to Polk, then south a mile or so to Woodland where we hung a right and veered towards Waterbury. Waterbury Road was palatial houses on hills. Everything there was abundant – mature trees, old money and new cars. We were streaking along a slight downgrade alongside the remnants of what might once have been a decent creek but by then was little more than a moist, mossy ravine. Suddenly a small dog came at us from the mayor's front yard, yipping and nipping at our wheels and heels. I slammed on my brakes [which were not hand-operated] to spare the obnoxious cur. It was close, but the critter survived. My bike, however, did not. As the rest of the peloton shrank away from me I tried vainly to get my pedals turning again. They wouldn't move. I tossed the only bike I'd ever owned into the Waterbury ravine and pouted home.

The recklessness of our comings and goings was balanced by the comparative safety of our destinations. Sure we careened about with no seat belts no bike helmets and no adult escorts to and from school, but we were much more quarantined from exposure to corruptive temptations than are today's kids.

~ The Days... ~

We were at the mercy of a television industry bound by puritanical codes mandating that married couples should have twin beds and permitted four letter words no tangier than, "gosh" and "darn." Movies weren't rated in the early 60's because there wasn't much likelihood of one being significantly more or less erotic or profane than another. When we went to the movies it was usually in hopes of being scared, not titillated [unless it was a James Bond movie starring Ursula Andress].

Tickets for the Saturday matinees at the Varsity were thirty-five cents. A buck was good for a ticket, some candy or popcorn and a soda. The Capri was the closest theater to home, just across University from the Uptown, but the Varsity, just east of the Drake campus on 25th Street, catered to kids on Saturdays with an assortment of Tarzan adventures and Vincent Price horror films. Plus, we could ring doorbells all the way home after the movie.

Once, a carload of us was dropped off by Mrs. O'Reilly. Have I mentioned the O'Reillys? They lived across Kingman from us. Tad was an assistant football coach at Drake. His wife Sharon was real loud. Their son Jerry was my age, with Andy and Kathie as younger siblings. Anyway, Sharon insisted that Jerry eat a peanut butter and honey sandwich en route to the movie. He threw it out the backseat window after hollering, "Mom, look out!" and pointing the other way; then, after she dropped us off, Jerry, with only fifty cents in his pocket, created a diversion so his four bits could all go towards treats. He appropriated a pooch aimlessly wandering the neighborhood and redirected it into the Varsity's lobby. In the ensuing scramble to capture the dog and get him back outside, Terry scooted unseen and uncharged into the theater.

The Saturday matinees even included prize drawings for lucky ticket stubs. When the Varsity had a look-alike contest to coincide with their showing of *The Adventures of Huckleberry Finn*, guess whose older brother and sister made him dress up in overalls and straw hat and go to the show barefoot? At least that get-up didn't include any of our mother's unmentionables.

The worst movie I ever saw at the Varsity was *Heidi*. Gary Turnbull, the son of *Register* sportswriter Buck, took a bunch of classmates there for his birthday in third grade. Gary was my opponent in one of the few schoolyard bouts of my youth; the only one I can ever remember clearly winning. We were in first grade then, and my sixth grade brother was impressed by the faint trickle of blood leaking from Gary's forehead when the contest was stopped, probably by Mr. McGuire. Perhaps *Heidi* was his long-awaited revenge on me, though to have inflicted her also upon the other innocent guests that day would have been uncalled for. All I know is that we were all promised a Wolfman movie all week at school before the party. Gary suffered the social consequences of that faux pas clear through high school, by which time he too was known as Buck and co-edited, with me, the sports section of *The Roosevelt Roundup.*

Besides the Varsity we did sometimes go to the Capri. I know I saw, *It's a Mad, Mad, Mad, Mad World* there. There was also the Ingersoll, located on the wide avenue of the same name, about a mile south of us, but it did not cater to our demographic. *The Sound of Music* had a run there in excess of a full year.

The most viable alternative to the Varsity for a Saturday movie outing was to go – cue the Petula Clark soundtrack – downtown.

An excursion downtown took more loot than I usually could muster, but was worth it if you had it.

We took the bus. We'd get off at City Drug, right next to the Greyhound bus depot and do some people watching before strolling to the Des Moines, the Paramount, or the Orpheum. They all had indefinitely closed balconies which made great bomb bays. Everything from spit to canned soup [simulated vomit – Jerry O'Reilly] was known to rain down from the forbidden upper reaches. Seats on the main floor were chosen with that in mind.

After the movie the next stop was Jimmy C's, a good old fashioned walk-up pool hall for an hour's worth of racks. The coup de grace was a stop at King's where we ordered Cheez Frencheez via the telephones all of the booths included, like the ones in big league dugouts that managers used to call the bullpen to tell relief pitchers to warm-up. Cheez Frencheez were deep-fried equilateral triangles of bread stuffed with molten yellow goo, sort of a volcanic grilled cheese sandwich. Sometimes it became necessary for the poor folks at King's to remind us it was about time we got home after we'd called the bullpen and ordered a couple dozen relief pitchers in addition to our Cheez Frencheez.

We were always home in time for dinner. Dinner was always at six; at least it was at our house. Surprisingly, we seldom ate dinner at each other's homes. Our family ate on the cheap, but our mom was a great cook. I don't know about Marsha Dean, Jean Leonard or Ella Donald. Once when mom was cooking for the Dean boys while Marsha was away she made them hot beef sandwiches from the previous night's leftover pot roast. I couldn't believe it when they all passed on the gravy! Gravy, the precious derivative of beef, pork and poultry, Gr on the culinary table of the elements, right up there with bacon grease [Bg].

Mom was Madame Leftover. Cold mashed potatoes were transformed into potato patties that featured a thin, golden brown skin courtesy of the saved bacon grease they sizzled in. Yesterday's extras could always be added to a white sauce and served over toast. One thing she insisted on was that brand names not be advertised on her table. If a ketchup bottle was required for the meal, she would remove the Heinz label with hot water. Other condiments were spooned from small serving dishes and beverages were filtered from their original containers through pitchers or decanters if they were provided more than a glassful at a time.

Besides poached eggs on toast, mom was big on oatmeal for breakfast. She thought the fact that it would "stick to your ribs" was a good thing, but in my mind's eye a vision of goop dripping from the cage that enclosed my heart and lungs wasn't appetizing. I would only eat the stuff after it was buried in the camouflage of butter, brown sugar, milk and syrup, and even then only on cold winter mornings.

I liked peanut buttered raisin toast. I'd plunk a couple of slices in the toaster and standby, peering inside as the heating element began to glow red hot. The scent of bread turning to toast was my cue to take up the knife and get ready to baste each slice with a primer coat of butter laid over as rapidly as possible with a slathering of peanut butter. Then I'd hold the almost finished product upside down, one slice over each slot, to use the residual heat from the toaster as a means of melting the yellow and brown butters into a breakfast plasma. I never really cared for straight raisins or raisin bran, but raisin toast is an extravagance of my youth that I expect to occasionally enjoy the rest of my way.

Bologna was known as lunchmeat. Somehow our mother could make a one slice of lunchmeat sandwich into something tasty and substantial. Partly it was the undercoat of butter. Partly it was her presentation. She'd quarter the sandwich and fan it across a small plate accessorized by apple wedges, carrot sticks, sweet pickles and a few chips. She wasn't much for cookies. Mom didn't do a lot of baking and when she occasionally brought home store-bought cookies they were invariably a bag of rather dry, small discs called Pecan Sandies. Sandy they were too. Sometimes when her mother was visiting from Slater they'd collaborate on batches of sugar cookies – sugar beat the hell out of sand – but Grandma Hillestad's notions about treats reflected a heavy Norwegian influence that resulted in a lot of kringla and lefsa. Kringla is sort of a bland, doughy pretzel and lefsa is like a buttered tortilla made from potatoes, sprinkled lightly with sugar and rolled up like a cigar. Not bad, but hardly the stuff of cobby-wobbles.

Slater was only about twenty miles north of Des Moines, a very small town where we lived before moving to Kingman Boulevard. We'd often go there for Sunday dinner at Grandma's dinky house where she lived alone, having been widowed in 1947. She lived on Story Street in Story County, next door to her sister and brother-in-law, Minerva and Harold. Her street wasn't paved. An annual or so coating of hot oil combined with what little traffic meandered by kept the gravel down. We'd eat stalks of wild rhubarb out of her yard while waiting to be called in for feasts of Swedish meatballs bathed in brown gravy. Mark swears I once downed more than fifty at one sitting. Maybe so – after all, they were bite-sized. Grandma made rice pudding and custard for dessert, neither of which would I eat. Mark especially loved her rice pudding. After dinner, which served mid-afternoon, someone was always sacrificed to Grandma at the checker board. None of us can recall that she was ever defeated. An otherwise gentle, quiet woman, Anna Hillestad was an assassin in checkers. Apparently she didn't believe it was in our best interests for her to tank a match the way adults often do when opposed by small children in parlor games. She would slaughter us, each in our turn, and then just grin as she cleared the board for the next game.

Her cooking talents and methods were in stark contrast to those of Grandma Wellman, who was a teacher and spent apparently little time in the kitchen. Grandma Wellman lived with Uncle West and his family when we were small and was as good at Scrabble as Grandma Hillestad was at Checkers. Sometimes she'd baby-sit the four of us and if such an assignment ran over the dinner hour, we had no choice but to resort to drastic measures. Grandma Wellman made French toast by forking a slice of battered bread and holding it over the open flame on our gas stove. So you can imagine why, if she was preparing an evening meal for us, we'd have to execute *Operation Ringback* as follows: One of us would be excused from the table, ostensibly to go to the bathroom. Once upstairs that person would lift the receiver on the upstairs phone, dial 1-1-9-1-1 and quickly hang up. That sequence was known as "dialing ringback," and when it made the phone ring, Grandma would get up from the table to answer the downstairs extension. While she was gone our plates were scraped into the garbage.

Grandma Wellman was small but hardy. After

moving from Uncle West's home to a small duplex a few blocks from there, she tilled and tended a substantial garden well into her eighties. Once in a while I'd mow her lawn with Uncle West's power mower. When I finished she'd fetch me a room temperature tumbler of yellow water she liked to call lemonade. It was no more refreshing than dishwater. As soon as she resumed weeding the garden with her trusty hatchet I'd dump my beverage in the freshly cut grass, half expecting it to wither and discolor on contact.

Sometimes I'd meet kids from other schools who'd had my grandmother as a substitute teacher. After many years in the public schools, she was mandatorily retired, so she started teaching in the parochial system even though she was a staunch Episcopalian, i.e., a Catholic as diluted as her lemonade. They invariably liked her, describing her as both firm and funny, a rare combination in a teacher, but a hallmark of the best ones. She didn't hear too well as the years passed. In church at St. Luke's her "whisper" could be heard from the back pews to the altar.

"Ward, there's Mrs. Oldbiddy. She's the one who inherited all that money and doesn't give any of it to the church."

I never knew either of my grandfathers. They had passed from the scene by the time I arrived upon it. But their widows managed long and well without them, each living into their nineties.

The cross that every Sunday leads the processional and recessional hymns at St. Luke's is kept near the altar there, mounted on the wall under a small plaque that points out it was donated in the name and memory of Grace Wellman. That seems a fitting reminder of a woman who faithfully walked a considerable distance to and from church until her sons grew up, bought cars and took turns driving her.

For all the shenanigans the neighborhood kids rolled in with one another throughout the week, we did not rinse off together at church on Sunday. Besides our six-pack of Episcopalians and the Leonards' Lutheran affiliation, the Deans and Donalds too were Protestant families. Lon Donald was a deacon at Plymouth Congregational, the high-profile church in the Roosevelt district where the elders dressed out in pilgrim getups every Thanksgiving. This was the second compromise that he and Ella came to between his Christian Science upbringing and hers as a Lutheran. Before moving to 43rd Street they'd attended Westminster Presbyterian where Carl and Marsha Dean were married and maintained a nominal membership.

I was often envious on Sunday mornings when we were piling into the car to head for church just as Wayne, Stu and Craig were piling out of the house to shoot baskets, ride bikes or just plain fight with each other. One Sunday morning as we sat in the car waiting for dad the rest of us watched through the wire fence that divided our driveway from the Deans' backyard as Craig relieved himself against the brick foundation of his house. If I'd been embarrassed in kindergarten when spotted whizzing on a tree by a lone stranger, it was nothing compared to what Craig must have felt when he shook his tallywhacker dry, zipped it back in his jeans and turned around to see the car-full of us grinning back at him.

Mom rarely accompanied us to church for reasons that were never clear to me. She was involved with the ladies guild there, the Episcopal Church Women, or ECW, and was of strong faith, but her primary offerings to St. Luke's were her children and escalloped potatoes with ham, always a popular dish at ECW potlucks.

St. Luke's began just over a century ago as a Sunday school outpost of a downtown church before it became a parish in its own right. Resolute and humble, the little church persists just west of the Drake campus, nestled modestly amidst the oak trees on Forest Avenue. It's right around the corner from Drake's fraternity and sorority row on 34th Street, an interesting juxtaposition of attitudes and lifestyles. For instance, one Sunday morning after church we passed a frat house where a sofa had been moved onto the front lawn during the weekend's festivities. Sprawled across the furniture, swaddled in beer bottles was a quenched but exhausted student, for whom there'd apparently been no room at the inn. Away in this manger with him, rounding out the crude nativity scene was a mascot of faithfulness, a mutt dog, lapping alternately at the student and the beer bottles.

I know that our folks were prayerful even though the only prayer our family regularly shared outside of the liturgy at church was the blessing we asked each night at the dinner table. Were it not for the umbrella of intercessory prayers that covered us, well...I lacked the sense to come in from the rain.

* * *

The Dean property was like having a private playground next door. Sometimes for baseball games one of the Dean boys would hop on the lawn tractor and cut the grass while the rest of us scattered to our respective homes to collect flour from our mothers to sprinkle on the freshly mowed grounds for baselines. Everyone would inscribe a white t-shirt with a number and scraps of plywood were requisitioned from garages and basements and fashioned into scoreboards. Marcus Leonard once forced postponement of an elaborately planned doubleheader when he imbalanced the rosters by stepping on a sharp stick with one of his bare feet while laying down a baseline and had to go for stitches and a tetanus shot.

Games were frequently interrupted when balls were fouled into the Wolfs' or Donalds' yards. Fences were quickly hurdled, the ball was retrieved and the game resumed. Sometimes fair balls would bounce into the shrubbery scattered along the fence-lines and get lost. That still happens in the big leagues at Wrigley Field with its vine-lined outfield walls. I love that aspect of that place.

Once in a while we even played golf at the Deans. We'd tee it up just outside their back door and aim toward the Leonard house which was just beyond the range of our best drives. One year we all dared each other to enter the city junior golf tournament. Only Stephen Leonard and I followed through. I think I was nine, so he would have been eleven when we showed up just after dawn at the Grand View municipal course on the east side. Where were the rest of the guys from the neighborhood and worse, what the hell were all my country club classmates doing there?

"Hey Wellman, I didn't know you played golf!"

Well, how could they? I'd only just played my first round earlier that summer, a smooth 63 over nine holes with my dad while we vacationed with relatives in Minnesota.

A small, curious and discerning gallery assembled when I was summoned to the first tee and fired my first shot in competition. The faint sensation of impact that managed to make it all the way from the very outermost edge of my club back to my hands was commensurate to that experienced when a bug too small to be visible alights on one's outermost extremities. It was thoroughly disproportionate to the force of my mighty swing. Surely to have missed the damn ball altogether wouldn't have been as embarrassing as the interminable time required for it to bounce pathetically away, skipping like a sissy, at a right angle from its intended line of flight into the adjacent parking lot. Still arriving contestants regarded it with a perplexity that the sight of a golf ball rarely produces on the premises of a golf course. Ordinarily, one struck in the direction of a group of people causes them to scatter frantically, but this time people casually stepped aside as it trickled past and rolled finally and feebly to a stop under a car. Crawling under to retrieve it wouldn't have been so bad if I could've just stayed there, at least until the country clubbers stopped laughing, lost interest and drifted away. But I had to fetch it back in bounds, back from concrete to grass, and swat it I don't know how many times until I finally crested the hill of the first fairway and left my gallery behind. Funny, I don't remember how Stephen did.

Since our driveway was graveled I particularly cherished the basketball hoop next door. It offered the additional appeal of being hidden from the view out the Dean picture window because it was mounted on the back of their garage. This was crucial on days when I feigned illness to stay home alone from school. After everybody was gone I'd sneak across the Dean backyard to the basketball court. There were even times in the winter when I'd shovel the court if I had to. Then I'd play an entire game, both teams, keeping score, tracking the stats in my head and announcing the play-by-play out loud as I went. When the bouncing of the ball coupled with my animated descriptions of the fantasy playing out on the cement slab of Dean Arena drew the attention of Marsha Dean I had a hard time explaining myself to her. I had an even harder time explaining myself to my parents.

The Leonards too had a hoop, and theirs was free-standing. The fact that the Deans' hoop was mounted flush on the garage wall made it tough to drive to the basket there, especially when defenders were involved. We'd check each other into the boards like hockey players do. But the Leonard hoop better approximated what you'd find in an actual gymnasium. Consequently I had some of my best imaginary games there. I think I made more baskets at Leonard Coliseum than all three of the Leonard boys combined.

Beneath the Deans' cherry tree was a waste area that we used primarily as a quarry for dirt clods, a kind of munitions depot when the border skirmish with the neighboring Payne militia flared up. When hostilities subsided we'd find other uses for the wallow. Short tunnels were sometimes dug. Occasionally we'd fashion dormant volcanoes out of the dirt and raid the pantries for vinegar and baking soda that would induce eruptions. Occasionally we'd manufacture a batch of clods for a parley with the girls. How better to express my attraction to Lynnette Donald, for instance, than to hurl things at her? Her hair was blacker than the dirt I pitched at her like woo, nighttime dark, and her eyes seemed never quite wide open. They were sultry in a twelve-year-old sort of way. Purposely errant clods, apples and walnuts I threw in her general direction went over her head like esoteric poetry.

As it was, we boys had little use for the girls in our midst except to fight with them. Sister Mary gave as good as she got with the Dean brothers, battering Stu with her lunch box all the way home from school one day to indirectly offset the broken collarbone she sustained when Craig shoved her to the ground in a rousing game of tag. Carrie Leonard too was grubby and tomboyish then, though looking back I can see that her Nordic prettiness was already emerging. Laura Donald kept above the fray as much as possible, sensing perhaps that such a vantage point would only get safer and smarter in the years to come. From an early age she helped out in the nursery at Plymouth Church, priming for a career as a teacher.

When I was still relatively alone in the neighborhood I played a lot of cowboy. Westerns were still a popular movie genre then and besides Matt Dillon there were the Lone Ranger and Roy Rogers taming the Wild West on television. My cowboy credibility got a real shot in the arm one day at the Roosevelt Bootery. We'd gone there for a new pair of Red Ball Jet sneakers, but instead I came out sporting a flamboyant pair of cowboy boots. After stopping off at the drugstore for a now more authentic than ever Marshall Matt Dillon rootin' tootin' root beer, I sauntered home practically daring some badlands bad-ass to mess with me. The Smythes next door were pouring a new driveway that day and invited me to leave my boot

prints in the wet cement, sort of like asking Gene
Autry for his autograph. Stepping in with both feet,
I paused to let my mark sink in good and deep and
give all the paparazzi a chance to get a good shot.
When I stepped out of the gooey, gray batter I came
also out of my boots. The stuff was like quicksand
and while I'd managed to free myself I left it to my
mother to go back and salvage the boots which were
already markedly depreciated. I was briefly distraught, but soon realized that the gaudy boots were
more Roy Rogers than Matt Dillon anyway. All
Rogers had that I wanted was the magnificent, brilliant and obedient Palomino named Trigger. Other
than that, and notwithstanding all the bad-guy butts
he kicked in every episode, I thought Rogers was a
little effeminate with his spurs that jingle-jangle-
jingled and his loud, look-at-me cowboy ensembles.
His sidekick Pat Brady paled next to Dillon's man
Festus, and when it came to Dale Evans versus Miss
Kitty, well, as Lyle Lovett was to later sing, "I
couldn't bring myself to marry no ol' Dale." Not
that I desired Miss Kitty in matrimonial ways. The
fantasy was more along the lines of sweeping the
beer mugs from the bar at the Long Branch and
knowing her right there in front of Chester, Doc and
the good people of Dodge City.

In lieu of a palomino, the Kingman cowboy had
his trusty dog. Homer was a black mutt unac-
countably named after the man who owned the
bootery. He would have been no match for Rogers'
German shepherd, Bullet, but he was as loved.

Naturally, Homer had his counterparts in the surrounding families. The Deans had a black cat inspiringly named Furry and the Mantle namesake, a black lab mix that answered to the call of Mickey. The Leonards had a wirehaired terrier they liked to call Frisky. The rest of us called her Shut-up! Shut-up/Frisky was kind of menacing, especially while the Leonards were still settling in. She was wary of anyone approaching their house. The closer you got the more her alarm-bell bark descended until finally it became a sinister sort of mad scientist evil grin with just a slight show of fangs, daring you to make a run for the door.

She was mostly Stephen's dog and spared outsiders because he told her to, but there was another side of her that we never got to see.

Before the Leonards moved from West Des Moines to California Drive, Frisky went missing one night. She was pregnant. The family fanned out in a wide but vain search for her. Finally Dr. Leonard had to call it off when it grew late and dark. Sometime after the kids had been forced to their beds, he called them excitedly to the basement where he'd discovered Frisky giving birth on a pile of laundry. One from the litter was lifeless; the doctor in the house went to work but there was nothing he could do. He put the apparently stillborn pup back down next to its mother and was explaining the unforgiving laws of the jungle to his own litter when Frisky resuscitated her runt with one fell swoop of her tongue across the newborn's chops.

For years afterwards the whole family made sport of the great medicine man, the great healer who was upstaged one night in his own home by his son's dog.

Homer ran away – disappeared anyhow - and was eventually replaced by Mitzie, a two-year old, pre-named black lab. We started her out on a lengthy chain in the backyard until she got familiar with her new turf. One afternoon she took off sprinting in pursuit of a squirrel. We watched helplessly from the dining room windows expecting that Mitzie's neck was about to be snapped when she got to the end of her chain. Instead the chain snapped without her ever breaking stride.

She was in fighting trim when she came to us, but soon sniffed her way to Doc Treloar's, a small takeout rib shack at the Roosevelt Shopping Center. When her timing was lucky she was rewarded with leftover slabs and carcasses out the back door that would otherwise have found their way to the dumpster. Instead Mitzie lugged them home where she'd plop down in the maple's shade and gorge herself. Too soon she became as inert as the Sidneys' obese lab that lived halfway up the block on 44th and went by the gross misnomer, Jet.

The Donalds were cat people [especially the feline Lynnette]. They already had one named Tiger when they moved in and would add another [Bobby] from "the cat lady" after they'd settled. The cat lady was old and lived solitarily next door to the Leonards. She was like a mysterious gargoyle perched on our neighborhood, alone except for the seemingly countless cats and kittens that shared her reclusion. The night that a bunch of us pitched a tent to camp out in Dean National Park was an other-worldly mix of spooky story-telling beneath a star-spangled sky accompanied by the tortured chorus of caterwauling coming from the cat lady's place. More than one of us surely "marked our laundry" that night, my dad's phrase for being scared to the point of wetting yourself.

It wasn't hard to imagine that Homer's runaway was really a careless wander into the cat lady's lair where he was transformed in some ceremonial séance devised for turning dogs into cats – something along the lines of the bite of the vampire.

Still, even in the shadow of the cat lady, nothing went leashed on the block. Kids, cats and dogs careened so freely and so fearlessly that a scary night spent outdoors was a thrilling change of pace.

Of course, no one went near the cat lady's house on Halloween. We did make our rounds in a pack, but we were a cappella in terms of adult oversight. Costumed canvassers went door to door fattening pillow cases by swapping somersaults and bad riddles for candy. Free-wheeling bands of teens basted cars with eggs and shaving cream.

One memorable Beggars' Night Mark sustained more damage to his teeth than years' worth of candy chewing could have done.

Mark and some adolescent associates were throwing crab apples at cars near an intersection that served as the gateway to Des Moines' "south of Grand" district where the money was even older than Waterbury's – not exactly a rough area. The true story is that some older teens took offense to their car being pelted with a hail of apples, stopped and gave foot chase. In the dark and away from the block that he knew like the back of his hand, Mark fled around a corner into the parking lot of an apartment house where he collided at full tilt with a pole that supported a section of the chain link fence around the perimeter of the lot. After he regained consciousness he walked home three teeth lighter.

At home the story that went into the record of that night omitted the parts about the apple throwing and the fence post and replaced them with a sad tale of purloined goodies and Halloween highwaymen punching an innocent kid's teeth out.

I think the rest of the family tolerated Mark's gross tricks at the dinner table with his false teeth for years to come because we wanted to see them as evidence of his unsinkability, a tough refusal to pout over a scarring we all believed had been inflicted by thugs upon an innocent, if mischievous, boy.

Greater Kingman Boulevard teemed with black cats and dogs, but there were virtually no black people in our experience. I remember a kid named Ronnie Welch from the early school days at Hubbell. Ricky Claytor and Bobbie Stanton were teammates during my last season of Little League. When Roosevelt won the state basketball championship in

1965 one of the main cogs was Ken Whitney, but besides being the only black player on that team, he was one of the very few blacks in the student body at what was then one of the largest high schools in the state.

So we didn't have much frame of reference when civil war broke out along racial lines in the early '60's. Passage of sweeping civil rights legislation in 1964 was too little too late to head off the racial strife, and by the summer of 1965, just after Martha graduated from high school, race riots started breaking out in cities across the country from Los Angeles to Detroit to Newark to Washington D.C. Des Moines, though, was still nicely air conditioned, too white to absorb much of the heat being thrown off by larger, blacker cities.

Probably one of the first black people our family ever dealt with directly was Luther Glanton, a local judge who would preside over the dispositions of some of the juvenile mischief perpetrated by first my brother and later, me. He was flamboyant, high-profile and well-regarded on our local scene, but not a civil rights activist beyond the example he may have been to Des Moines' relatively small black population.

I am quite certain that I never heard either of my parents use the word nigger. They never said or did anything that disparaged another race or betrayed any sort of bigotry lurking in them. Neither, though, did they instruct us as to how we should relate to and treat people who looked overtly different from us. Such instruction would have been almost entirely theoretical since, as a practical matter, pretty much everyone we saw everywhere we went looked pretty much the same as we all did. I really had no idea what was going on out there except a vague notion that blacks were a downtrodden people. The ones I was most acutely aware of were athletes like Ernie Banks and Billy Williams on the Cubs, or Iowa Hawkeyes like Larry Ferguson in football and Chris Pervall in basketball. It didn't occur or matter to me that they were black, but I remember an example of someone else taking notice of Ferguson's, uh, uniform.

Iowa's colors are old gold and black. The story that I remember about the radio broadcast of a Hawkeye game was probably apocryphal since I cannot document it, but I remember hearing it told many times. The announcer was Al Coupee, a former Hawkeye himself who'd been a member of the school's famed "Ironmen" squad of 1939, a team that included Iowa's lone Heisman Trophy winner, Nile Kinnick. Ferguson fielded a kickoff during the game and began weaving through traffic until he found an opening and turned on the speed. As he raced toward the goal line Coupee, whose son Eddie had been the star slugger on Mark's county championship little league team incidentally, got increasingly excited counting down Ferguson's sprint toward the end zone: "He's at the 50, the 40, the 30...Jesus Christ folks, look at that black---*jersey* go!"

Coupee's better judgment just barely managed to throw a career-saving block and Ferguson scored unslurred.

Racial upheaval was one of the tributaries of the great river of change flowing throughout the land and reshaping American life as profoundly as the Missouri and Mississippi rivers that carve Iowa's western and eastern borders. Strong currents were developing that would sweep even kids on Kingman Boulevard into an unprecedented mainstream.

Somewhere in the shuffle of assassinations, space flights and racial warfare the Beatles sneaked into the American consciousness. Our family didn't make a regular point of watching variety show television, but I know we were tuned in the night Ed Sullivan introduced John, Paul, George and Ringo to immortality. The next morning I walked to school down 43rd Street with Wayne, Stu and Craig Dean. We were joined by Marcus Leonard when we got to the island. From there to Hubbell we all sang, *I Wanna Hold Your Hand,* plodding through the February slush, stocking caps atop the crew cuts that would soon begin to disappear.

It's hard to overstate the impact of the Beatles. Even carpets got shaggy in the wake of their emergence as a force of popular culture, if not nature itself. Beatles trading cards competed with baseball cards for shelf space. The boys from Liverpool drove a second wedge into the steadily widening "generation gap" first opened by Elvis Presley, the musical terrorist of the '50's. Girls began squealing uncontrollably and teachers like Mr. McGuire felt they had no choice but to arm themselves with scissors in defense against the growing menace of growing hair.

At our house we stood fairly firm in the face of this first wave of sea change. I wasn't about to forego the half a buck I got every time mom touched me up with her shears and Mark's butch wax had no place on a Beatles cut. Martha kept playing Ricky Nelson and Neil Sedaka 45's on her phonograph for the most part and Mary was more into Nancy Sinatra go-go boots, the ones made for walkin', than she was into shrieking at the sight of the "fab four."

Calmly presiding over our little corner of the changing landscape were Ward and Mildred. When mom started working as a librarian dad began taking the bus to work since we had just the station wagon. On Fridays after work he'd get off the bus at the Roosevelt Shopping Center and stop at the florist there to get mom a single rose before walking the last couple blocks home. He always made a point of complimenting her meals and thanking her for preparing them, and he expected us kids to do likewise.

Our mother thought no less of our father than he did of her. She used to say that everybody should have the chance to stand next to dad at a ballgame when the national anthem was played. He wasn't one to just go through the motions of anything. He kept his politics and patriotism as private as his faith, and it was not his way to judge others on the basis of their leanings in these areas, but his reverence at appropriate times and places made clear his appreciation for the blessings and duties that he believed attended his own life.

They so obviously loved one another that it never quite fit to notice that they didn't share even the same bedroom, let alone the same bed. Even allowing for the fact that the prevailing TV standards forbid married couples like Ward and June Cleaver or Ozzie and Harriet Nelson to have anything in their bedrooms more carnally accommodating than twin beds, our parents' chastity seemed odd to me. Once when I spent the night at a classmate's house in fourth grade I was awakened in the middle of the night to see the naked silhouettes of his parents stealing down the hallway. I had never seen the likes of this at home. Of course, we all knew that dad snored like a Harley and that mom kept strange hours, reading her beloved books deep into the night. For all their mutual devotion they may simply have been nocturnally incompatible. Perhaps dad even had a touch of guilt-induced E.D. He wanted life to be easier and more comfortable for his family than he'd been able to arrange. But if that anxiety manifested in a flaccid marriage it was just their tough luck to have married at a time before television commercials began spreading the good news of pharmaceutical excitations. Too bad for all of us; I would have loved to hear dad's commentary when a couple appeared on-screen, luxuriating out in the yard in their twin tubs, gazing stupidly into each other's eyes while the post-coital sun sets in concert with the recession of the man's magic wand.

If I didn't always understand the private dynamics of our parents' relationship, I was always securely blanketed by their belief in each other and our family.

Dad taught us to play Cribbage. I liked to watch him shuffle the cards. Even though he wasn't a big man his hands were oaken and venous. I have a memory of him once using them and nothing else to halve an apple that I'm not sure could have happened. He fondled the deck gently and the way he shuffled – loosely; like the cards were fragile; very unmilitarily - didn't fit with the way he did everything else.

When Mark would contrive some transparent cheat by *accidentally* dropping cards on the floor, dad would wink at me while Mark retrieved and rearranged them beneath the table.

Mom's game was Scrabble. She could have been the Grandma Hillestad of the Scrabble board, but instead insisted on staying out of the games to kibitz. We never knew which contestant would be the beneficiary of her patented late-game seven-tile, triple word score, triple letter Q, tide-turner that invariably decided the game. She'd carry one of us to a dramatic, come from behind win and then wander off to finish washing the dishes leaving the rest of the family to marvel and argue about her consultations.

Besides their children the great collaboration of our parents was *The New York Times* crossword puzzle that was reprinted in the *Register* every Sunday. In both contexts their partnership was a seven letter word for ardent that starts with d.

Our good early years together are perfectly rendered in a black-and-white snapshot taken on the occasion of my fourth birthday. I have the chicken pox and am gamely holding up four fingers to the camera. Next to me, Mark is pulling the tip of his nose up and back with an index finger making his nostrils appear cavernous and porcine. Mary's mouth is open wide, probably singing *Happy Birthday* to the brother she was then closest to in all ways. Martha looks guarded, enjoying herself, but only tentatively. Dad is in the foreground, facing the camera with a wide-eyed look of bewildered pleading on his face. All of us are wearing ill-fitting party hats. Mom is out of frame. She took the picture.

Martha's presence in that photo is an exception to her general absence from my album of childhood memories. Seniority was also obscurity for the most part. But there are some notable exceptions to the bit part she generally played in my formative years.

She was the protagonist in one of dad's rare outbursts of temper when she refused to comply with his order to relinquish the comics at the breakfast table one morning. One thing led to another and she ended up fleeing the scene with dad in pursuit. When he reached to grab her from behind in the front hallway, she eluded his lunge and his arm

went through one of the glass panes in the front
door, severely gashing his forearm. Seeing him
bleed so freely was an unsettling revelation of his
mortality that now ranks right alongside the first
time I saw him shed tears when he was out of work
for a time a couple years later.

Martha inadvertently wounded dad again when
she was learning to drive several years later. Always petite, she was having a hard time mastering
the subtleties of a lumbering Chevy station wagon
with a manual transmission. As if that weren't
enough to deal with, she had to contend with Mary
and I as back seat passengers one day when dad was
giving her some pointers while she attempted to
drive the car the short distance up the driveway,
around the back of the house. With Mary and I
howling in her ear Martha panicked when she realized she was on a collision course with our tether
ball pole. "Step on the brake!" dad hollered several
times. "Where is it?" Martha cried, pulling her
hands off the steering wheel and covering her eyes
in a desperately vain attempt to disengage herself
from what was about to happen. Just in time, dad
reached down and across the front seat and plunged
the brake pedal to the floorboard with his hand. We
stopped so suddenly and abruptly that he pitched
forward into the dashboard and chipped a tooth.
Mary and I were practically applauding. Martha was
so distraught that she wouldn't obtain her driver's
license until many years later, well after she'd
graduated college, flown as a trans-oceanic stew-

ardess, married and was starting a family.

In the fall of 1965 Martha left for the University of Iowa and Mark returned from Shattuck to rejoin his classmates, including Fred Donald, at Roosevelt as a junior. I was a sixth grader at Windsor and Mary was still at Hubbell along with Stu and Craig Dean, Phil and Carrie Leonard and Laura Donald. Wayne Dean, Stephen Leonard and Lynnette Donald were all at Merrill. The built-in pecking order of the schools was beginning to sift and separate us. Besides the handy affiliations of the block, each of us was gradually finding pals elsewhere. My friendship with Tim Gebhart was becoming a primary one for me and the elders of the pack were naturally exploring across gender lines. Shenanigans that hadn't previously exceeded, say, sneaking into the Home Carpet store at the Uptown Shopping Center to hide inside the giant rolls of rug and snipe customers with pea shooters now began tiptoeing into areas with darker implications and potentials.

Tim and I sneaked a couple of his dad's L&M's one day only to have Tim preemptively confess that we'd been smoking, unprovoked by any suspicion or interrogation from his parents whatsoever. Speak for yourself pal, I remember thinking.

Another time when he was sleeping over, we'd just gone to bed after watching the late scary movie [I think it was *The Wasp Woman* – about a scientist with the head of a bee, not a white lady] when Mark arrived home. He came into our shared bedroom with mom right behind him, interrogating. Mark sat down on the side of his bed, heavily scented breath bellowing across the room, kicked off his shoes and fell over on the floor.

Tim and I played possum, just like I tried to do every Sunday morning when dad made the bedroom rounds to rouse us for church. Given the little success I ever had trying to avoid anything this way, it's been a surprisingly persistent technique of mine.

Not only were the older friends and siblings figuring out the various ways that boys and girls, uh, connected, they were also starting to drive and get jobs. Mark drove me to little league practice at Raccoon Valley like a New York cabbie, reaching speeds I didn't think the Chevy wagon was capable of, careening round corners by clutching and downshifting, rarely bothering with the brakes. He was becoming increasingly an object of both fear and curiosity for me.

He also got a summer job as a lifeguard at Ashworth, the public pool in Greenwood Park. Ashworth was the place where couples would rendezvous to entwine and float about in the simmering, shallow waters of young lust while squirts tried to splash the lifeguards with "can openers" off the diving board. I can picture myself bobbing along nose to nose with one of the local mermaids almost like a Cialis commercial with adolescent actors. When I was in my Ashworth prime I fancied myself Mike Nelson, the hero of a TV drama called, *Sea Hunt*. Nelson was played by Lloyd Bridges and he wore polo shirts with the collars up to keep his neck from sunburning. It was just a bonus that they looked cool that way. Nelson/Bridges must have been the greatest aqua-pugilist to ever scuba dive into the ring, possessed of a devastating short right hand that, even underwater, rivaled the punch Cassius Clay used to knock out Sonny Liston in 1964 and win the heavyweight championship. He was the captain and one-man crew of a charter boat who somehow got mixed up in every episode with malevolent smugglers and treasure hunters. His voice narrated the underwater action scenes and his trademark line was, "suddenly my air hose was cut!" No matter; knives and spear guns were no match for this amphibious stud.

In winter the skating rink that was fashioned every year on a plateaued portion of the fifteenth fairway at Waveland became the neighborhood's youth parlor. Afternoon hockey games gave way to a floodlit night sky above the rink and warming house, fogged a deep blue-gray by cigarette smoke and hormonal steam. Cold, dry winds combined with awkward, novice kisses to chap lots of lips. I went many times to the rink at Waveland and I still have never been on skates in my life.

* * *

It was circa '65 when we had our great barn fire. The out-building behind our house truly was a barn. Its interior was floor-planned into stalls and a hay-loft. Sometimes when the Ahrold clubhouse was unavailable after one of our Playboy capers, we'd repair to the barn and unfurl the centerfold in the hayloft. Otherwise it wasn't used for much besides serving as an oversized tool shed.

Late one afternoon, a school day it was, smoke suddenly began billowing from the roof of the barn. KIOA, a local radio station popular with teenagers whose frequency was 940, had a promo running whereby anyone who called in a hot news tip won $9.40. Mark was the first on the scene, and he hollered at me to run inside and call KIOA and the fire department, probably in that order, while he advanced toward the fire with our garden hose. Mom ran outside screaming at Mark to stay back and almost immediately it seemed like the whole neighborhood had surrounded our house. Since it was only the barn ablaze and not the house I reveled in the fiery spotlight unfettered by worries about where we would live and what would become of us. The firemen finally managed to maneuver an engine within spitting distance of the flames and extinguished them. In the aftermath of the great event, their only explanation as to the cause of the blaze was that a squirrel had possibly carried a smoldering butt into the loft and dropped it in a pile of old leaves. That begged the question of how prevalent smoking was among rodents, which went unanswered.

The argument between Mark and I as to the split of the KIOA news tip proceeds was rendered moot when we were trumped by someone else with a

more spectacular story than "Squirrel Sets Boulevard Barn Ablaze." Maybe if I had shared my sus-
picions about the origin of the fire and the fact that
Mark had once torched a field in rural Slater before
we moved to Des Moines I could have gotten all of
the money to myself. But $9.40 wasn't enough,
even that long ago, to sell him out in an expose:
"My Brother the Barnburner."

The 1965/66 school year also included my con-
firmation at St. Luke's. Father Elmer Johnson, our
kindly Rector who was Christ-like right down to the
carpentry sideline, presided over my preparation for
that ceremony. Recollections of my spiritual condition at that stage are murky beyond the dread with
which I approached the obligatory memorization of
the books of the Bible. The first half dozen or so are
all that I can still rattle off in proper sequence, a de-
cline that I trust is offset by resumed church attendance that is no longer compulsory.

It was about this same time when I attended my
first Annual Meeting of the parish. I had no real interest in the proceedings, but the meeting was held
right after the Sunday service and dad was going.
Since it was February and I had no other ride home,
I went with him. One of the routine orders of business was the election of new members for the Vestry, which is Episcopalian for Board of Directors.
I've forgotten who the other nominees were, but I
was incredulous that my dad wasn't among them.
No offense to the rest of you, I thought, but my dad
is just about the most faithful man here. I rose to

place his name in nomination. The roomful of adults smiled sweetly, but the outgoing Senior Warden [Episcopalian for Chairman of the Board] made the point of order that, by diocesan rule, I was too young to participate on the record. Fortunately, one of the elderly parishioners that have always been plentiful at St. Luke's rallied to my cause and nominated my dad by proxy. Naturally he was swept into office by acclamation. By the time we left several people had approached and remarked on how proud dad must have been to have been nominated to the Vestry by his son. I think he was. I know that many times in the forthcoming years I fell back on that singular highlight of our relationship whenever I was besieged by waves of reflection on all the ways that I'd dishonored both of my parents.

Church was sort of the secret hideout for a lot of my feelings. At home love was abundantly demonstrated but rarely declared. The Cubs were a major artery for the circulation of affection between my father and me but not as easy to monitor then as they are now. Very few games were televised in Des Moines and none of the local radio stations were affiliates of the Cubs' radio network. Only occasionally were we able to tune in flagship station WGN all the way from Chicago. During the summers when the Cubs were on a homestand at Wrigley Field where all the games were still played in the afternoon, I'd call the sports desk at *The Register & Tribune* for updates on the score and highlights of the day's game. There was nothing I liked better than to greet my dad coming home from work with the news that the Cubs had won, flourished with details like home runs from some combination of Ernie Banks, Ron Santo and Billy Williams. Inasmuch as it was the Cubs we pinned our hopes on, there were never enough of those good news days in a given season to suit us, but over the course of many years the cumulative effect of the team on father-son batteries like us was profound. The Cubs were the perfect mascot for the unconditionality and permanence of our relationship. In lieu of an actual and public ceremony where parents and children pledge the sort of for-better-or-worse commitment that spouses proclaim at weddings, shared support of a cause as lost as the Cubs becomes part of the cement that bonds one generation to the next.

The Cubs' haplessness struck me as contributory to our also-ran status in the neighborhood. The Deans' superficial adoration of the vaunted Yankees was a direct result; I was sure, of the team's seemingly perennial appearance in the World Series. The Yanks were also fixtures on national "game-of-the-week" telecasts on Saturdays which tended to pit them versus a rotation of American League palookas. As a consequence of the Yankees' traditional success, their high TV profile and the Cubs' propensity for settling near the bottom of the National League standings, the Dean boys had plenty of ammo to lob over the fence at us losers. There they sat watching Mantle and Maris in first place, in living color, while we struggled to hear live accounts of the Cubs' inevitable defeat through the static of a faraway radio broadcast. They were just next door but they were in the penthouse and we were in the basement.

I think it was the summer of 1964 when I was to have a rare shot at some oneupsmanship on the Dean boys. Our family vacation, as usual, was a trip to Minnesota to visit relatives on our mother's side. The itinerary included two exciting side trips: the first was a day spent frolicking at the confluence of the Mississippi and the St. Croix rivers from our cousins' houseboat. After spending the night on the boat my Dad and I were supposed to go see the Minnesota Twins and Camilio Pascual take on the Yankees and Ralph Terry in a battle of ace pitchers! I fell asleep that night on the boat like a commodore on his yacht with visions of my first big league ballgame dancing in my head. I awakened in the middle of the night with badly swollen glands. Instead of heading to Minneapolis the next morning my dad and I headed home to Des Moines where I was diagnosed with a bad case of the mumps.

When CBS bought the Yankees in 1965 there was no reason to expect any meaningful change in what had become baseball's natural order of things. But not even baseball, not even the New York Yankees – the very logo of dynastic America – would weather the unraveling that marked the remainder of the decade.

In the fall of 1966 I moved on to junior high

school at Merrill. Merrill reunited me with old
school chums from my Hubbell days. Seventh grade
meant expansion of athletic programs. Up until then
Raccoon Valley had been about it. The rest of our
sports were staged mostly on our sandlots and
driveways. Outdoor basketball had been hampered
in-season by the cold, deflating air that took the
bounce out of balls. We used to always keep a
warm backup ball right inside the door at Tim
Gebhart's house so we could switch when a ball got
so cold it became like dribbling a stone with frost-
bitten fingers. Now we could play indoors in shorts
for the glory of Merrill! There was also "rec."

"Rec" was an open gym program offered at the
school on Monday and Wednesday nights and Saturday mornings. We flocked to it so we could practice dodgeball, basketball, smoking and making out.
It was an upgrade in terms of intimacy from
Ashworth and the skating rink. There was nothing
like branding your target in the gym during dodgeball while working yourself into an adolescent
lather, then slipping outside for orthodontic
smooches followed by a ceremonial smoke. We
took deep breaths of an atmosphere comprised of
perspiration, pheromones, tobacco smoke and Jade
East cologne. Here the profuse sweating that began
on or about my first day at Merrill and continued
unabated like a flood of biblical proportions
throughout the junior high years was an acceptable
sign of masculine vigor, not the dead giveaway of
pubescent self-consciousness that my sopping arm-

pits were in third period English.

More and more of us began pairing off in couples and going steady for durations approximating the life expectancy of a tsetse fly. Boy-girl parties started breaking out like acne in darkened basements. After a few minutes of nervous chip dipping and soda swigging, off went the lights and on went the music. You had to be officially linked to someone to get invited to these orgies. My personal record was a kiss that lasted the entire length of the song "Cherish," by The Association. By the time it was over most of the other couples had broken up with one another.

While I was just beginning my apprenticeship as a marathon kisser, Mark, five years up ahead on the road to sexual fulfillment, was going too far. Early in his senior year at Roosevelt the news broke that he was going to be a father. There was a wedding at St. Luke's after which Mark and his bride Marcia took up residence in what had been known as our attic, but now suddenly became "the third floor." Marcia was a sweet and talented girl who paid a high price for her acquiescence to my brother's charms. She was only a junior and not permitted to continue at Roosevelt as an expectant mother. She transferred to "Tech," the common name for the now defunct Des Moines Technical High School. Near the end of that school year, on May 24, 1967, Christopher Mark Wellman was born. His father, a co-captain of the Roosevelt High School baseball team, missed a ballgame on account of the birth.

Mark's counterpart at second base for that day's opponent made All-City; Mark was named to the 2nd team.

Against all odds the marriage of Christopher's parents would last about five years. One of the many happy byproducts of it, beyond Christopher's life itself, was the closeness he grew into with his paternal grandparents and, for that matter, his paternal aunts and uncle.

One night in June of 1968 I was hired to baby-sit my nephew. By then his parents had moved out of our house to an apartment not far away. Christopher was awakened by a soggy diaper which I felt both obliged and unqualified to change. I laid him on the bed to remove his wet pants and turned away to get a replacement. While I fumbled around the room for where the hell did they keep the diapers!?, I began to hear a splattering sound behind me. I turned around to see my naked nephew spouting like a fountain in the town square, much to his infantile delight and my dismay. Frantically, I stemmed the flow and adorned him in a new loincloth. As soon as I held him aloft it fell away onto the floor. Right on cue I heard Mark and Marcia slamming car doors in the parking lot outside the open second floor window. I couldn't wait to give them the news: "Christopher just peed all over the bed!" I announced out the window. They were so proud. I put him back in his crib and walked out of the bedroom to unlock the front door, oblivious to the television blaring loudly in the living room with news from California.

Bobby Kennedy had been shot.

Kennedy's assassination followed that of Dr. Martin Luther King by only a couple of months. When King was shot down in Memphis, it fell to Kennedy to break the news to a mostly black crowd in Indianapolis where he'd gone planning to make a campaign speech in his bid for the Democratic presidential nomination. He was advised by local officials to cancel his appearance in Indianapolis rather than put his safety at risk when word of King's murder inevitably exploded in his audience. Instead Kennedy himself delivered that sad, crushing news in a six minute speech that was actually interrupted a couple of times by applause. Some said that Bobby Kennedy was the only white man in America that would have been safe in that crowd that night. Ironically some sixty days later an adoring throng of his own most ardent supporters, wound as tightly around him as the fruit of a seed, was penetrated by a lone deranged hater who somehow drew near enough to kill him. Kennedy's life lay suddenly and unbelievably draining into a pool of hope and tears; another bloody mess on America's floor.

No wonder 1968 was the year that our sturdy father was stricken by a heart attack. He came home one night from a vestry meeting at church – in fact it was April Fool's Day – and after briefing mom on the local version of God's agenda [is there ever really any "new" business at church?] he started complaining that his chest and arms ached. I was upstairs in bed and I could hear him. I remember hoping that he was trying some lame prank owing to the date but when the ambulance pulled in the driveway I realized that downstairs someone might be dying that I'd once thought was indestructible. I was fortified when he refused to lie down on the gurney and insisted on walking out of the house for the ride to the hospital but he'd blown his last smoke ring.

There was smoke but never much drinking in our house when the kids were kids. Dad's obligatory beer after yard work was about it. Sometimes he'd let us take a sip if we asked and we'd always knot our faces at the taste. Our parents didn't entertain much and rarely went out. Occasionally dad's brother, our Uncle Russ, would drop by on a Saturday afternoon. His visits were unannounced but somewhat predictable. He was very taciturn, but given to wide, genuine grins and firm handshakes that combined to give me the real feeling of affection. Uncle Russ was in the insurance business and he loved to fish. He always brought with him some flavored brandy as an additive for the coffee his youngest brother served him. The third brother, West, was more garrulous than Russ. He'd pester me from behind in church into blasphemous games of tic-tac-toe while his brother, my dad, was in the pulpit delivering the readings. But West and Russ had fatherly tragedy in common. Before John Wellman was blinded and nearly killed by that shotgun blast in 1959, Russ and Aunt Pete [her given name was Frances, but everybody knew her as Pete, a fond abridgement of her maiden name, Petrie; along with mom's sister, Henrietta, who was known as Henry, we had two avuncular aunts] lost their son Rusty to illness in 1957 when he was nine years old and I was only three. I never knew him.

Dad and Uncle Russ would sit opposite one another, but their heads practically met in the middle when they'd lean across the table on their forearms to sip from each other's troubles in hushed tones; one mourning a son who never saw high school and the other perhaps calculating his accountability for a son who fathered a child before he graduated. But they never swallowed too much - just a wistful, brandied coffee or two at a time. They managed. Years later when I'd hear Uncle West speak of, "the Wellman curse" I understood better why it was always just dad and Uncle Russ at the Saturday tables. No matter what, I think those two felt themselves blessed.

There were sometimes sorrows at our house, but never one drowned.

Against a backdrop of racial unrest, generational strife, a big war in a small place and what felt like the slaughter of American leadership our astronauts kept banging away at the door to the moon until Neil Armstrong opened it and stepped across the threshold of science fiction in July of 1969. For real, we had lassoed the moon just like Jimmy Stewart promised Donna Reed he'd do for her in,

It's a Wonderful Life.

One night in the midst of all the confusion arising from heart attacks and babies and assassinations
and riots and protests and blastoffs I slipped away
from Kingman Boulevard and the first people I ever
knew. I wandered over to Waterbury Road, to practically the very spot where I'd tossed my balky,
clownish bike into the shallow ravine that trickled
through a neighborhood where everything else
flowed affluently.

By then Pandora's temptings came also in aluminum cans and opened with the pfoossht of a pop
top. Three of us shared a twelve-pack of Schlitz before taking to the streets. We marauded merrily
through the night ringing doorbells and cheerfully
fingering motorists who honked at us to get out of
the middle of the road. I remember having a tug-of-
war with my watch serving as the rope until it unraveled and had to be discarded much as my bike
had been another time. Wheeee!

I was fourteen.

In the aftermath of that experience I feared I'd
taken the first step down a path my brother seemed
lost on. At the same time I excused it as an almost
inevitable rite of passage for adolescents everywhere. In the months to come I actually took heart
when my first few attempts at encore performances
were thwarted when I couldn't drink enough beer to
produce the desired effects. I literally couldn't
stomach the stuff. The thought occurred during that
time that I was being led from temptation. But I

persevered and managed finally to acquire a taste for alcohol, little knowing that I'd first acquired an allergy to it.

As the decade wound down other cracks started to appear in the foundation. The Deans moved to a home on the stylish fringes of the Waterbury district in 1968. Stephen Leonard went from Boy Scout to rum-runner, smuggling contraband across state lines [Coors wasn't yet available in Iowa so trunks were filled with it on ski trips to Colorado]. If the Beatles were breaking up how the hell was our troupe of chums supposed to stay together? Wayne Dean, Marcus Leonard and I all played football on a team coached by Bill Reichardt, the gridiron hero turned clothier, but we were just random faces in the team picture. We were being absorbed by the wider world around us. As all-encompassing as the Dean backyard had been when first it opened to us, we'd all but abandoned it by the time that family moved. No longer hiking about our network of backyard, back-alley routes and shortcuts, I was thumbing rides to school on Polk Boulevard before I finished junior high. Instead of swiping a buck for baseball cards I was grabbing a pack of Winstons from mom's stash to share after school with the trendy crowd of rebels I was edging toward while writing eighth grade essays about my plans to get an athletic scholarship to college.

In ninth grade I was swept into office as Student Council President after bringing down the house with a smart-ass speech full of wisecracks. I also had the best campaign posters, all of them done by Mark's wife Marcia.

After pushing through a measure calling for pre-game introductions of the starting lineups at all home basketball games I got suspended from the team and almost run out of office when a school-skipping scandal dating back to that year's World Series caught up with me. A batch of parental notes for doctor and dental appointments I'd forged for a whole squad of classmates had been exposed.

I was eventually disgraced when my brother and dad showed up at Merrill to watch the battle of un-beatens between us and Franklin, the other junior high that fed Roosevelt. I wasn't even suited up. Sitting through this red light moment of my life at the intersection of wise and dumb I was ashamed and embarrassed but trying hard to spin myself as a spirited, causeless rebel. Rebellion was especially hip then but what did I have to rebel against? In lieu of any legitimate grievance I effectively decided to overthrow myself. The light changed and I went straight ahead on Dumb Street.

Just who were my new sidekicks as we crossed the threshold of high school? None of my previous mates ever really fell into disfavor – we were all just wandering the social woods, keeping each other within earshot while we explored new affiliations. Two of mine that emerged during the Merrill years were Robbie Farris and Jan Long.

Robbie and I met in the homeroom of Senor White, Merrill's Spanish teacher. Robbie was a

Cardinal fan so we were bonded in rivalry. We played many whiffleball games, one-on-one, where he was Bob Gibson and Lou Brock and I was Fergie Jenkins and Billy Williams. One of them was particularly memorable. Our backyard was dressed out as Wrigley Field. We'd even contrived a scoreboard which hung from the swing set. Home plate was at the back of our lot so the batter was hitting toward the house.

I clouted one up on the roof to break up a taut pitchers' duel. The ball almost crept over the peak toward the front yard but instead rolled back down before lodging in one of the gutters. No problem, I figured. I'll just get a step ladder, place it on the balcony and climb up on the roof to fetch the ball; nothing to it. Everything went as planned until I reached the roof and was reminded, in one terrible instant, of my acrophobia. I clung to a ventilation exhaust pipe that poked from the shingles, looking enviously down at Robbie standing smugly on the ground far below and laughing up at me. I was sure that if I released my grip on the pipe that I would slide over the edge and into the void. So steep seemed the pitch of the roof that I couldn't even tell where the balcony and the ladder were positioned beneath me. I was doomed. Robbie went inside and told mom that I was trapped in tense but hilarious limbo atop the house. She called the fire department. Soon there were as many emergency vehicles on our property as were summoned on the occasion of the great barn blaze. An amused crowd assembled giving rise in me to a strange mix of abject fear and profound self-consciousness. A policeman made his way onto the balcony, mounted the step ladder, stuck out an arm and basically ordered me to come down. I decided to go quietly rather than re-sist arrest and risk a rooftop struggle with the cops, but he'd be sorry, I knew, when I slid right past his grasp to an untimely death in full view of the whole neighborhood. Reluctantly I let go of the pipe and dug my nails into the shingles as a drag on my plummet. Next thing I knew I was standing sheep-ishly on the balcony while the officer admonished me not to make him come back there ever again. And so I didn't, but Robbie and I may well have met him elsewhere in contexts to come.

Jan Long lived in the house on the Waterbury hill where three of us first quenched our curiosity about alcohol. He was burly and competitive. We played lots of basketball games in his driveway, splashing shot after shot through the chain net that hung from the hoop in the back. Jan liked to host card games in his basement for small stakes. His parents stocked Frostie root beer by the case and Jan charged his guests a quarter per bottle when we gathered there to play cards. He called his rotund dad "pard" [short for partner] because they were great friends. They loved to hunt and play golf to-gether. Jan and Ned were best pals as much, maybe more, than they were father and son.

Robbie's father had died by the time we met. He too lived in the Waterbury area, though more modestly than the Longs. The three of us figured we'd be sixty per cent of the starting lineup when Roosevelt won the state title in basketball while we were there, just as the school had in 1965 when my sister Martha was a senior. I remember one night as ninth graders when we ran the hills at Waveland, swigging beer and puffing Swisher Sweets, chanting "RI-DER POW-ER!" [Roosevelt teams were the "Roughriders"], a cocky ode to the high school exploits we reasonably imagined were in store for us.

The summer of '69 before I started high school began so promisingly. The Cubs were in first of all places when Armstrong made his giant leap in July. That a man was actually walking on the moon made all things possible, even a notion as outlandish as the Cubs winning the pennant. In August Robbie Farris and I listened on the radio as Ken Holtzman threw a no-hitter against the Braves that included a blast by the great Hank Aaron into the teeth of a wind that spat the ball back into Billy Williams' glove on the left-field warning track at Wrigley Field.

When I reported for football practice at Roosevelt later that month I was excited about the prospect of someday playing for Lon Donald. I didn't expect someday to arrive so soon. During two-a-day drills before school started Coach Donald took me aside and said that I was being considered for the varsity but he wanted some assurance that I wouldn't screw up like my brother had. He told me that Mark was a fine athlete who wasted his chance to play quarterback at Roosevelt and instead wound up playing for the All-Center Bums, an informal social fraternity that was headquartered at the Roosevelt Shopping Center just east of the school grounds. I gave Coach Donald the assurance he sought and by the time school opened I was one of only three sophomores on the varsity, second-string quarterback behind a senior co-captain. I'd caught the eye of Barb Reichardt, daughter of Bill, and best friend of Lynnette Donald. Barb and Lynnette were both cheerleaders and they seemed anxious to cheer for me in particular. Lots of people were.

Life was straddling the line between pointless and purposeful. My bluff was being called. People were paying attention, and this time it wasn't because I fell out of a tree, or our barn was on fire, or dad had a heart attack or I was marooned on the roof.

The Wellmans, the Deans, the Leonards and the Donalds broke our huddle and took up positions that were new for us all.

Four
The Night...

Football players at Roosevelt in the late '60's all wore their hair short. On game days we wore a necktie to school to further the point. When Mark was on the team and I was still in grade school I watched him dress for school on football Fridays, both figuratively and literally looking up at him from my bed in our shared room. There was a blue and white "rep" silk tie that he liked to wear that almost certainly came from Reichardt's. I wore it too now that I was a Roughrider. I was about 6'1" and 175 lbs. as an entering sophomore and I felt quite special strutting through the corridors. I was sure that I cut a fine figure on the sidelines during games, dressed out resplendently in my #17 uniform.

I was not called upon in either of the season's first two games and didn't expect to be in the third. So my reaction was something of a double-take when suddenly I heard Coach Donald bellow, "WELLMAN" midway through our game with Des Moines Lincoln. The offense was struggling, so the veteran coach summoned the raw rookie from just around the corner to shake things up. I have no idea what he said to me as he ushered me into the fray. I'm sure he offered a play that I might suggest in the huddle as an ice-breaker. I remember not feeling the ground beneath my feet as I trotted from the sideline toward the huddle and also that some strapping Railsplitter called me out as an untested soph as I pranced skittishly onto the field. Now the white parts of my uniform were fairly glowing, a neon fabric shining like a beacon to guide defensive players to their target – me! The paralytic mix of fear and self-consciousness from my rooftop stalemate washed over me again and dripped from beneath my suddenly cumbersome helmet in the form of cold sweat. Somehow I stammered out a play call and made my way to the line of scrimmage, even managing to insert my trembling hands beneath the right pair of buttocks in our offensive line. I squealed out a cadence, the ball was hiked and away we went. I completed some sort of a fluttering screen pass to our fullback, a senior who was a close pal of the kid I'd replaced and probably just as anxious as the Railsplitters to dig postholes with me. Later in that series I lofted a long one that

Chuck Sears – another senior, the best player on the team and a hellion who treated me well – somehow came down with. We eventually scored on that drive, our only points in a losing effort, but I had done enough to shake up the depth chart.

On Sunday afternoons during the season the team gathered in the Donalds' basement to watch game film. Watching replays of my own exploits the Sunday after the Lincoln game was a disembodying sensation. Enough wisecracks punctured the darkness of the room that I knew I'd earned some respect and acceptance from the upperclassmen. The next day at school my name was posted on the locker room bulletin board as the first string quarterback heading into the next game with Hoover.

Hoover was named after the only native Iowan to rise to the presidency, Herbert Hoover. It had only been open a couple of years but was a natural rival for Roosevelt because it split the west side of town and siphoned off part of Roosevelt's attendance base. Roosevelt's days as one of the two or three largest high schools in the state ended with the construction of Hoover. The school chose Huskies for its nickname. Apparently the feeling was that nothing about Hoover's presidency lent itself to sports jerseys and headlines the way Roughriders and Railsplitters did in the case of the city's other two presidential high schools. Given that Hoover's term in the White House coincided with the Great Depression, what were they gonna call the school's athletic teams, "The Crash?"

Des Moines at the time only had three football stadiums to accommodate eight area high schools, the six public ones in Des Moines plus Valley, the public school in West Des Moines and Dowling, the area parochial school. That meant that every week three games were played on Friday night and one was deferred until Saturday. The Hoover game was slated for Saturday night. Practice went pretty well during the week as far as I can recall. I was soaking up attention as word spread that I was going to start the big game. It wasn't until I arose on Saturday morning - game day - that I started running a fear fever. I sought treatment for it with some guys that let's just say weren't on the football team. By lunchtime I'd broken the fever with several cans of a cold beverage. Unfortunately there were side effects including slurred speech, impaired judgment and loss of coordination. By mid-afternoon I'd been passed into the custody of Barb Reichardt who set about trying to sober me up before I had to report to school and suit up for the bus ride to the game. I tried to hold my breath the whole time my ankles were being taped in the locker room.

We lost the game 8-6. Our try for a two-point conversion that would have tied the game failed when my pass to Chuck Sears was batted away. I sort of whimpered all the way back to school on the team bus. When we got back and unloaded into the locker room to shower one of the assistant coaches took me aside. I figured he was going to console me and slap me on the butt and make me feel better. Instead he chewed me out good, more or less for being a crybaby. But he didn't ask me anything about how I'd spent the day preparing for my big chance – no one ever did. At the time I actually thought I'd gotten away with something that never would have happened anyway if we'd just played on Friday night, right?

I settled back in as second-string after that. We alternated between winning and losing and I still got a share of playing time, even throwing a long touchdown pass in the Tech game. The last memorable thing that happened with that team occurred in the middle of the season.

In mid-October protestors against the war in Viet Nam organized a worldwide moratorium day. Marches and demonstrations were staged nationwide and, indeed, around the globe. In Des Moines, the full context of this event would have to include the background of Tinker v. Des Moines Independent Community School District.

In 1965 three Des Moines high school students – John Tinker, his sister Mary Beth and their friend Christopher Eckhardt – wore black armbands to school in symbolic protest against the war. They were suspended and their parents sued. Eventually their case percolated all the way to the U.S. Supreme Court. On my birthday, February 24, in 1969 the court ruled 7-2 in favor of the students and their parents.

That was the backdrop against which one of my

teammates trotted onto the field for practice after school on Moratorium Day in October of the same year with a black armband accessorizing his football gear.

We were all assembled and loosening up for practice when Coach Donald arrived on the scene and began reviewing his troops, strolling between the evenly spaced rows of his regiment as we went through the humdrum of our routine calisthenics. Suddenly something caught his eye. He huffed into his whistle as though all the movement was a candle he was blowing out. Everything, everyone stopped. Coach Donald strode toward the armband like a dart to a bullseye. "Hell's bells Murphy," he hollered, "what the hell is that?" pointing at the offending article as though it were a section of used toilet paper.

"It's an armband sir." stammered Murphy timidly.

"What's it for?" demanded Coach Donald.

"I'm protesting, sir." Murphy countered as he backpedaled into the ropes.

"Protesting what?" Coach Donald probed.

"The war, sir." Murphy mumbled, more like a timid child than a robust young man outfitted in a full suit of football pads.

"Get the hell off of my football field!" thundered Coach Donald, and Murphy was gone before the count got close to ten. His case never saw the light of day.

My dalliance with Barb Reichardt, who was a

junior by the way, lasted through Homecoming. But by the time football gave way to basketball I was swimming in senior waters. Much to my surprise the girl I thought Roosevelt's most popular and desirable had taken an interest in me. She too was a cheerleader, not to mention a gymnast and a comely blonde, and I gladly risked the enmity of the senior class guys to get at her. I was smitten but good and a relationship ensued that ranks still as the best part of my high school years. We spent a lot of time in her mother's Cadillac and one of the things I learned there was how to drive. She was popular for good reasons in addition to the usual, superficial ones. She was bright and funny and kind to everybody so everybody liked her, including my parents. I was convinced then that I'd found the girl who would be the woman of my life. I suppose it's not uncommon for high school romances to hit that hard before someday being recalled with a chuckle. But I did love Jane.

We went together to the school's winter dance where I emerged from the bathroom with the zipper on my suit pants broken. Had I been sober I imagine I'd have also been embarrassed, but I wasn't, so I wasn't. In the spring she asked me to the "Spinsters' Spree," and if I'd forgotten that I was drunk on that occasion too, the picture that we had taken at the dance would remind me.

Of course I was not the lone drinker at Roosevelt. There were plenty of jocks who drank, for instance, just not too many besides me that drank on the day of a game.

During the basketball season there was a game during which mom sat right behind our bench passing Certs to Robbie Farris and me to camouflage our beer breath. I'd forgotten that. Now the memory of a real experience feels false upon retrieval. Many things that I know happened feel dream-like now, and countless more have sunk forever into an abyss of blackout.

I was arrested for the first time before that basketball season ended and launched a prolific career in juvenile court. The charge was "illegal possession of beer" and the consequences were twofold: six weeks' suspension from the basketball team [which in turn prevented a promotion to the varsity for post-season tournament play] and a sentence to attend Saturday morning court classes. Penalties imposed at home didn't go beyond roundtable discussions between me and my parents.

The court classes were sessions where teens caught drinking sat in the gallery while the Friday night "drunk tank" was dumped out in open court for arraignment. It was a good concept: show the party punks what kind of fire they're playing with. But it didn't have the intended effect, at least not in my experience. The kids made sport of the poor denizens from skid row, snickering when one of them said, "under a bridge" in response to the court's request for an address. When Judge Glanton asked the sot to be more specific we figured we were supposed to laugh at his reply of, "down by the river."

I was an alcoholic before I was old enough to drive and the incongruity of that sequence of milestones in my life blends pretty well with the times in retrospect.

America itself was out of order. Drugs were the emerging menace. It didn't occur to anyone, especially my parents and me that a red-blooded fifteen year-old kid who was good at sports and standardized tests and girls might also, and most notably, be a drunk.

Once mom showed me an article from some academic journal she'd found reprinted in Reader's Digest. It asserted that only a very confident, secure and focused teenager could abstain from drugs during those times. Pap like that inflamed her denial of a growing problem. When mom cited that research she was still right as to my abstinence from "real" drugs [alcohol and nicotine were generally excused from classification as drugs by the thirsty, smoky masses], but otherwise she and Reader's Digest couldn't have been further from my truth.

The days of bellying up to the soda fountain at the Roosevelt Pharmacy for a Marshall Dillon mug of root beer had passed. Now pods of teens clustered at dusk across the street from the shopping center in the parking lot of Matulef's, the neighborhood's family owned grocery. Any young adults that pulled in were tentatively accosted as they emerged from their cars and beseeched to buy beer for us. Someone often obliged, even to the point of taking orders for six-packs in assorted flavors: a case of Schlitz, a twelve-pack of Hamm's, random six-packs of Grain Belt and Drewrey's. Sometimes a cartful of beer came to the checkout counter with so many different brands that even Julius, the normally asleep-at-the-wheel, balding old patriarch of the store would ask if the beer was for the kids gathered outside, in a tone suggesting that his customer hadn't gotten up early enough that morning to slip one past the sentinel of the beer cooler.

Occasionally when a buyer didn't materialize, a delegation was dispatched inside to shoplift an order. One kid, Harvey Michaels, was so brazen that he'd walk inside, wave to Julius and tell him that he was there to steal some beer and cigarettes. Julius would chuckle and shake his head, then wait at the checkout for Harvey to file through, paying for a pack of gum or a Salted Nut Roll before clanking out the door with half a dozen quarts of beer and a couple cartons of smokes arrayed on his person which he proceeded to bootleg at bargain prices outside behind the store.

Harvey was an enterprising youngster who also earned money by selling tickets to keggers out in the boondocks and eating live fish and cows' eyes in public events that staged in the parking lot behind the Roosevelt Shopping Center. After a hat was passed to generate enough incentive Harvey would climb atop the roof of someone's car and hold his gruesome meal aloft while the crowd chanted like bloodthirsty fans at the coliseum. Then he would down it while the teenaged throng cheered wildly. He also once rode his motorcycle through the shopping center naked for nothing more than the hell of it.

The up-front costs of our early drinking escapades were cheap – I'd snatch a pack of smokes from my mom's carton at home, scrounge two or three bucks and be flush for a night's provisions of six beers topped off by a nightcap of cheeseburgers at the McDonald's that sat just beyond the woods at the southwest edge of Waterbury.

It was right in the middle of my sophomore year of high school that the last page of the epic '60's was torn from the calendar, though themes established in that decade would color outside its lines into the next. Eventually, after Watergate assassinated Nixon's presidency and America ignominiously fled Viet Nam, things calmed down. Music too returned from the revolution to pimp in discos for the libidos of guys clad in leisure suits who'd neither fought nor protested the war. But as one decade ended and another began strong winds of change were still buffeting the country, sweeping from coast to coast and gathering momentum on the straight-aways of the Great Plains.

In May of 1970, just as America's schools were about to adjourn for the summer, four students were shot and killed by the Ohio National Guard during an anti-war protest at Kent State University. The nation's first draft lottery since WWII had been instituted late in 1969, and now the war in Southeast

Asia was being expanded into Cambodia by President Nixon, who'd pledged to end it when he was elected in 1968. The shootings at Kent State were followed by what amounted to a nationwide student strike at schools ranging from junior highs to colleges. The protest of young people was now widespread and multi-faceted. Locally, Greenwood Park, the woodsy home of Ashworth Pool, the Des Moines Art Center and family picnic grounds, was becoming a hotbed of skirmishes that came to be known as, "cops and kids," as in, "let's go down to the park and play 'cops and kids.'"

It became fashionable to drink there, and the aroma of burning cannabis was often on the breeze. LSD was also coming into vogue, although its usage was less conspicuous than that of both beer and pot save for the occasional wood nymph scampering naked through the trees. Inevitably the police would be summoned to disperse the restless malcontents but it wouldn't be until the summer of 1971 that a full-throated protest was staged at Greenwood, one that struck especially close to home for the alumni of our neighborhood.

Still abstinent from drugs, but already a documented illegal possessor of beer, I finished my first year of high school and prepared for a summer job mowing and otherwise maintaining the grounds of the state capitol complex in Des Moines.

Whatever local outcry arose in the wake of the Kent State killings, I was not part of. I was too self-absorbed and too busy. Though I'd been eligible for a driver's license since turning sixteen in February, I hadn't found room in my class schedule for Driver's Ed. So I was enrolled in a summer school session that began each morning at 6:30. After class it was off to work. As that summer opened I was also on the JV baseball team. Game-days required changing from work clothes into uniform in the back seat of the car on the way from work to the game. One day early in the season our coach over-heard me grousing about my daily grind during the pre-game warm-ups. He approached and proceeded to upbraid me as, among other things, a "never-sweat" in front of my teammates. I'd never heard that term before and I've never heard it since, but I was pretty sure that it didn't apply to me, just infer-ring from the context. I may have been a budding alcoholic, but certainly not a never-sweat.

After starting in the outfield and holding my own for the first couple of games, I was embarrass-ingly benched and branded that day. I showed him. I quit the last baseball team I would ever be a part of and devoted the rest of my summer to Jane, driv-ing and drinking – in no particular order; sometimes in combination.

A couple of significant things happened on the job that summer. One day another summer hire and I were dispatched to one of the state driver's license stations to clean up and organize the basement of the undersized facility. We quickly discovered that most of the mess was invalidated driver's licenses. Most of them had words like, REVOKED or EX-

PIRED or, SUSPENDED stamped on them in big red letters. But there were some where the stamp just grazed the edge, and some of those had birth-dates on them that would qualify the holder to buy and drink beer legally. We smuggled several boxes full of the discarded licenses out of the building and drove our state pickup truck to the home of my col-league's girlfriend where we spent most of the af-ternoon hatching a plan to become distributors of fake ID's. The days of soliciting someone to con-tribute to the delinquency of minors in the Matulef's parking lot were over.

The other lowlight of my first stretch of paid manual labor occurred during my last week on the job. It was a rainy day so we were again reassigned from our usual duty of mowing. I'd come to enjoy mowing, by the way, as never before. Not only was I getting paid for it, but all of the equipment was motorized. Often we were deployed mounted on riding mowers, unsupervised on vast state proper-ties. Some of the hillier state grounds offered irre-sistible opportunities to crest a hill, slip your tractor into neutral and race down steep inclines screaming like roller coaster passengers. Once I carelessly let a walk-behind get away from me while I stopped to mop my brow. I watched with vivid premonition as it bounced down the hillside toward a street teeming with mid-day traffic. Somehow it crossed the four-lane avenue and bumped up over the curb on the far side without collision, as unlikely an outcome as a blindfolded man strolling unscathed through a minefield. This beat the hell out of cutting the grass at home with gear endorsed by Fred Flintstone.

But rainy days resulted in contrived indoor duties. So it was that we found ourselves one day that August moving office furniture from one floor to another in one of the many buildings that comprised the capitol complex. Scrambling up a flight of stairs with a desk chair in each arm I stumbled, pitching forward and breaking my fall and my wrist with my outstretched right arm.

When football practice opened the next week I was sidelined with a cast that wasn't slated to come off until mid-season. Into the breach at quarterback stepped a sophomore named Doug Reichardt, son of former Big Ten MVP Bill and younger brother of my former steady Barb.

In the space of about a year I'd made an almost meteoric descent from incoming sophomore varsity quarterback dating older cheerleaders to sidelined, washed-up junior never-sweat. Jane had graduated and was resuming a gymnastics career across town at Grand View College that she'd set aside when her family moved to Des Moines. As a young girl in Huntington Beach, California both she and her older sister Patty competed alongside Cathy Rigby.

Even though she was still in town we faced obstacles that are inherent to couples split between high school and college. Sometime during that season we agreed upon the "date other people" strategy.

In the latter half of the season I shed my cast

and played just enough to letter again, but after the last game of the year Coach Donald suggested to me that, looking ahead, maybe I should be thinking of a position switch. What? I don't even know if I went to the team banquet. The year before that event was the occasion where I was one of only three sophs to be awarded a letter. I was so proud, and I promptly went down to Van Ginkel's Sporting Goods to get my white R sewn on my navy blue sweater. The first night I wore it was the first time I ever got drunk on wine. The wine was red and after I threw it up all over myself the R had kind of a pink cast to it.

I awoke from that escapade in my underwear beneath a blanket on the couch at my brother and Marcia's apartment. I had no recollection of how I'd gotten there or how my sweater and other clothes had gotten into their bathtub where I found them soaking in a broth of puke and tap water. I vaguely recall Mark taking the occasion to caution me that I was blowing my shot at lots of good things that were already out of his picture at twenty, a rather premature age of foreclosure. Whatever he had to say apparently took no root because the letter I was awarded after my junior season of football was the last one Roosevelt ever bestowed upon me.

A school of thought sprang up whereby I was the victim of the Reichardts' undue influence on the Roosevelt athletic department. The truth was that a broken wrist and broken training made it easy for Doug to supplant me on the football team. The fact that I had people in my corner perpetuating the myth that I was somehow getting screwed enabled me to opt out even more from the high school career I'd imagined all those years on the gridirons, diamonds and courts of the Dean yard, the island and the Leonard driveway.

I didn't even go out for basketball in my junior year, a decision that I can't recall ever discussing with anyone, either at school or at home. Given the abduction of Mark's future by drinking and unplanned parenthood, you'd think my parents would have seized a more despotic control of my life. But they didn't – or couldn't. They'd pulled out all the stops in dispatching Mark to Shattuck as a high school sophomore, a move they could not possibly have afforded financially and would not have undertaken unless they realized the stakes were getting high.

I have no doubt that earnest intercessory prayer was always at work on my behalf and, indeed, ultimately salvaged my life if not my high school athletic daydreams.

By now the old Kingman bunch had fanned out into assorted social circles. We were all exploring and experimenting with various toxins of the times, but strangely, almost never together in any combination. I was still solidly in the beer drinking camp, as I think were the Leonard brothers. News from the cutting edge had it that Wayne Dean was often there, squarely in the forefront of the mushrooming, shall we say, drug culture. The eldest scion of Roosevelt's erstwhile royal couple never put on the school's colors in any sport, nor would any of his three brothers in the years to come.

* * *

My first driving mishap was in February of 1970, just days before I reached sixteen, but still several months prior to acquisition of a driver's license. Three of us had a buddy's car while he was bussing tables at his job in a West Des Moines restaurant. While he was working we were drinking. His car was pretty nice for a teenmobile; a navy blue Chevy Malibu – not too old, clean and well-maintained. We took turns at the wheel while we killed time and six-packs, cruising around, singing along with the radio. By the time we headed out to grab Pete from work I was driving. We were careening west on the freeway when I abruptly cranked the steering wheel clockwise upon our realization that we were almost abreast of our intended exit. We scraped past the sign marking the ramp like a skier missing a gate in an Olympic downhill, leaving a jagged sort of racing stripe along one side of Pete's car. I don't know what time that happened, but police records show that by 11:30 that night the four of us were arrested at McDonald's when Pete tried to walk through a window instead of the door after fetching a sack of burgers for us. The report of the incident also says that an unnamed passenger in the car mentioned to the

arresting officer that there had been an accident earlier in the evening. I don't know who that was or in
what spirit that information was offered up – probably just an awkward attempt at making conversation
with the officer.

In November of that year, by then a licensed
driver, I crashed Mark's '69 Mustang into the back
of a car that had the misfortune of being on the
same street at the same time. Reports on that incident were filed by a police officer who noted that
his car too was nearly struck by mine when I hit the
brakes to slow my speeding car upon noticing him.
My passengers, who'd been dispatched with me
from a party to get more beer, jumped out and ran
and went unidentified by me, according to the report. Improbably, the driver and passenger of the
other car sustained only minor injuries. My fogged
recollection of the moments just before the crash
includes someone excitedly exclaiming from the
back seat that we were going almost ninety [down-
hill]. It was raining. I had no idea that we were
roughly a block from the house where my father
lived as a young boy.

The disposition of both of those cases was referral to the Saturday morning court classes, a program
started by Judge Ray Harrison, himself a recovering
alcoholic. My entry into the judicial system also
coincided with the passing of Iowa's gubernatorial
torch from Harold Hughes to our neighbor, Robert
Ray. Hughes too was in recovery from alcoholism,
and much admired for it. Despite these germinating

seeds of treatment for substance abuse it was still not yet fashionable to suggest that a high school kid was a drunk, steadily mounting evidence to the contrary notwithstanding. Consequently, January 9, 1971 happened this way in my life…

There was a Roosevelt basketball game that night. I think Robbie Farris and I listened to some of it on the radio while we drove around drinking in his mom's Plymouth. We should have been playing in it but our basketball careers were already over. By the time the game ended we were out of smokes and feeling irresistible to girls so we headed for the Pizza Hut on Grand Ave., just across the street from the McDonald's where we'd both registered our first arrests not quite a year before.

We expected to find classmates there and weren't disappointed; the place was full of them when we entered and began scavenging for loose change to plunk in the cigarette machine that stood in the foyer. Our behavior would have been annoying to strangers, but many there knew us and found it amusingly typical for us two. The police officer hired by the Pizza Hut to work off-duty security must have figured that this pot of teenagers might come to a boil if we weren't dialed down, so he advised us that we'd have to leave. He wasn't in uniform, but he did identify himself as a police officer. We protested briefly that we just wanted to scrounge a pack of smokes, but he was adamant that we leave immediately, so we did. The Plymouth was parked just outside the door and right after we'd gotten in, a pair of brothers we knew from school ran out and asked for a ride home. Robbie said sure, and they hopped in the back. There was a steady snow falling atop what already lay on the ground like the head on a glass of beer.

We started backing up and sensed a slight shrug at the back of the car. Robbie stopped, opened his door and looked out to the rear. He'd bumped fenders with a girl from school who was just arriving in her Dodge Challenger. She was a friend, and she looked at her bumper before she told Robbie to go ahead, there was no damage. As soon as he started forward the cop, who'd apparently been watching through the glass door of the restaurant, rushed out, opened the driver's door and ordered Robbie to stop – at gunpoint! Robbie panicked. Instead of stopping he took off. We spun around the rear of the building and started fishtailing through the snow toward the street. I remember a sound like a wadding piece of paper behind me. I looked back to see that half of the back window was gone and watched the remainder of it fall away as the realization that we were being shot at barged through the beers into my consciousness. I yelled something to that effect. Robbie yelled something back. Our passengers were yelling too. We spun out of the parking lot and got stuck on a snow bank. All four of us jumped out and fled across Grand, one of Des Moines' longest and busiest streets, blindly trying to escape a nightmare that was unfolding faster than we could process.

I made it to the next corner and jumped into the

back seat of a car I recognized at the stop sign there. The other occupants were more Roosevelt students who knew me, but had no idea what they'd driven into. I pleaded with the driver to take off, but we were blocked by a squad car and I was apprehended by an officer who jumped out of it. He handcuffed me and walked me back down the street where I was reunited with Robbie and both of us were handcuffed to his mother's perforated car.

By then the scene was surreal – a fleet of strobing police lights reddening the snowy landscape; us shackled to the complementary white sedan with a red interior. I was wearing a heavy, woolen, below-the-waist winter coat that helped soften the blows one officer was uppercutting between my legs while another was macing us. I couldn't understand what we'd done that warranted gunfire and a dragnet.

The two brothers we'd promised a ride home were also rounded up, but they were excused from rough stuff beyond the gunfire and sent on their way.

Incredibly, none of the four bullets that struck the car hit any of its passengers. Besides the shot-out back window, there were two bullet holes in the driver's side of the car. Formerly one who scoffed at movie chase scenes where every bullet fired at the protagonist[s] just barely missed, I now had to acknowledge some plausibility there.

Once we'd been handcuffed, beaten and maced into submission, we were transported downtown to the police station and our parents were summoned to retrieve us. My dad and I had ridden the first few blocks in silence before he asked me how I felt about what had happened. I stammered that I was scared and angry. He wondered what I had to be angry about and I wondered why he wasn't angry too about the fact that we'd been shot at. He didn't know.

Robbie's mom, Ellen Farris was alone in this. She'd been widowed by the death of Robbie's father before Robbie and I ever met at Merrill and Robbie's older sisters were out of the house. He lived on Waterbury Circle with his mom and younger brother, more modestly than most of their neighbors.

A bit of shit hit the fan.

The following day, Sunday, was spent in strategy sessions before Robbie and I returned to school on Monday like combat survivors. People didn't know whether to treat us like we were cool or radioactive.

It was ten days before any mention of the incident appeared in *The Des Moines Register*. On January 19 a story ran below the fold on the front page – no byline – that focused on the convening of a police advisory board to probe the use of deadly force by an off-duty officer. The article mentioned that unspecified charges had been filed against two of the four youths involved in the incident.

The charge against me was public intoxication. The proverbial book was being thrown at Robbie. Since the police department's official policy on deadly force was that guns should be used only when an officer had probable cause to believe a felony had been committed, the officer who fired at us told the advisory board that he believed Robbie had deliberately tried to run him down in the Pizza Hut parking lot [assault with intent to do great bodily harm on a police officer]. He also said that the shots he fired were aimed at the car tires. Zero out of four.

Both of our families lawyered up. Reporters started calling our homes. We followed our legal advice to say nothing. I remember our lawyer seemed to think that eventually we would go public with our version of events and that we had great leverage on the city and Pizza Hut for an eventual lawsuit.

On January 24 Donald Kaul, who wrote a popular column called *Over the Coffee* which my mother read religiously, ran an installment sympathetic to us which amounted to a thinly veiled adaptation of the incident couched in a Sherlock Holmes context. On January 26 the *Register* ran a copyrighted story disclosing that the police advisory board was expected to recommend a suspension of several days for the shooter. The ultimate decision rested with the police chief.

The advisory board was comprised entirely of law enforcement officers, including the chief. It had no subpoena power, so everyone who appeared before it did so voluntarily. Robbie and I did, of course. So did some other kids, but I can't remember who. I do remember that most refused on the grounds that their parents wanted nothing to do with the whole mess.

When all was said and done, the punishment imposed on the plain-clothed, off-duty policeman who fired four shots on a snowy night at a fleeing carload of kids heading toward a busy street, two of whom he suspected had been drinking and panhandling feloniously, was a brief suspension from off-duty assignments like the one at the Pizza Hut which officers liked to use to supplement their meager municipal salaries.

In exchange for the assurance that neither family would sue, all of the charges arrayed against Robbie were dropped, as was my referral to juvenile court. The gathering storm of scandal, injustice, controversy, brutality and attention just dissipated like a sneeze that never quite discharged. The bullets we'd literally dodged were reduced to metaphors when the deal was made to spare Robbie from defense against serious charges.

I remember sitting at the table with the panel of policemen, a circle of paddy wagons, a sixteen year-old kid telling a bunch of cops a story about their colleague shooting at my friends and me and other colleagues handcuffing us to a car before hitting us in the nuts with saps and spraying mace in our faces. I remember when I'd estimate a distance at, say, fifty yards, how they'd wonder if I meant to say a hundred and fifty feet. I remember the name of the man who shot at us for interrupting his easygoing, do-nothing off-duty shift at the Pizza Hut – he's dead now. I remember the police chief of my home-town where I'd lived all my life glaring menacingly at me from across that table like a bothered head-master dealing with a mischievous brat. I remember his ruling that the man who shot at us did use exces-sive force when he fired his gun but was not guilty of brutality when he used his sap and mace on teen-agers handcuffed to a car. I remember realizing that it wasn't always old age that did people in. And I remember that when the dust all settled I had to use an assumed name once when I went to pick up a date because who would let their daughter go out with the nice-looking, polite young guy shaking their hand if they knew he was one of the Pizza Hut desperados?

But I don't remember much about what hap-pened next.

* * *

Stephen Leonard was finishing his freshman year at the University of Iowa in the spring of 1971 and he wanted a motorcycle. His parents, Ed and Jean, were at odds on the subject – she was op-posed; too dangerous. But she was also outnum-bered and by the time Stephen came home to work a summer job and reconnect with high school pals, he and his dad had prevailed.

By this time Greenwood Park had become a quasi-reservation for west-side hippies and was more of a sanctuary for wine-swigging, dope-smoking flower children than it was for picnicking families. On June 1, 1971 a small article in *The Des Moines Register* was headlined, "Police Nab Seven in Greenwood." It detailed the Memorial Day arrests of a squad ranging in age from seventeen to twenty who were in the park after the 10:30 P.M. curfew smoking pot and drinking when the police cruised through and told them to disperse. The kids' response, according to the article, was a hail of bottles and jeers.

Another article on June 13 described the previous day's rock concert at the park, the second of the season. It painted a picture of an idyllic Saturday festival that attracted a young, enthused crowd of about 2,000 to Greenwood and noted that the next such event was slated for July 11. I'd forgotten this series of mini-Woodstocks ever took place. I don't think I attended them. I don't know if Stephen Leonard did or not, but I can pinpoint the date and time of his last visit to Greenwood Park.

There was a party the night of Monday June 14th at the Sidneys' house. When we first moved to Kingman Boulevard the Sidneys lived diagonally across the street from us, but soon moved around the corner, midway up the elm-canopied block of 44th that formed the primrose path between Kingman and University Ave.

My recollection of the Sidney party is generic – it was well-attended, loud and drunken. I was there and Stephen Leonard was too. I learned after the fact that at some point the party got loud enough to attract the attention and arouse the curiosity of my mother who ventured about half the distance between our house and the Sidneys' to determine where the ruckus was coming from.

Between leaving the party and dropping off a friend, Stephen Leonard stopped briefly at home on California Drive and spoke with his mother. Then he took off on his motorcycle, delivered his buddy safely home and, just after midnight, steered his bike toward Greenwood Park.

The park unfurls without fanfare south of Grand Ave. You're on 45th ST., passing by a handful of stately, hilltop homes on the east and a dense wooded area on the west, the road bends and there's an outdoor amphitheatre and a lagoon that was fished some in the summer and served as a skating rink in the wintertime. The road forks uphill to a wading pool, basketball and tennis courts, and a picnic area. Further ahead on the flatter main road is Ashworth, the municipal pool. Just southwest of the corner of 45th and Grand are the building and grounds of the Des Moines Art Center. The other access road for the park forms the western boundary of the Art Center premises and across it are a shelter house and still more picnic areas.

The grounds and facilities are ample but they blend seamlessly into a woodsy residential area and in the summer of 1971 there was but a small sign or two mumbling that a park threshold was being crossed at the point where 45th ST. became Greenwood; where Nottingham became Sherwood Forest.

Stephen knew where he was – after all, his family had moved to this neighborhood almost a decade before. But he didn't know that, by order of the same police chief who presided over the Pizza Hut advisory board, a chain was being strung across the park entrance at curfew every night in response to the rowdiness that had become commonplace there.

That stretch of the road is wide and it was empty that night but for Stephen so it's easy to suppose that he was going fast – why not? He was nineteen at midnight on a summer evening with the wind in his hair, the world in his pocket and probably a grin on his face before he skidded into the chain that was meant to turn people back.

The next night what the *Register* described as a "minor disturbance" was put down when police chased a group estimated at fifty to seventy-five people out of the park at curfew. They were there to mourn and rail against chains. Between fifteen and twenty of them were arrested.

The night after that hundreds of young people massed in the park. I was there that night. So was the police chief. He brought enough troops to close a six-block stretch of Grand Ave. and push the mob back out of the park with riot gear and bullhorned promises to meet the next day with representatives of the protesters. That meeting resulted in a relaxed park curfew of 1:00 A.M., effective immediately, and the *Register* reported that the kids in the park Thursday night were elated about that development.

Their grievances had been addressed almost before the Leonards' grieving had begun.

Stephen's funeral was the day after the institution of the new curfew. I can't remember it, but it's the event I referred to earlier as perhaps the first one that drew all of the Leonards, Wellmans, Deans and Donalds to the same place at the same time. I don't even know who first told me Stephen was dead or how I reacted. I don't know if I even briefly considered turning back.

Marcus Leonard remembers those wrenching days in much greater detail. He remembers that the church was overflowing. And he remembers that the relatively new pastor there, the one whose retired predecessor confirmed Stephen and truly knew him, used the occasion to deliver a sermon that moralized about a wayward generation and cast Stephen's death as some sort of toll that had to be paid on the highway to hell. The family thought the service was a defamatory effigy of Stephen that reduced him to a tragic mascot for the times. They went home reeling from what amounted to the aftershock that follows an earthquake. Two days later was Father's Day.

The first-born child is in many ways the linchpin of a household. After all, two's a couple, three's a family. So it was with the renaissance kid and the Leonards. Marcus was suddenly yanked from Stephen's shadow, a spot where he'd been comfortable, just as our senior year of high school loomed. Within his family he ascended through tragic attrition to the rank of eldest sibling and he found also that some of Stephen's many friends looked to him now for help he didn't know how to give.

Although they'd disagreed about Stephen's motorcycle, Ed and Jean knew it wasn't what had killed him, so that potential wedge did not split them. The pediatrician who'd lost his own first child went on with his life's work like the deafened Beethoven went about composing music, but the wounds inflicted upon his own self and family were more than he and his wife could heal.

They did the best they could.

* * *

When school started I appeared to be a new, uh, man. Both my hair and weight were growing unchecked. For the first time my locks were beyond drip-dry length. The beer and cheeseburgers lifestyle started catching up with me as soon as the brake of athletics was released. Instead of playing football I covered the team for the school newspaper. Like a congressman defeated in a re-election bid who parlays connections into a lobbyist teat, I posed myself as an insider uniquely qualified to get and deliver the real story.

Midway through our senior year one of our buddies enlisted in the Marines. His induction was delayed until after graduation, so the rest of the year, whenever we were out cruising around drinking and had to stop for a pee, he'd get out of the car and pretend that his stream was a spray of gunfire mowing down 'gooks' while he supplied little boy machine gun sound effects to make his piss sound more lethal.

On Groundhog Day, 1972 [February 2], what would be the last of the selective service draft lotteries was held for young men born in 1953, the year ahead of us. No one subject to that lottery was ever drafted into the military due to the gradual withdrawal of American troops that began early in 1973 in accordance with the Paris peace talks and culminated with the collapse of Saigon in the spring of 1975.

Some of Mark's classmates were drafted and served in Viet Nam. Mark himself was not classified 1A until after he and Marcia divorced, eventually drawing a number high enough to save him from conscription.

Even luckier than the guys born in '53 was my buddy Wilson James who enlisted in the Marines and pretended that he couldn't wait to go to war. We were in the same homeroom and he used to get turned on while scanning the morning paper by Abby Spencer, the wealthy and curvaceous playmate of Sam Driver from the *Judge Parker* comic strip. That she was a cartoon character, not to mention already spoken for, mattered not to him. He surely would have been killed in Viet Nam.

Realizing that mobile drinking exposed us too much to patrolling cops, a group of us undertook to rent premises where we could socialize more leisurely and comfortably before graduation scattered us forever. We took an apartment in an underprivileged neighborhood that was very comfortable compared to the Waterbury woods in winter. It was a good start, but became quickly too popular and so, too small. We moved on, closer to home. Somehow we rented an entire two-story frame house in a quiet residential area mere blocks from Roosevelt. Robbie Farris was pulling down a buck an hour tearing tickets on a part-time basis at the Ingersoll movie theater. I was making twice that setting up the patients' dinner trays after school everyday at Iowa Methodist Hospital. The rest of our real estate syndicate had less stable income streams, so understandably only Robbie and I approached our parents and declared our readiness to move away from home. While the rest of the bunch contributed to an ongoing open house, for Robbie and me, be it ever so trashed and smelly and crowded, it was home. I have surmised in retrospect that my parents only acquiesced to my premature exit from the nest in a spirit of letting me learn through experience. After a couple weeks of panhandling in the school parking lot for milk and egg money so that all of our wages could go towards the essentials of beer and cigarettes, we both limped home with tails between legs. Space flights by then were lasting as long as our experiment in independent living.

One of the Saturdays while I was supporting myself was the day for me to take the ACT exam. I came to after capping off a long night of cramming [beers] with a couple hours of shut-eye. There was just enough time to fill my quiver with sharpened #2's and race to school, but not enough to shower, brush teeth and swap last night's rumpled clothes for a fresh set. I rolled into the testing center/cafeteria like a keg and endured a long, dotted morning. I flunked the self-examination part.

The following week I followed basically the same protocol in advance of posing for my senior pictures. There I sat outfitted in my Reichardt's uniform of worsted navy blazer, rep striped silk tie and all-cotton blue button-down; bloodshot blue eyes peering out from beneath a wavy, rolling helmet of thick brown hair; the very portrait of promise. All the cracks were either out-of-frame or more than skin-deep.

The home away from home went down spectacularly when we stormed the delicatessen owned and operated by our landlord, loudly announcing during business hours that we knew he was selling beer out the back door on Sundays [at that time, Sunday sale of alcoholic beverages was still illegal in Iowa] and if we didn't get what we wanted, we would call the cops on him. I can't remember what it was that we wanted, but I do remember that he called our bluff by calling the cops on us, right then and there! He told us to get the hell out of the house immediately and we raced back there just far enough ahead of the squad cars to permit a final flourish of trashing, grab our laundry and beat it. Oddly, the signatories to whatever sort of lease had given us access to the premises included neither of the two mature young men who were playing house there. In the end our whole platoon cleaned up the place and all parties agreed to leave things at that.

With less than a semester of high school remaining my parents welcomed the younger of their two sons home. It was time to plan for college.

* * *

Both Martha and our father were graduates of the University of Iowa. Mark had briefly attended Grand View across town, but he was carrying more luggage than could be lugged even that far. My mother was still an unabashed disciple of St. Olaf even though she'd never been able to return there and graduate.

Aside from the collegiate influences of my immediate family, the eldest pups from the Kingman pack were wandering away from home by now. I didn't know it then, but Dr. Leonard had long hoped that Stephen would attend St. Olaf based on what he'd learned about the school as a boy growing up in Minnesota. Fred Donald was so bright that he'd graduated from Roosevelt a year early and found his way to Grinnell, a small liberal arts college in central Iowa that continues to rank as one of the best in America. Roosevelt was the last school Wayne Dean was ever enrolled in and Lynnette Donald headed to Iowa City upon graduation.

I applied only to St. Olaf and Iowa. In an administrative upset that must have cost somebody in the admissions office their job, I was accepted to St. Olaf. Actually, I suspect that my Uncle Orv had more to do with my acceptance than did my checkered high school transcripts. He was married to my mom's sister Jean, a St. Olaf grad, and owned the most popular clothing store in Northfield. He was also on the school's Board of Bigshots at the time and perhaps in a position to yank some strings. I felt somehow that by going to St. Olaf I could make some things up to my mother, if not both of my parents. I wasn't sure how I'd survive there since I almost never brought a book home during high school and had no idea how to study. I pictured the place as a study hall on a hill where the only sustenance was food for thought and I would be quickly exposed as a delinquent imposter from south of the border; neither a Lutheran nor a scholar – uff da! I resolved to make the most of my last summer with pals.

For the season of our last hurrah a group from the Roosevelt class of '72 took an apartment on Ingersoll Ave., not far from the one where I'd been diapering my nephew the night Bobby Kennedy was slain. My dad had arranged a summer at hard labor for me at Pittsburgh-Des Moines Steel where he worked in an administrative capacity. My job was in the steel plant. I was paid $2.71 per hour. Every day I came out of the plant blackened. It was a goggles/hard hat/steel-toed boots job. Every one of the massive machines contrived to fabricate and bend steel had a small chalkboard posted near it which was used to record the date of the last injury that occurred at that post. They might as well have had a skull and cross bones on them.

The man I was assigned to help all summer on a monolithic set of jaws that bent massive steel plates to specification was missing a total of three fingers. I noticed that about him right away and that's all I remember about him now.

Every morning my dad would awaken me for work. Usually I had a hangover which intensified my dread of a return to the plant where overhead cranes ran the length of the building all day. The cranes were always beeping loud warnings so nobody wandered beneath them. My septopus mentor told me about the time an oblivious peon like me was literally cloven in two when something huge slipped from the crane's talons and dropped on him like a bomb.

Every morning, usually as we headed south on 35th Street past the big Dahl's grocery store in our white Ford Pinto, the song *Brandy* about the fine girl who worked as an alewife for sailors would come on the car radio. That song became so linked in my memory with the worst job I ever had that even now when I hear it I start ducking like one of Pavlov's dogs.

The only part of my workday that I enjoyed was lunch. Lunchtime was quiet and safe and I would usually walk up to the offices and eat with my dad. Our brown bags were stuffed with lunchmeat sand-wiches made grand by their pairing with mom's potato salad, the finest ever concocted, and I always washed everything down with a chugged bottle of Pepsi from the office vending machine. Even a packed lunch eaten in the field was like an act of surgery for my meticulous father. Nary a crumb escaped from the place setting he improvised on his desktop, eating with a plebe's precision while I gorged, belched and regaled him with my daily reflections on the plight of the Cubs. He grinned at me and listened and I think he allowed himself to envision his son becoming a man, working hard at a summer job before leaving home for college and the rest of his beckoning life.

I couldn't wait to be done forever with that place, but I knew I would miss lunching with my dad when I left for school in August.

Despite all of my shenanigans and the disappointment, worry and stress they wrought upon my folks, my relationship with them was never stormy. There was no local battle of the then raging generational war being fought in our house; maybe there needed to be an occasional skirmish, who can say? But I know, and perhaps our parents did too, that more discipline could not have changed who my brother and I were.

By the time we drove to Northfield to deliver me to St. Olaf, Martha was living in New York City and working as an international stewardess for TWA. She was fluent in both Spanish and French and had found a good base of operations for a young woman with an aversion to driving. Mark by then was divorced from the first of what would become a quintet of wives. I left Mary behind at home to finish high school. After sixteen years as the youngest of four, she was now an only child as far as her day-to-day living arrangements were concerned.

If I didn't arrive on campus completely squared away for my insertion into the perfectly round hole I imagined St. Olaf to be, the corners were soon sharpened.

One of the traditional activities during the freshman orientation week was an event that randomly paired incoming boys and girls for a campus concert and dance. I drew the company of a plain, prim young thing who could as well have been my babysitter. The band headlining the concert ["Climax"] had a hit song then current called, *Precious and Few*. The lyrics included the sappy declaration, "quiet and blue like the sky, I'm hung over you..." I'm hung over too, I thought. Another line asserted, "If I can't find my way back home, it just wouldn't be fair." Yeah, they had that right. The refrain moaned that, "precious and few are the moments we two can share." That wasn't exactly my mood and the feeling was clearly mutual. After my companion learned that I was not planning to audition for any of the school's renowned choral ensembles, maternal history there notwithstanding, she bluntly opined that, "no offense, but you look like the beer drinking type."

My God, had it become that obvious?

Reeling with homesickness, I nevertheless resolved to study hard for the first time and keep up in school. Every day after morning classes I'd race to my PO Box in the student union in hopes of finding mail there. Besides my weekly allowance check in the amount of twenty bucks, I got occasional mail from scattered friends. Sometimes I got letters of encouragement from home. My mother's handwriting was elegant, practically calligraphic. My dad wrote as a southpaw, though he threw right-handed, and his letters were always signed, "Your Lucky Dad." He wrote so firmly that when he sat at the dining room table doing our taxes it wobbled. His signature was proud and legible and looked like it belonged on important documents that certified historic events. Each capital 'W' finished with an upward flourish that suggested the tip of a flame to me.

As the semester unfolded I discovered that the dorm floor I lived on [seventh floor, Mohn Hall] had quickly acquired a reputation as perhaps the rowdiest on campus despite virtually no contribution from me. There were several ardent and enterprising druggists on our floor of freshmen, and it was St. Olaf of all places where I first accented my drinking with anything stronger than Winstons.

I remember the first time I got high. A bunch of us gathered in a darkened dorm room and passed around a bong with Led Zeppelin blaring the soundtrack. When I excused myself to go to the communal bathroom down the hall I suddenly realized, much to my amusement, while standing at a urinal and staring at the wall in front of me that I couldn't remember if I'd unzipped my pants before I opened the spigot and couldn't deduce the answer without looking [I had]. What fun!

Once I'd been mainstreamed at school, I soon abandoned my practice of getting drunk on Friday nights, wandering out to highway 19 that bordered the campus and hitchhiking home for weekends. The first time I tried that a guy picked me up around midnight and when I told him I was headed for Interstate 35 to catch a ride south to Des Moines he hit the brakes, told me I was headed the wrong direction, and dropped me a few miles further from home than when I started. Eventually I got a shotgun seat with a man bound for Los Angeles. He was road-weary and asked if I'd mind driving for a spell while he got some sleep. Sure thing; the least I could do in return for the lift home. That was the only time I ever drove a car a hundred miles an hour. It was still dark when I came knocking on the door at 4322 Kingman around 4:30 A.M. Saturday morning. I don't know if my mom was glad to see me or not. She was definitely surprised.

When I came home for Thanksgiving I traveled more conventionally. I had a pre-arranged ride with a fellow Iowan, we left right after lunch, I packed a suitcase and I was sober. I also had a midterm grade report that detailed my 3.0 GPA, of which I was rather proud. I was feeling pretty good. St. Olaf was not the monastery I'd envisioned. The cafeteria food was plentiful and tasty, beer and pot were readily available and I was getting decent grades. I'd started the year with two roommates, one from a Minneapolis suburb and one from Sioux Falls, but the South Dakotan had returned home to be with his girlfriend. The reduction of our triple room to a double made even the sequestered portions of life in the dorms reasonably livable, so I returned home for my first collegiate holiday somewhat reasonably adjusted. What began triumphantly turned somber on Thanksgiving night.

Mary and I had both gone out, she to her boyfriend's and I to the Greenwood Lounge to reconnect with high school chums. Mom had probably fallen asleep with a good book, leaving dad alone in an upstairs bedroom that had been converted to a TV parlor as offspring attrition took its toll on the household. Downstairs was Mitzie, our beloved and faithful pooch. Mitzie by then was probably eight years old. During her six years with us she went from natural born hunter to slothful beggar, figuring, why chase squirrels when they're giving away pork slabs down at the corner? She had become prematurely hobbled to the point where she never ventured up to the second floor of the house anymore, so dad was taken aback when he looked up from the television to see Mitzie standing in the doorway, staring at him and panting to regain her breath. Unable to answer dad's question as to why she'd made the effort to come upstairs and see him, Mitzie then turned and plodded away. A short time later, when dad went downstairs to freshen his coffee, he found our dog lying dead beside her food and water bowls in the kitchen. It was left to him to relay her good-bye to the rest of the family.

I received the news of Mitzie's death while in an altered state, but I don't know if that cushioned or intensified the initial blow. It's likely that the next morning throbbed doubly when I awoke to both a hangover and the realization that there'd be no dog waiting to fetch my childhood for me when I returned home for Christmas in less than a month.

Almost as soon as my freshman year had begun I decided that I would transfer to the University of Iowa as a sophomore. Early in the second semester I hitchhiked from Northfield to Iowa City for a Grateful Dead concert that was held on my nineteenth birthday, February 24, 1973. At home I had come of age since, as of July 1, 1972, the legal drinking age had been lowered from twenty-one to nineteen. No more busts for illegal possession of beer! My problems were over, or so I wanted to believe. The truth was I'd not seen anything yet.

My second and last semester on the hill at St. Olaf passed without incident.

One day I came in from a rousing game of broomball on the rink behind the dorm to take a phone call from Robbie Farris in Hawaii. My old cellmate had joined the Navy but it wasn't working out and he was looking for the exits. As far as either of us knew, security at the Pizza Hut back home was no longer an issue now that we were both out of town.

I came home in the spring after racking up a 3.3 GPA for the second semester, a 3.15 for the year. I was a college student. Drinking was as much a part of the routine as cramming for finals. And when I crossed the border back into Iowa I was also an adult. My drinking was legal as long as I stayed out of drivers' seats and public places, but no less pathological. All that really changed was the nature of the charges.

I spent that summer unloading railcars at Capp Homes on the industrial northeast edge of Des Moines. It was just as physically demanding as the steel plant had been, but less overtly dangerous and there was more outdoor time too.

Martha was married in June to Bob Conley, eldest son of a Catholic undertaker and a Viet Nam vet who was just getting started in the hotel business. He was a quipster happy to share his gift of gab with anyone so long as the subject never turned to his war experience.

I was anxious to head for Iowa City and rejoin old high school classmates, one of whom was Bob's younger brother, Paul.

Whether or not it was a factor in my anticipation, the truth was that my lifestyle would be less conspicuous at Iowa than it had been at St. Olaf. Iowa City had been a hotbed of campus unrest as the antiwar movement came to a boil and offered just the sort of anarchic environment I sought but didn't need.

~ The Night... ~

When I arrived on campus I was consigned to a temporary barracks in the basement of Currier Hall. The dorms were overflowing and so my first home in Iowa City was no more than a bottom bunk. No matter – all I needed was a place to pass out after a night of carousing downtown. Hell, classes hadn't even started. At first, legal drinking was a mixed privilege. Sure it was a relief to be able to flash your actual driver's license in bars, but assumed identities had resulted in a lot of laughs over the years – who could forget the times when we guessed wrong when quizzed as to our middle names or birthdates by savvy bartenders and grocery clerks? We got used to it. Iowa City was Shangri-La as far I was concerned. But bad news soon arrived from Des Moines.

Over the Labor Day weekend my old friend Tim Gebhart had gotten engaged. Tim paved my way into a new school in fifth grade. His family took me on a trip to Chicago that included my first visit to Wrigley Field. We were twelve and I remember being astonished at how savage a mere single was in the big leagues when I saw Hank Aaron line one to leftfield there. There were a couple of years at the height of our friendship when Kim was more of a brother and roommate to me than Mark was.

The Gebharts were up at Lake Okoboji in northwest Iowa for the holiday. Tim hadn't gone off to college from Roosevelt. He was working fulltime at the Firestone plant in Des Moines, making good money for his age at a stable, unionized job.

He proposed to his girlfriend Dawn on Saturday night and she accepted. They celebrated together before driving around the lake to share the good news with Tim's parents. Later, after dropping Dawn off at her cabin, Tim missed a bend in the road and rolled his Jeep.

I rode back to Des Moines with Darcy Pomeroy who'd been Tim's girlfriend for a good portion of high school. When we got into town we went straight to the hospital and were ushered quickly in to see Tim in the intensive care unit. The early prognosis was not promising. There wasn't a scratch on him, no visible, obvious wounds or injuries to indicate that he was barely alive as he lay there on display for the procession of friends that flowed quickly to his bedside like water towards a drain. Tim looked to be snoozing, just like during our countless sleepovers as schoolboys when I'd fire a good night fart at him across a darkened bedroom and drift off to the sound of his irrepressible giggling.

There were discussions with Tim's parents as to pallbearers and a visit to the apartment he'd taken for himself in West Des Moines to gather remnants of his apparently dwindling life. But his irrepressibility ran deeper than a giggle and something in him dug in and held on. All of us at the bedside were adjourned back to the lives from whence we'd gathered while Tim slept on.

He slept all through that autumn while I was figuring out that I could carouse more and study less in Iowa City than I had in Northfield without damaging the GPA.

The Iowa football team put together a winless season that was nevertheless well-attended. It was in the student section at the football games that flasks of schnapps and bottles of industrial strength nectars like "Mad Dog" were passed freely about. Mad Dog was a rabid strain of wine known to induce episodes of frothing, the customary treatment for which was a painful series of shots, usually Jack Daniels.

One Saturday night after a home game I found myself at a kegger on the outskirts of Iowa City. My loud, rambling diatribe on that afternoon's game in particular and the hapless team in general was abruptly ended when one of the other guests, who happened also to be a captain of the football team, took offense to my inebriated monologue and flattened me. The count was way past ten when I got to my feet and set about finding my way back to campus. After conventional hitchhiking failed to get me a ride, I wobbled to the middle of the road and took to flagging down the oncoming traffic. It worked. A police car arrived and offered to give me a lift. I got in and announced that I was headed for Iowa City. In that case, said my driver, we better turn around - Iowa City's the other way. My poor sense of direction was really getting to be an embarrassment!

Shortly after the football season ended I rode home again with Darcy Pomeroy for Thanksgiving. Again we went first to the hospital to check in on Tim. There'd been encouraging news recently of an awakening and progress. We were excited as we parked the car and hustled through the lobby to the elevator that took us up to Tim's floor. The bell dinged to signal the end of our ascent, the doors parted and there in a wheelchair sat what had actually happened that night at Lake Okoboji when a bend in the road became a bend in a life.

Staring back at us, slumped and wide-eyed, was an emaciated, atrophied rendition of Tim. It was a residue really; the shell a cicada leaves behind when it buzzes noisily off into the sky or the spent stage of a rocket that falls away when its fuel is gone. We had no idea what to say to this impostor. It had been easier when he was asleep.

Slowly in those bleak, grim days a remarkable rehabilitation began. Doggedly, Tim resolved that he would walk again. Eventually he did. But instead of leaving home to become a husband and father and whatever else might one day have been, he remained mostly his parents' son and his sister's brother.

He also made many new acquaintances and gained lots of admirers over a period of years through his agonizing walks to and from bus rides that took him back and forth from daily workouts at the downtown YMCA. Gradually a modified version of his signature giggle returned. Life would probably have been swifter and easier for Tim if piloted from a wheelchair, but he turned out to be at least as tough as my brother had tried to make me, as tough as my cousin John.

His pace was slow and mechanical, almost ro-
botic, but there was also a relentless rhythm about
it. One of his arms was stiffly curled and clutched
against his torso which made everything he insisted
on doing even more laborious.

Our friendship had already receded from the
high tides of elementary school by the time Tim
was so gravely injured, and his accident relegated
him to the wayside of most of his peers' lives. After
slowing down for a look-see most of us whizzed on
past.

That first year in Iowa City brought me back in
touch with Marcus Leonard. One of his roommates
in Burge Hall across the street from Currier [where
I'd finally been assigned to Room N-30] was Paul
Conley, a sometimes drinking buddy from high
school and the younger brother of my new brother-
in-law. Marcus and I became part of an amorphous
social group based in the dorms on the eastside of
the campus. Our pack included Jon Aiello who
lived down the hall from me in Currier and was also
a Roosevelt grad. Jon was one of the test pilots in
the drug scene at Roosevelt and was in fact attend-
ing college on some sort of a vocational rehab
scholarship that had been presented to him as an
alternative to a jail sentence in the disposition of a
drug possession charge he incurred during high
school. In time the program would have its intended
effect on Jon's life, but not right away. He was in-
strumental in the maintenance of what was becoming my daily habit of getting high, usually by

smoking fairly garden variety cannabis, but occasionally more exotic strains like Thai Sticks or sensimilian or, when we were really lucky, hashish [aka, "chunks"] or hash oil.

Sometimes on Sundays a bunch of us would head for the Amana Colonies about a half hour's drive west of Iowa City for dinner at Zuber's, one of the many family style restaurants the area was noted for. We'd pass joints around on the ride to fuel our appetites and then gorge ourselves on homey meals like roast beef and unlimited helpings of the trimmings; mashed potatoes & gravy, vegetables, rolls & butter, etc. Then we'd drive back to campus, getting stoned again for dessert. It was all very quaint.

So it was that we set out one idyllic spring Sunday. When we returned to the dorms we noticed that canoes were being rented from the boathouse on the banks of the Iowa River, just behind and below Currier and Burge Hall. It was a beautiful late afternoon, so we decided to go for a row. Once on the water our flotilla was soon engaged in a good-natured naval battle that resulted in my canoe capsizing. I surfaced and decided to swim ashore rather than risk capsizing one of the other vessels by trying to go aboard. I was a strong swimmer in pools when straight and clad in swimming trunks so I thought nothing of what looked from my vantage point like a relatively short sprint to the boathouse dock. But I was high and fully dressed, including long pants and a woolen sweater, and this wasn't a pool. In fact there was a fairly swift current whisking me downstream. Every time I paused to check my progress towards the boathouse I seemed to be further from it. I started to worry. While still stroking I began calling to my fellow sailors just in case I went under but they thought I was clowning. I reached the point where drowning seemed imminent and I started looking for the newsreel of my life to begin flashing before me. Desperately I kicked off my brand new shoes to lighten my flippers and just as my noodled arms made the last thrash at the water they could have managed, my toes barely brushed the muddy river bottom. I staggered from the shallows and flopped exhausted onto the slimy riverbank. I felt at once nearly dead and unprecedentedly alive. It was the most competitive swim of my life and narrowly, I won.

That year was the only one of three in Iowa City that was spent in a dormitory. In the fall of '74 I moved off-campus with Jon Aiello and another fellow whose name and face I can't recall. At home Mark's second marriage to Pam Fletcher had already given way to a third. He was twenty-five when he married Pam Dikis in our living room on Kingman Boulevard.

Jon became the head of a student organization called the Hancher Entertainment Commission, a group responsible for booking and staging concerts in Hancher Auditorium, the relatively new and state-of-the-art performing arts venue on the Iowa campus. Since I was Jon's roommate I was in show business!

He made me a roadie for all the shows he booked over the next two years, ranging from Bonnie Raitt to Bruce Springsteen. I had never heard of Springsteen when Jon called during the summer of '75 to tell me that he'd landed him for a show in the fall that would coincide with the release of the album, *Born to Run*.

"Wait and see" Jon predicted. "He's gonna be big!" About a month after he played Hancher, Springsteen appeared simultaneously on the covers of *Time* and *Newsweek*. The Hancher gig was probably one of his last pre-arena shows.

Jon was an audiophile who schooled me on the merits of components like Dual turntables and Advent speakers, though I never put together my own stereo system; I just listened to his.

Early in our shared housekeeping an acquaintance of Jon's came knocking one night. The heat was on, he said, and he needed to lower his profile. Would Jon mind holding some stuff for him until things cooled off? Sure, said my roommate, no problem. So we took possession of a lawn & leaf bag full of high-quality pot with the understanding that it was cool for Jon to "keep the house high" until Cheech or Chong or whoever he was returned to fetch his inventory. There wasn't much left when he finally came back in the spring.

Jon had another pal in Iowa City who was a robotics genius with a part-time job in a lab at the renowned University Hospital complex. One day he was assigned to organize and inventory a store of chemicals that had fallen into disarray after a long period of neglect, sort of like the driver's license clean-up I'd been assigned a few years prior during my summer job working for the state.

Once Matty realized that nobody knew how much of what was in the facility he helped himself to a large jar of barbital, one about the size of a #5 jug of mayonnaise. He set about the tedious work of portioning the pixie dust into capsules like the Sandman run amok. There was a Hancher concert coming up featuring Doc Watson and Bill Monroe & the Bluegrass Boys. Lots of friends from Des Moines and elsewhere were coming to town and Matt prepared to throw them free caps of pixie dust like candy tossed from a parade float.

Barbital had first been marketed under the name Veronal, a nod to Verona, the town where Romeo & Juliet fell asleep. The barbiturates were first synthesized from a distillate of animal urine and apple juice by a German guy who won the Nobel Prize for chemistry early in the twentieth century. He knew he had something when he observed that his concoction put dogs right to sleep. He could never have imagined the pack of wild dogs that was sedated that weekend in Iowa City.

Jon delegated Matty to emcee the Watson/Monroe concert and even the blind Watson could see that Matty was, uh, impaired when he oozed onstage and slurred out an introduction modulated at about sixteen rpm. People were falling down and hurting themselves all around me. Running strictly on booze and reefers, I stood out as practically caffeinated. Some of the out-of-towners had to stay over an extra day until their personal fogs lifted enough to give them a good shot at completing the hundred mile journey back to Des Moines.

I can't say exactly why I didn't gobble any of the magic beans. By that point I think I knew on some level that I had come equipped with an accelerator but no brake. The prospect of what I regarded as real, true drugs – actual chemicals – frightened me enough that I recoiled from them as I had from the edge of our roof the day I fetched that whiffleball.

Iowa City had hosted many anti-war demonstrations in the late sixties when Martha was there, but now as the war wound down students took to the streets to undress instead of protest. Streaking was in vogue. The closest I ever came was walking back from campus one night after making the rounds of the downtown bars. A small group of us, both genders, stopped at an intersection and traded dares until we were all standing there shirtless with pants around our ankles. We didn't streak. We would have been tripped up by our own underwear. We just stood there like dopes playing that variation of poker where cards are slapped against foreheads so each player can see what everyone else has got but not what they're holding themselves. The light changed and we pulled up our pants.

I guess this was my rock 'n roll phase. Besides

my affiliation with Jon, the Iowa City impresario, I
was also able to land backstage grunt work in Des
Moines every summer at the "Iowa Jams" that were
staged at the State Fairgrounds by Steve [Whizzer]
White, a good friend and fellow All Center Bum of
my brother's. Whizzer owned a small record store
called Music Circuit, but he really made a name for
himself as a promoter. His annual summer holiday
orgies at the fairgrounds were major events with
headliners over the years that ranged from the
Grateful Dead to the Eagles to ZZ Top to Journey.
One year Boz Scaggs was on the undercard. Boz's
unique blend of pop vocals with bluesy, jazzy layers
to them had found a devoted audience in my circle
of friends about that time, so I was pumped when
Whizzer dispatched me to the Des Moines airport to
pick him up on the rainy, muddy morning of the
show and deliver him to the fairgrounds. The residual cool from hauling Springsteen's equipment off
the truck in Iowa City was about gone, so this one-
on-one with Boz would restore my façade as someone with connections to the music scene. I drove to
the airport flashing back on all the times in the
dorms we passed around bongs with Boz's *Freedom
for the Stallion* wafting in the background about justice and greed and, "Lord, you got to help us find a
way." I was in an idolatrous stupor by the time I got
there, but came abruptly out of it upon meeting my
Muse. Boz must have been having a bad day because he was rude and boorish and didn't seem to
care that he was riding shotgun with the individual

who probably had a greater appreciation for his music than anybody anywhere. By the time I dumped the prima donna off I felt like a stiffed cabby. He got out and told me I could keep the disillusionment.

I spent the summer of '75 subletting an efficiency apartment in Iowa City that was to be Jon's home when school started in the fall. I took a writing course that was being taught by John Irving, an alum of Iowa's famed Writer's Workshop who was back temporarily as an author-in-residence. He was at work on what would become *The World According to Garp,* and read excerpts from it in class. Each of us had the chance for a private audience with Irving, and I came to mine armed with some pages about the Pizza Hut caper I'd been working on. He read them assuming they described a fiction and told me the story was too implausible to be taken seriously. I think I got a C in the class.

That summer was otherwise constructive. I had ballooned by then to a ponderous weight of about 235 lbs. I took advantage of the relative isolation to ration myself to one meal a day at the student union and dropped a lot of weight. Before the summer was over I made arrangements to share an apartment on the outskirts of campus with Marcus Leonard come fall.

There is a portrait in my mind's eye of Marcus standing with his bare feet rolled onto their outer edges, clad in a tartan flannel bathrobe with a cup of coffee in one hand and a lit cigarette in the other.

He is grinning, probably amused by some misadventure or tantrum of mine.

That was his uniform and posture; those were his accessories. He was taking business courses; I was focused in Journalism and English, although the degree I would earn was a Bachelor of General Studies. I think I balked at taking another lab science beyond biology that would have qualified me for a B.A. Marcus was neither a morning person nor a driven student. I used to think he should have majored in psychology or philosophy because he was always an astute observer and a deep thinker. He was also a talented artist but he never struck me as a businessman. His old roomie, on the other hand, Paul Conley, had partnered up with John Lore, an ex-Raccoon Valley Oriole like Wayne Dean and me, and gone into business. Still students, they opened *That Deli* and tried to make sandwiches, money and grades, all at the same time - tough juggling act.

It was four years since Stephen's death when Marcus and I moved in together. Surely we talked that year about the good old days in the Kingman neighborhood. Surely we talked about the tragic night in Greenwood Park and its aftermath. But if we did it was probably when one or both of us had been drinking and, for my part, most of whatever we shared besides a mailing address was stored in blackout.

Marcus was driving a red MG that year and I do vividly remember riding home to Des Moines with him once the morning after a snowstorm had blown through the Iowa City area. It was a clear, sunny day, but the interstate was pocked with random patches of black ice. We had just passed a semi when we hit one. The car went into a series of 360's and I braced for the impact of the just-passed semi that I was sure would finish us off. I guess it missed us. We came to a stop in the highway median facing back from whence we'd come. I gulped my innards back into place and looked over at Marcus. He was grinning at me, just like he used to when we were poised to leap off the Deans' garage roof. He laughed at the whiter shade of pale I'd turned.

Most people knew the wise guy facade I used to fend them off. But I told you Marcus was good at observation. I think he'd always known that I was scared.

My sister Mary was also in Iowa City that year taking her obligatory stab at college. She was cute and the kind of girl that guys liked to have as a friend even if they could have nothing more. It was good for her to leave Des Moines and get beyond a relationship that had consumed most of her high school years. Somehow she'd fallen under the sway of a guy several years older than her who'd been a wrestler at Roosevelt before graduating and becoming a connoisseur of cannabis and an employee of Carl Dean. The house he shared with his mother had become a gathering spot for a lot of us, including Wayne, Stu and Craig Dean. There was an endless renovation of the attic begun that became the ostensible reason for convening to get high, play pitch and listen to Boz Scaggs at high volume.

Mary had worked all through high school at a mall record store. She was always a better worker than student. For her Iowa City became the place where she wandered into a career in restaurant management when she took a job at a pizza joint in Coralville, just outside Iowa City, following her one and only year of college.

I took eighteen hours worth of class in the fall semester of my last year in school and got straight A's for the one and only time in my life. I wanted the spring and final semester to be as feathery as possible, so I front-loaded the year, although my pursuit of a liberal arts degree with no major permitted me to cherry-pick the course catalog for classes that suited me best. One was a focus on the works of Fitzgerald and Hemmingway; another, the complete works of Shakespeare. Finding great literature well-stocked with drunkards and rascals was reassuring to me, as were the Old Testament accounts of spectacular lust and wantonness that triggered lively discussions in a theology class. Somewhere in the college years I learned the word, *agnostic*, and I applied it to myself now in faint hope that it might lend an air of academia to my heathen ways.

One morning in May of 1976 I came to somewhere in Des Moines with someone who cared no more for me than I did for her as my dad waited in Iowa City for my name to be announced at commencement. Now what?

* * *

Dad arranged a job hunting safari for me in Chicago. He had a couple of old Army buddies there, one of whom worked for the *Sun-Times* and another who was a big shot in the PR department for a corporation based there. They both granted me interviews as courtesies to my father. I went alone, riding the bus and staying at a hotel in the suburb of Oak Brook, compliments of my brother-in-law who was working his way around America in the hotel business. When I rode the El downtown to my interviews I was scared to the point of laundry-marking that the trains were going to topple off the tracks. Thank God no job offers came my way – how would I have explained that I had no intention of throwing myself into the furnace of a big city like Chicago?

Once safely back in Des Moines I sought out jobs at small town newspapers and was offered a couple, but I turned them down on the grounds that rural Iowa was as too-small/too-boring as Chicago was too-big/too-scary. What I needed was something in between those extremes, a city like, well, my hometown. As summer's end neared I was planning to return to Iowa City, enroll in grad school and take a job as the Assistant Sports Editor for *The Daily Iowan*, the university's student newspaper. I'd had a part-time job as a staff writer in the sports department the previous year. I got paid a hundred bucks a month, mostly to cover intramurals, but occasionally I got to write a feature article or cover Big Ten sports events. Once I traveled with the football team to Evanston, Illinois to cover the Hawkeyes' game with Northwestern and felt important when I was brought food and stat sheets in the press box just like the real sportswriters. Another time I covered a home basketball game versus Purdue at the venerable Iowa Fieldhouse in lieu of the DI Sports Editor, who usually reserved the major stuff for himself.

Sports writing seemed like a natural and perfect marriage of two of my chief interests, and a return to Iowa City was also appealing since life there could be managed on foot and through free rides on Cambus, the intra-campus transit system.

As I was packing to move back to school I heard about an entry level opening in the sports department at *The Des Moines Register.* I applied. Leighton Housh was the Sports Editor. He called me in for an interview. Also present was Michael Gartner, then Editor of the *Register*, future head of NBC News and still later a Pulitzer Prize winning writer of editorials. At the time he was writing an occasional column on etymology, so I was duly flattered when I was offered a job on the nighttime sports desk, at least in part because they'd both noted my correct use of the word, *emphases* on my resume [as in, Bachelor of General Studies [B.G.S] from the University of Iowa; emphases in Journalism and English].

Newspapers then were just making the transition from typewriters to computers. I was assigned to someone from the paper's in-house geek squad to learn how the *Register's* system worked. At least I think that's more or less what they had in mind for me if I'd hung around. I was assigned hours something like three to eleven, and I quickly realized that, while this job was a great opportunity to break in and start a career as a journalist, I would be way behind my friends on the partying curve by the time I got off work every night. Also, I was intimidated by the computer system and afraid of having my poor typing skills exposed. Couldn't I just go to ballgames and write a syndicated column from home? The stereotyped sportswriter who filed game stories from the press box and did his investigative research in hotel bars – that's where I saw myself starting out.

It took me all of a week to tell opportunity to get lost. The first night after I quit I was out on the grounds at Waveland with a bunch of friends. We had a buddy who was a greenskeeper there and he sometimes worked overnight running the sprinkler system. He knew the layout like the back of his hand and we'd tear around from hole to hole in his Cushman by the light of nothing more than the joints we passed back and forth.

Des Moines had a police helicopter doing a lot of nighttime surveillance of trouble spots like the parks that summer; anyplace that kids were gathering to get drunk, stoned and loud. In this case, though, we were few in number and trying at least to be discreet. I still don't know what drew the eye in the sky to us, but suddenly there it was, hovering loudly above the municipal observatory behind the seventeenth green where Stephen Leonard had led us to look at stars. A spotlight knocked a big hole in the night. We scurried like roaches for the dark, but bullhorned orders from on high swatted us in our tracks like the wrath of God.

Every time I cue it up the scene of that helicopter landing amongst us that night on our neighborhood golf course/sledding hill plays back like an episode of, *The Twilight Zone.*

John, the greenskeeper and an ass-kisser in the style of Eddie Haskell from *Leave it to Beaver*, approached the officers and explained his presence there as the night watchman. We couldn't hear whatever he said that prevented the rest of us from going to jail. I was expecting either my first ride in an airborne paddy wagon or to see a phalanx of backup squad cars hustling onto the scene via the blacktopped maintenance road that wound through the course. Neither happened, but I was sure nothing came across the sports desk that night at the *Register* anywhere nearly as exciting as watching the grass grow at Waveland.

Maybe I convinced myself that there would be other jobs. Maybe I convinced myself that I deserved to start out as a full-fledged sportswriter, not a desk jockey manning the phones. Maybe I convinced myself that landing a job fresh out of college for the sports section that literally rubbed off on me almost every morning of my life wasn't really such a big deal after all. Maybe I convinced myself that getting drunk and stoned and lucky was more important than getting on with my life. And maybe I convinced myself that I was alright. I guess I must have.

I was right about there being other jobs. There were lots of them. I was a mailman for a few days and a night stocker at a grocery store for a few more. Occasionally I'd help some friends who were small-time contractors put in a new sidewalk or driveway. Of course I was back on Kingman Boulevard living with my parents and I think it was more or less during this sedentary period that my mother, who ordinarily served up a steady diet of enabling, offered me a small but potent portion of honest appraisal.

"Michael, you're dissipating," she told me one day. She said it evenly despite the fact that it must have hurt and angered her and my father to subsidize my lifestyle. Besides their emotional stake in me they'd both grown up in the Depression when, "Thou shalt not waste" became the unwritten eleventh commandment. Dad's constant admonitions about turning off lights in vacant rooms and using both sides of a sheet of paper before wadding and tossing it weren't borne of an avant-garde concern for the environment, but of a childhood of deprivation and hardship. My parents hadn't the means to spoil their children in the usual, material sense, but neither did they have the wisdom or experience it would have taken to avoid enabling the addictions of their sons. So increasingly obvious and public were those, in fact, that it was easy to ignore the very private cans of beer that mom was now stashing on the kitchen counter behind a slightly unfurled roll of paper towels while she hummed her old choral anthems and stirred until she was placid.

* * *

Martha's marriage to Bob wasn't the first occasion when the Wellmans and the Conleys hoisted glasses together. Records of the two families joined in celebration go back as far as 1970 when Paul and I were rounded up in the afore-referenced bust at McDonald's that was triggered by an attempt to walk out of a window instead of the door.

Paul was friendly and gregarious, a credit to his Irish heritage. He was a good swimmer in high school and had what it took to start his own business while still in college. We used to joke about the dangerous mixing of gene pools when our older siblings took up with one another and eventually married.

Paul was a good guy bound for success when he went out to celebrate St. Patrick's Day in 1977. March 17th rivaled December 25th in the Conley clan. Bob was one of the founders of the local chapter of The Friendly Sons of St. Patrick. Even Marshall, his close Jewish friend, had a touch o' the Irish in him – his surname was Green.

I think I was in the same joint as Paul at some point that night, but he was alone after he dropped a girl off in the wee hours and headed for his parents' home in Ankeny, a suburb north of Des Moines where they'd recently moved. During high school the family's address was right across the street from Roosevelt on Polk Boulevard.

Paul never made it to Ankeny. He died in a one-car crash on a sloping, winding road on the north-side of town. Until Marcus Leonard dug up his copy of the funeral program I'd lost the fact that both Marcus and I were among the pallbearers that day when the Irish Catholic undertaker buried a young son lost on St. Patrick's Day.

Paul's death was the third major accident that had whizzed too close for comfort in less than six years, to say nothing of the Pizza Hut shootout and my own traffic mishaps. Was I paying no attention? Was there nothing I couldn't shrug off?

* * *

Sometime late in the '70's Jane reappeared in my life. She was about to start coaching gymnastics at Drake University when our paths re-crossed and had by then gotten into and out of an ill-fated marriage. Feelings that had never really been extinguished between us rekindled quickly and we were soon essentially living together. These were strange days. I got a job at Reichardt's of all places and was suiting up everyday to accessorize expensive Southwick suits with complementary shirts and ties for the customers in Men's Furnishings. I was a haberdasher at the store where I hadn't been able to afford the vaunted burnt ivories as a boy, suddenly in the employ of the family that many thought had used its high profile and influence to pull the rug from beneath me at Roosevelt. But I knew that wasn't the case and, besides, I liked the 50% employee discount.

Working for Bill Reichardt was a far cry from my summer in the steel plant. He was one of the strongest personalities in town; a man not anxious to relinquish the spotlight that first shined on him during his football days. On one of my first days working for him he took me along downtown where he was to give a talk to a bunch of farm wives in the city for an agricultural symposium. He used me like a living mannequin, an anti-scarecrow, draping my outstretched arms with assorted neckties – clubs, reps, foulards – and sending me out amongst his audience so they could feel the silks while he demonstrated the four-in-hand knot from the podium that I remembered from Sunday mornings as a small boy. His remarks ranged widely from serious instruction on the nuance of men's fashion to a comedic monologue in the style of Red Skelton. He had the ladies eating out of his hand and lining up to get their husbands measured for a Southwick befitting of an agri-businessman.

Reichardt's TV advertising was based on the slogan, "…because I'm here. I'm Bill Reichardt [pause; grin], and I own the store." It was genius. Everybody who came in the store asked for him by first name. When he was pinned down by someone he'd never met or couldn't remember that seemed to know him he'd resort to hand signals that we, his subordinates, were supposed to be on the lookout for. If we saw him scratch his nose it meant that we were to casually approach and drop the mystery person's name into the conversation so Bill could invoke it later as though he'd known it all along.

He was intimidating and I always thought he bore both a physical and emotional resemblance to Burt Lancaster. Once he came upstairs to our department to sign off on an order for a trendy line of merchandise placed by my manager, a young guy from the other side of town about my age who already had a wife and child. He took one look at the Henley styled casual shirts and overruled the entire buy.

"But Mr. Reichardt, these are popular." Ken protested. "We could sell a lot of them."

"God damn it, Lucas! McDonald's could sell a lot of spaghetti, but they don't, and we don't sell shit like this!"

He went on to make clear that he thought the garments weren't sufficiently masculine and left for his daily handball match. Ken was embarrassed but the rep that just lost the big sale was amused.

I don't know that Bill Reichardt and my father

ever formally met. Dad certainly never was a customer at the store. He rarely bought himself any
clothes anywhere for that matter [he'd hold aloft a
pair of underwear that he was looking through like a
window and say, "Mildred, I knew when I bought
these twenty years ago they wouldn't last..."].
Probably one of the few establishments they had in
common was Wellman's Pub. Bill became a fairly
regular customer there and liked to tell his company
a story about how he promised his son Doug a new
car in high school if he beat me out for quarterback
at Roosevelt. Hell, he should have given me the car.

When Bill Reichardt died in 2004 an overflow
crowd that included me rightly gathered in review
of his many accomplishments: football star, suc-
cessful entrepreneur, state legislator, gubernatorial
candidate, youth advocate, etc.

When my father died the sum of his fit on a
laminated card he carried in his wallet that his children now carry in theirs.

* * *

After several months of this house-playing arrangement Jane got a roundabout job opportunity
that required relocation to Seattle. It was a ground
floor deal with a company that would be selling
eyeglass frames. The coaching job at Drake paid
meagerly by comparison and I was in no position to
make her life easier and the decision tougher, so she
accepted the job. We softened the mutual emotional

blow with some half-ass plan for me to join her after she settled in the northwest.

It was the fall of 1979 when I left Des Moines and flew to Seattle to rejoin Jane. I took full advantage of my employee discount at Reichardt's before I left, loading up on business attire on the off chance that I'd grow up some day and land the proverbial "real job."

My dad took me to the airport the day I left; just him and me. It was a very Episcopalian sendoff – he nearly buckled me with his handshake and he was looking deep inside me, eye to eye. There was no hugging, no declaration of feelings. Neither of us thought there needed to be. A few hours later, after buzzing the summit of Mount Rainier, I landed in the arms of someone else I loved.

Jane had an apartment in Kirkland, a Seattle suburb on the shores of Lake Washington. The relative lack of sunshine didn't matter much at first; the postcard views from the balcony out toward the lake were simply black and white instead of color. Down the winding street a ways were the training facilities of the NFL Seattle Seahawks. The Sonics were en route to winning the NBA championship. Jane's job provided her an MG convertible and there was also a temporary but legitimate need for me to hold down the fort at the fledgling company's office so their few employees could all be in the field selling. In between taking the orders they'd call in to me I was blanketing the Pacific Northwest with what passed for my resume. The whole thing had potential.

I started to go for morning runs along the lake-
front, down past the Seahawks' training compound.
Life there was both opulent and organic; more of a
latte-da hike than a rat race. Microsoft and Star-
bucks and Nike and Boeing were convincing America that it wasn't necessary to stop and smell roses –
take a virtual sniff on the jog or jet to work. "Joe"
copped an attitude and went from porcelain mugs
into disposable Styrofoam. There was a rampant
consumerism masquerading as conservation; a run
on outdoor gear so the masses could get back to nature and trash it.

Me, I was just looking to go to an occasional
ballgame and find my way to Neverland. Big league
football and basketball were both played in the
Kingdome. I attended an NBA playoff game that
looked like a laboratory observation of mitosis from
my perch in the upper reaches.

I don't know that I ever broke loose and got
really inebriated in Seattle; I didn't want to embar-
rass Jane in the eyes of her colleagues, most of
whom were men – still youngish entrepreneurs who
looked good in the fashion frames they peddled. I
began to chafe at this imposed moderation. Months
passed and I had no job. The grayness in the view
from the balcony was deepening. When word
reached me from Des Moines that Stu Dean was
putting together a softball team for the coming season, I knew what I had to do. What meant love in
the face of a chance to play second base for the
Greenwood Lounge? Besides, I had responsibilities

back home as an uncle. My niece Carlye, daughter of Mark and Pam, would be starting school in the fall. They were back in town after trying for a time to make a go of it in the San Francisco area. Martha and Bob had Grace and Joe by then and their family too was coming back home after stops in the Detroit and Washington D.C. areas while Bob climbed the ladder as a hotelier. Mary too would soon be coming back to Des Moines to further her developing career in the hospitality industry as the general manager of a splashy new restaurant being planned by her employer from the Iowa City area.

So strong apparently was the gravitational pull of our childhoods that we were all coming back home – or in my case it could have been that I just needed somebody to drink with me.

Jane took me to the airport early in 1980 to send me back where I'd come from. I was ping-ponging between loved ones; between childhood and adulthood. When I'd left my father at the airport in Des Moines several months earlier I was afraid. Now I was just sad. The flight back was a little like the last time I drove home from St. Olaf at the end of my year there; in both cases I sensed that I was abandoning a good thing that I simply wasn't up to.

I had a good season for the Greenwood softball team, but 1980 was otherwise not a very good year.

Very early on February 29, 1980 I drove my older sister's VW wagon through a stop sign at the intersection of 31st & Kingman. It would be more to the point to set the time as very late on the night of

February 28th. What were the odds that a car driven by a young nurse on her way home from work would arrive at that intersection just as I did on my way home from closing the bars? She had the right of way – no stop sign – when she broadsided me and knocked my car on its side. I remember climbing out of the shattered window in the driver's side door but I had to buy a copy of the police report in 2008 to find out that I was wearing Levi's, white socks, dirty bucks, a light blue shirt and a blue nylon jacket. Oh, and that my blood-alcohol content was .22. Apparently I told the officers on the scene that I had started drinking at 5:00 P.M. on the 28th and stopped just after midnight, a period of time over which I estimated that I'd had six beers. The report further notes that I failed two field sobriety tests and was very cooperative and talkative throughout the arrest and booking process, repeatedly asking the same questions which are not detailed.

Five days after turning twenty-six I had at least my third accident while driving drunk and was arrested for drunk driving for the first time.

I awakened on that extra day of 1980 feeling sorer than usual and also with the vague, unfocused sense of remorse that had become a routine hangover symptom by then. On this occasion I recalled an accident but little else.

It's a difficult thing to describe the experience of coming to after a blackout. The easiest way to put it is simply to say that I remember not remembering, over and over again. It became axiomatic for me that gaps in my memory were always like expletives deleted from the record of my behavior. Even if the blanks were filled in by friends or witnesses with accounts that they thought amusing and harmless, their stories described a person that I was embarrassed and ashamed of and didn't want to be.

My parents often had questions that I was powerless to answer, and this morning was an extreme example of that. I got in the car with my dad to drive down to the police impound facility where the carcass of the VW had been towed. I was not prepared for what I saw. The car was demolished, and it was only because a mere Renault had toppled it that I'd survived. Remarkably, the driver of the Renault had sustained nothing more than a slight knee injury.

I was shaken and scared, but only to the point of resignation about my ultimate fate. My campus agnosticism had given way to an acknowledgement that God did exist and would justifiably see to it that I got what I had coming to me. Chronology is problematic when reconstructing sustained periods of time marked by memory loss, but I believe it was the disposition of this arrest that included my referral to an agency called Lutheran Social Services for an alcohol assessment. I was interviewed and subjected to a standardized psychological battery. I still believe that I tried to be as forthright as I was able in anticipation of the relief that might come with an expert telling me officially what was wrong with me. The diagnosis was that I was not alcoholic, but did have vocational and family issues arising from my transient employment history since graduating from college. I was pretty sure that I was a drunk, but I certainly didn't want to be, so who was I to argue with the professionals? I took the diagnosis as a license to keep drinking and addressed the vocational issues by getting a job bartending at the Greenwood.

The sentence on my drunk driving conviction was deferred on the condition that I not repeat the offense during the next year, at which point the blot would be expunged from my record. I couldn't do it. In August I re-offended and only strings pulled by an attorney pal of Bob Conley's spared me the just consequences of that arrest.

Heretofore nights on the town typically culminated with a fine meal like the Bootlegger Combo [cheeseburger and fries] at Country Kitchen or a hot beef sandwich at the Y-Not Grill after the bars closed. But then came cocaine.

The great thing about cocaine was that it made it possible to keep on drinking. When my circle first sampled it we all agreed that it was good stuff but, given its cost of a hundred bucks per gram, we determined that it should be held in reserve for special occasions. Very soon any given weekend was accorded that status.

We had a distributor in our midst whose home we'd often repair to now in lieu of the greasy spoons at closing time. He lived in the same condo complex as the County Sheriff, so anyone who was too noisy in the lobby, elevators or hallways was fined 'bad boy points' by our host and supplier, a sort of demerit that was assessed in the form of withheld "lines" during the all-night after-parties.

Trivial Pursuit was a favorite game between closing time and dawn, when a chirping bird would signal the end of the party like an obnoxious buzzer ending a basketball game.

Sometimes we scanned the parking lot for pickups so we could wager on produce tossed from the fifth-floor balcony at the bed of the truck – target practice. We also played card games like pitch and poker for exorbitant stakes beyond the means of the players. Someone would lose in excess of four figures and we'd play all night until they either recouped or the creditor forgave the debt and slunk home at dawn.

I moved into a small house in a quiet residential block on the west side of Des Moines with three other guys who were more or less as aberrant as I. There went that neighborhood.

We had no business living amongst decent, civilized taxpayers. Fireworks, in every sense of the word, sprayed from our address on a regular basis. Those of us who lived there fired them upon one another as a display of affection. A shower might be interrupted by an incoming bottle rocket. Sometimes we were under fire just backing out of the driveway. Once a small missile launched from the front stoop went straight up, ricocheted off the aluminum awning, dove to the sidewalk and then made a diagonal beeline along the lawn straight toward the car of the elderly next door neighbor who was pulling away with his wife and granddaughter as passengers. Their lives flashed before our eyes just as the projectile scooted beneath their car and exploded. We had fled inside for asylum, not unlike the tactics we employed as young snowballers when the driver of a pelted vehicle stopped and gave chase. It surprises me still that the enraged driver, who we referred to as Mr. Puddles [his beagle was named Puddles], didn't gather a mob to come and drive us from the block with torches and pitchforks. We were man-sized kids with drugs and booze and cars and an animal house [which we named Big Steve in the middle of one long night when the discussion turned to a children's book about Steve the Steam Shovel] making a nightmare of our neighbors' peaceful American dreams.

By the summer of 1982 my brother's third marriage was in the rear-view mirror and the fourth was just up ahead. Mark and Michelle took joint interest in a commercial property a few blocks down Ingersoll Ave. from the Greenwood Lounge. The premises had been a series of restaurants and bars. In fact, it was during its incarnation as a supper club called The Captain's Cabin that Martha and Bob had first met while she was a waitress there. Most recently it had been The Silver Bullet Saloon. In September that year it reopened as Wellman's Pub. My relationship with my brother took on a new dimension.

Mark became my employer after nearly thirty years as my older brother. I was part of the crew that worked day and night to refurbish the interior of the property on a shoestring as we readied for the grand opening. Mark and Michelle considered naming the place Whiskeyman's Pub which would have been a mistake on multiple levels. Besides sounding like shit it would have failed to capitalize on a potentially big asset – our name. The Wellman family was deeply rooted in Des Moines, and for all of our misadventures along the way, Mark and I both were widely known "Good Time Charlies." If we'd been opening an accounting firm there might have been skepticism, but it made some sense to imagine having a good time in a saloon owned and operated by the Wellman boys. I was to be the general manager of the place. On the afternoon of September 29 we were literally nailing barn siding salvaged from a defunct farm into place on the interior walls as city inspectors trailed us about waiting to sign off on the necessary licensure so we could open the doors. When we finally did there were people lined up outside waiting to get in. The place was immediately and consistently packed. Working there was exhausting and exhilarating, a little like defending The Alamo with food and beverage for munitions.

For all my imbibing, I had never been one to drink before or during work, even if the workplace was a bar. When I drank it was wholeheartedly, not on the sly, so early on there were many long, hard days and nights followed by raucous, rowdy wind-downs that routinely spilled into the following day. Had it not been so loud all the time we might have heard the ticking of a time bomb.

Mark's friends were given access to the back of the house where various malfeasances went on during business hours. He and Michelle, not yet married but soon to be, were living "south of Grand," that part of Des Moines with the same cache as the "south of France." After our first few months in business the pub's staff gathered at their home for a Christmas party. As the joyous night wore on we were polled as to what would be our preferred holiday bonus. The unanimous vote was that we get a quantity of cocaine immediately and shovel it into the party like coal into a locomotive.

And so it went. One night after hours Mark and I brawled behind the bar. Another time we came to in the morning uncertain as to the whereabouts of the previous night's considerable revenues. The SOP at first was to take the day's proceeds home each night and deposit them at the bank the next morning. On this occasion nobody could recall who had left them where. Mark was all over me like George Bailey on Uncle Billy if you can imagine Jimmy Stewart and Co. scrambling around trying to dodge drug and alcohol induced bankruptcy. Luckily when we got to the pub the canvas bag full of cash was right where it had apparently been left – on the floor in the [oops] *unlocked* foyer!

We were prosperous both because of and despite our debauched lifestyle. Our respective social circles were a steady source of both clientele and staff. Wellman's was a trendy hot spot and lots of people wanted to play AND work there. Not long after it opened as strictly a pub, foodservice was added and the place quickly became a popular lunch spot too. Soon a patio was added [or 'outdoor service area -OSA - as the licensing authorities labeled it] at a time when virtually no comparable establishments in the market had one and we were on our way. If my last name came up in the course of some transaction, writing a check at the grocery store maybe, the usual reaction was, "Oh, do you own Wellman's Pub?" Close enough, I thought. Being Little Wellman was the best it had been since my batboy days. Mark got himself appointed to the Steering Committee of the Iowa Cubs, the local professional baseball team; Triple A affiliate of the Chicago Cubs. He was practically in the big leagues!

If only we hadn't been such inebriates. My brother and I had started in the bar business like kids in a candy store but we were actually asthmatics in a coal mine.

Mark first went into outpatient treatment for substance abuse in 1983. It wasn't long before, as my employer, he gave me the choice of going to rehab myself or losing my job. I went to treatment. It was, for the record, the first time I ever identified myself out loud in the company of others as an alcoholic. By the time this finally happened it was as obvious as Marilyn Monroe standing in Times

Square and declaring herself a woman. We'll never know how many people, upon reading the headline, "WELLMAN BROTHERS ARE ALCOHOLICS!" would have muttered "no shit" in response.

My first bout of sobriety lasted for all of maybe six weeks in the aftermath of my four-week outpatient treatment program. Not only did I continue to work in the belly of the beast, I kept hanging around the same old places and people in my free time. I imagined that my friends regarded me admiringly, impressed by my forbearance in the face of my condition. Actually my presence in their midst was more like that of a priest at an orgy. It was selfish to make them squirm. I did the kind thing and rejoined the party.

Drinking for an admitted, relapsed alcoholic is like eating without benefit of taste buds. You do it because you must, but it's joyless as never before. There isn't the cover anymore of chalking up misadventures to boyish oat sowing. I was thirty years old and subordinate to my brother as both sibling and employee when the latter relationship came undone. Jobless and sharing half of a duplex across the street from the pub with a reprobate who still worked there, I was plucked from the scrap heap by Serge Garrison.

Serge was in charge of a non-partisan bureau that provided staffing support for the state legislature. He was a stoic North Dakotan with a grim countenance behind which hid the fact that he was really quite a nice guy. His son Bill had worked at the pub during the summers of his college years so, in a spirit of reciprocity I suppose, Serge hired me as a Research Analyst to work at the statehouse. My job was to take minutes of legislative committee meetings, draft proposed legislation as requested by legislators and otherwise grease the gears of Iowa's branch of the USA.

It wasn't easy fashioning the confused deliberations of a bunch of part-time statesmen into documents worthy of the Founding Fathers, but I tried. I finally had need of the business wardrobe I'd amassed on my way out the door at Reichardt's. I looked like a white collar working stiff when I'd drop in at Wellman's after a hard day at the seat of government with my sleeves rolled up and my tie loosened. I'd enjoy a few beers and a few racks of pool while dropping the names of the movers and shakers in state government I'd spent the day advising.

What a pose! I lasted a couple of years only because the legislature was in session maybe a third of the year. The rest of the time was known as "The Interim," during which I basically played hide-and-seek with my superiors, bluffing and dodging my way around the cavernous Capitol building.

I was a complete novice at our office's variation on the three martini lunch. There was one spectacular occasion when a group of us went downtown at noon to eat. Everyone had a beer or a glass of wine or two with their meal before heading back up the hill to finish the day. I never made it back. All I know is that by sundown I was by myself at a "gentleman's club" [one of the great euphemisms of our time] on the northern outskirts of town. At some point I left there and got lost on the freeway system, eventually running out of gas and passing out on the shoulder of the interstate somewhere south of Des Moines. I was awakened by a state trooper early the next morning who drove me to the next exit where I called in sick for work and used my watch as collateral for enough gas to get home. I was at low ebb, living now with my sister Mary who was in the throes of a short-lived marriage. She and the rest of my family collaborated on an intervention in my life, telling me in effect that they would individually and collectively shun me if I didn't accept help. I was tricked into attendance at this summit conference, of course, the way a person is tricked into attendance at their own surprise birthday party. The way I recall feeling at the time is extremely loved and lucky and relieved. My patient records describe me as angry and depressed. Only later would I reflect on the fact that I drank to the point where people who loved me might resolve not to, both for their own sake and for mine. It becomes difficult to feel lovable when those who've been there are looking for a way out.

Back I went for a second round of rehab. If I didn't necessarily enjoy it, I accepted my need for it, just as I had before. I embraced the program and resolved to better follow the advice that came along with my ticket back to life in the real world. I changed my social patterns and networks, a wise strategy that was probably negated when I resigned my post as a legislative staffer to reprise my role at Wellman's Pub after an absence of two-plus years.

* * *

By 1986 when I returned from Capitol Hill to the pub, the old Kingman squad had long since splintered, in some cases to far-flung outposts. Marcus Leonard had done a stint in the Peace Corps, serving from 1982–84 in Kenya before coming home and moving west to California. The youngest three of the four Dean boys were still in the Des Moines area, but Wayne was adrift and out of contact, whereabouts usually unknown. Fred Donald had found his way to Iowa City at some point and been unable to break free of the expansive drug culture he found there. All eight of the backyard parents were still alive and all four of the marriages they constituted were intact. Only the Deans had moved from the old neighborhood, but even they still lived within Roosevelt's reach.

It seems too bad now that none of us fully realized how much we still shared at a point when our lives appeared to have gone separate ways. The loss of Stephen Leonard had been sudden and violent. The loss of Wayne Dean was more figurative and ambiguous – a missing child versus a dead one – while the arrested alcoholism of my brother and I was analogous to children with a potentially fatal disease going into remission. Fred Donald was alone, fighting for his life and losing.

There was plenty of heartache to go around but each household hoarded its own share. I didn't know then that my maternal grandfather had a problem with the drink. In contrast, Jean Leonard had shared with her son Marcus that there was alcohol in his bloodline whether he took a drink or not. Whatever the respective families' histories and internal policies on their disclosure, when the neighborhood mothers gathered it was less to commiserate and support one another than to posture in the context of a bridge game.

Pretending that innocence still ran the boulevards in blue jeans and sneakers was easier than mourning it.

* * *

The pub still bustled. Sales rose every year as the management increased in efficiency and lowered its profile. For an unusually sustained period Wellman's was busier than any comparable establishment in town. It was almost two distinct clienteles merged in one enterprise, catering to a predominantly white collar, tea-sipping crowd at lunchtime that yielded the night to young howlers who took their fluids by the shot. Regulars ran the gamut from prominent state legislators and local business leaders to down-and-outers who'd regurgitate their night's purchases in the parking lot for us to hose away the next morning - a shower rinsing off the building's hangover from a hard day's commerce.

For a time I prospered too. If my job brought me daily too close to the flame of booze and drugs, my lifestyle was otherwise healthier than it had been since I began high school. I started running almost every day and eventually entered and completed a half-marathon. My weight steadily dropped before leveling off around the 175 lbs. I carried into high school. I still have a picture of myself that was snapped near the end of my one road race. I look almost too thin, but vigorous, with short hair and nothing on except running shoes and a pair of panty-sized nylon shorts, a sweat-soaked purple Wellman's Pub t-shirt balled up in one hand. I had come a long ways from careening recklessly through the streets by night to running them practically naked first thing in the morning – no wonder I looked so tired!

I'd always figured that my smoking and drinking were linked inextricably; that without one, the other would fall away. Not quite. I stopped drinking, smoking pot and using cocaine, but I found that a smoke after a meal still satisfied. I continued smoking about a pack per week, a vestige of a formerly vice-ridden way of life that I felt entitled to keep as a souvenir.

One afternoon in the spring of 1987 I was at work when a middle-aged man and a young woman walked in and proceeded to take themselves on an unescorted tour of the premises. They didn't take a seat at a table or approach the bar, just walked around and checked the place out. Right away I resented them without knowing the slightest thing about them.

They were Rick Middleton, an old softball opponent of Mark's, and his twenty year-old daughter, Chris. The Middletons were just moved back to Des Moines from Springfield, Illinois and Mark had apparently agreed to hire Chris to work that summer at the pub before she started classes at Drake in the fall. Besides her attitude she had naturally curly blonde hair. She was more inclined to smile than speak, the first indicator that my immediate impression of her might have been off the mark. I was to be her boss. That was the plan.

Chris was a good volleyball player. I noticed that when she joined the pub's coed team that played in a sand volleyball league on Sundays. She was reluctant to make that obvious as the staff newcomer and generally deferential, but she nevertheless managed to get across the point that she was interested in me. Overriding the thirteen year disparity in our ages must have been a narrower gap in maturity levels.

Chris was undeterred not only by my seniority and staff rank, but also by the fact that I was already philandering with another subordinate colleague. Despite the fracturing marriage of her own parents Chris exuded a powerful domesticity. I kidded her that she reminded me of Mrs. Ingalls from *Little*

House on the Prairie. After we started dating I imagined that this was a girl who'd really get me squared away and organized. Laughable now is the notion that she would, for instance, bring balance to my checkbook. Less so is my remembered hope that she would stabilize my non-financial affairs.

She transferred credits from Eastern Illinois to Drake and enrolled there as a junior to study art and graphic design while continuing to work at Wellman's part-time. At some point in 1988 her parents split up and we took an apartment together in West Des Moines. I was not drinking but still occasionally behaving in ways that conflicted with my values, a classic alcoholic tendency. On the one hand I was drawn to Chris in lasting ways; on the other I resisted the fidelity that came with full commitment. One by one I resumed my libertine ways, including intemperance.

Predictably our relationship foundered and Chris moved out, leaving me by myself, an arrangement I'd only attempted once before when I stayed in Iowa City for summer school. But that situation was temporary; this was indefinite and unsettling. I soon realized that I preferred life with Chris to life without her and set about convincing her to come back. She was more insistent that I abstain from other company than from alcohol, a demand that was reasonable and which I contritely agreed to. We may even have toasted to our reunion. I went shopping for an engagement ring which was presented upon her acceptance of my proposal on Christmas morning, 1988.

I was thirty-four, nearly old enough to run for president. She was twenty-one and fresh off her first vote in a presidential election. We were not otherwise as far apart as those numbers.

As a matter of fact, I was quite surprised to learn that we even had the old Kingman neighborhood in common. When Chris was a little girl she and her family had lived for a time at 1010 43rd ST., right around the corner from us. About the time I was trolling the halls of Roosevelt my future wife was toddling around in her backyard that was separated from mine by a section of chain link fence. Happily the aberrance of my teen years didn't include taking any notice whatsoever of Chris' presence then at the perimeter of my life.

Planning began for an August wedding. While Chris and her mother Joyce collaborated on that front, Mary and I entered negotiations to buy the pub from our brother and his wife Michelle. We took over the still-thriving business in April of 1989.

My relationship with Mary had always been closer than those with my older siblings. Martha was too chronologically distant and Mark was too lots of things – too scary, too dangerous...too married! But Mary always had my back. More than the other girls in the neighborhood, she held her own in snowball and dirt clod fights. After my hand-me-down clunker bike locked up on me and was discarded into the Waterbury creek bed, it was Mary's sporty blue Schwinn Tornado that I used to try and keep up with the Deans on their Stingrays. Later it was the second-hand Volkswagen Beetle she bought with money earned at her part-time high school job that I'd borrow when I was home during my first years of college. Eventually she even gave me a place to live. She was always a harder worker than me, but not as lucky in love. When she accompanied me during one of my two rounds of outpatient treatment for substance abuse as my "concerned person," she was told by one of the counselors that she suffered from the "wounded pigeon" syndrome. She liked to take guys in that needed help, whether it was a drunken brother, a fatherless boyfriend or a chronically stoned husband.

Mary was a natural for the hospitality business; she'd always been accommodating people. As for me, I was just lucky that Mark's enterprise had blazed a trail for me from barfly at the long-standing Greenwood Lounge to saloonkeeper at a thriving new pub just down the street. I literally stumbled into the business.

1989 was shaping up as a promising year. Besides my new partnerships in business and matrimony, the long-lost Cubs rose improbably to the top of the standings.

World Series refugees since 1945, our boys had advanced to the very brink of the Fall Classic in 1984 only to become the first team with a 2-0 lead in the best-of-five playoff format to lose three straight. The last game in that unprecedented collapse had begun expectantly for our family with all of us gathered back at the house on Kingman. We closed ranks around dad as the Cubs broke in front, anxious to celebrate with him when the Cubs secured their first National League pennant in nearly four decades. But it was not to be. As the game unraveled the room emptied. One by one we fell away. No one spoke. The last two in the room were dad and me. I wished the Cubs would come through for him sometime before it was too late. I wished that I would too. I felt sad for him that day as I followed him downstairs for a grim supper.

Mark was four years sober by the time he and Michelle sold the pub. In 1985, just a few months after he completed a treatment program at Hazelden, the famed facility in Minnesota, they were vacationing with friends at Lake Vermilion in the northern part of that state. There was an explosion during a boat refueling and Mark, Michelle and Whizzer – the concert promoter – were all burned, Michelle most severely. Everyone survived, but Mark and Michelle's marriage would not. It was failing by the time the sale of the pub dissolved their business partnership. Several months later Mark took a job as a paper salesman with Carl Dean.

The summer run-up to our wedding was frantic.

Martha was hospitalized with Crohn's Disease, a chronic and serious intestinal illness. Her malady was reminiscent of our mother's troubles when we were kids; troubles diagnosed as ulcers that resulted in the removal of most of mom's stomach.

Chris' grandmother was battling cancer and ultimately passed away in July, just after Chris' birthday and less than a month prior to the wedding.

In the midst of it all we managed, with my parents' help, to buy a small house on 63rd ST., a four-lane autobahn that was a main north-south artery and I-235 tributary on Des Moines' west side.

On August 12 we were married at St. Luke's. My support team included my brother and my nephews, Christopher and Joe. Dad was my best man, an idea first suggested by Mary, one that I wished I'd thought of first. Dad also did the readings during the ceremony as I stood by channeling the guards at Buckingham Palace while nervous perspiration snaked from my scalp down my face and inside the tuxedo that swaddled me like a strait jacket.

Mary, Chris' younger sister Sara, and my nieces Carlye, Grace and Gretchen were also part of the wedding between the young woman fleeing a broken home and a thirty-five year-old boy. It's probably accurate to say that God took the marriage more seriously than did many of the guests in attendance that day.

After a reception at the clubhouse of the apartment complex where we first lived together we were off for a honeymoon on the shores of the Gulf of Mexico, courtesy of my Uncle Jim and Aunt Sonja whose Florida condo was at our disposal. We almost got up at a karaoke bar in Tampa and sang,

~ The Night... ~

We've Only Just Begun – almost.

We set up housekeeping on Route 63. Instead of enrolling at Drake for the fall term Chris had taken a job with the state that completely muffled her artistic skills. In exchange for attendance to her bureaucratic chores she got a meager salary and a nice bag of benefits.

In September the Cubs roared into the playoffs as my honeymoon continued before ending with a thud when the San Francisco Giants ran them off the road to the World Series. At least the pub was packed for the games. Life was good and getting better. I embraced the commitments of matrimony and the responsibilities of entrepreneurship. Smoking pot and snorting cocaine were long gone and drinking had been modified, the traditional folly of a drunkard. Instead of carousing until the rooster crowed with my single friends, I might work late at the pub, lock up, have a few belts alone, then bring some beer home to complete the wind-down from a long night. When I drank in public Chris was usually there. If her presence didn't always inhibit my thirst, well, she could always chaperone.

The first real intrusion on the beginner's luck that marked my debut in the role of grownup came when mom got sick.

Actually she got sicker. From the time of her ulcers and stomach surgery when I was seven or so she was never quite well. Her shrunken stomach made eating much impossible. She smoked a pack or more a day, first unfiltered Chesterfields; then

Winstons. And somewhere along the way she acquired a taste for beer. It only took a can or two before you'd notice the silly smiles that didn't fit what she was talking about or the gesticulations that marked even her telephone conversations. Drinking didn't really alter her routines, it just became part of them.

After the Deans moved from the neighborhood mom and Marsha Dean developed a more symbiotic relationship than they'd had when they were next door neighbors. Marsha often went to the grocery store for mom, who was the elder of the two by a dozen years or so, and she'd stay and pour out her troubles to a sympathetic ear after she delivered the order. Topics came up for discussion between just the two of them that never did around the bridge tables.

Underneath our mother's short-cropped gray hair, glasses and ill-advised coping strategies was always the vivacious brunette with twinkling blue eyes and a deep-seated faith. Nothing she did ever struck me as a betrayal of what she proclaimed. If there were many nights in her latter years that she fell more quickly and easily asleep after a few beers, I am certain that she still made a point of prayer, and that most of it was on behalf of others. I have no choice but to believe that my mother's prayers were a primary instrument of my salvation, wrapped as tightly around me when I was vomiting up whiskey as her arms had been when I had a case of the cobbywobbles.

She looks pretty and pleased in pictures from our wedding – and healthy. But she was soon diagnosed with an ovarian cancer that was to kill her. Bedridden when the new decade began, she was hospitalized and dying by February. At first I thought she was going too gently. Death had visited our neighborhood but never our home, and I did not want to take a good look at it. But she made me; she made us all. Her last days were almost celebratory. She was emaciated but radiant; a withering body that still housed a joyous, expectant soul that blazed through her eyes and smile like leaves in autumn signaling a change of seasons.

Each of us was summoned for a private turn at her bedside. She told me, again, about the day I was born; how sunny it was, and she told me how glad she was that I had come to live with them. There was no advice, no parting wisdom for my future reference after she was gone. She simply made clear her feelings for me and her anticipation of what was about to happen. It was as though we had all accompanied her to a depot and were awaiting her transportation for a journey she would be taking without us.

She died and left on February 11th, five days past her 47th wedding anniversary. She was buried on Valentine's Day. She was seventy.

Ever since I have remembered the experience of watching my mother die as the most compelling example of faith I've ever witnessed, with the possible exception of watching my father live.

~ Far From the Trees ~

Alone now in the house on Kingman Boulevard,
dad went through the motions. He was retired to the
same modest means he'd always lived by and not
about to impose himself upon his children and their
families. We were all living in Des Moines. Later
that year Mark married for the fifth time in a ceremony at City Hall with dad in attendance as one of
the witnesses the law required. His bride was Jackie
Boldes who'd been one of Chris' attendants at our
wedding. Mary was engaged to Dave Tasler.

Dad continued his custom of daily walks, man-
dated by his doctor in the wake of his heart attack
some twenty years earlier. But he strolled aimlessly
about an area where he'd lived for decades. Instead
of the walking shoes and warm-ups that were trendy
by then he wandered about in flannel trousers, old
wingtips, light jacket and the style of Stetson made
popular by Hollywood's leading men in the 1940's.
Hands pocketed, he'd pass the island, Roosevelt, all
the old playgrounds, pausing occasionally to stoop
and pick up a long discarded coin or tennis ball or
random litter that had found its way to the curb. I
doubt that his heart ever quickened on these rounds
after he was left a widower, which was to be their
purpose. I think it just hurt.

The house that sometimes wasn't big enough for
six of us was probably too big for just him and
thirty-five years' worth of memories.

Luckily dad's culinary tastes were primitive
[remember the fridge junk sandwiches] because he
didn't cook [the son of the open-flame toaster]. We

all took turns hosting him which was always more privilege than obligation – he still made for fun company – but he refused to let himself become someone's chore. If it's possible he was gracious to a fault. He lived mostly under a self-imposed house arrest.

It wasn't long after my mother's death before Chris and I decided to try and balance the teeter-totter by having a baby. Early attempts having been fruitless, we started to explore possible reasons why. On a couple of occasions I had to produce a sample of fertilizer, then race it across town to the lab for analysis. There's nothing quite like bursting into a doctor's office carrying the stuff of life in a brown bag like a tuna sandwich. Talk about making an entrance – all heads turn to the breathless courier and flash the knowing glare that says, "I know what you've got in there, mister, and I know how you got it!"

Happily, there were no deficiencies in my legions, a fact borne out when Chris announced in November that she was pregnant. The next time I had to race across town with the next generation in a sac was the following summer.

On the evening of July 9, 1991, I was sitting in the living room watching the baseball All-Star game. Andre Dawson of the Cubs had just homered off of Roger Clemens when Chris intruded to declare that she was in labor. Early in the morning of July 10, with considerable support and encouragement from me, she delivered our son. My knees buckled the first time I saw him coming straight for me like a fuzzy torpedo from the future.

We named him Max [after his maternal grandfather, Max Middleton] Jacob [after his paternal great-grandfather, Hans Jacob Hillestad] and branded him with the same monogram as his grandmother who died the year before his birth [Mildred Jeanette]. I'm glad that I didn't know until later that Andre Dawson was also born on July 10, in the same year as me, 1954. Andre Dawson Wellman would never have sounded as good to Max's mother as it might have to his father around dawn on July 10, 1991 if I'd been aware of all the potential omens at work that morning.

Chris didn't go back to work after Max was born. The two of them stayed home together with our dogs, Ruby and Maggie. Life on Route 63 became unacceptably dangerous for us now that we were parents – too much traffic moving too fast - so we soon moved to a bigger, older house on Harwood Drive in hopes and prayers that there were more where Max had come from. Our new neighborhood was just south of Roosevelt and the freeway and dotted with islands like the ones I'd grown up around on Kingman. This block too was more rounded than grid-like and I was surprised, frankly, to find myself living there. I owned a prosperous business and a home in a comfortable area. I had a pretty, devoted wife and now a beautiful, healthy child too. I felt both blessed and strangely fraudulent.

~ The Night... ~

As my 20 year high school reunion approached I was plagued by regret since I regarded that period of my life as one marked by frittered opportunity. I found myself thinking about Tim Gebhart and feeling undeserving of the good fortune that had visited my life versus the tragedy that defined his. Falling asleep one night, sober by the way, I hatched a plan to use the occasion of the reunion for establishment of a scholarship in Tim's name. It was a good idea that was badly conveyed when I read the resolution announcing it during the reunion festivities. I was drunk, of course, as I had been throughout the weekend. Anxious I suppose to make up for all the things I'd failed to accomplish while actually in high school, I overdid the whole occasion. I got so drunk Friday night that I still was when I arrived late for the golf outing that I'd organized on Saturday morning. At some point on Saturday night a sizeable group went to the pub, but I couldn't tell you if it included me or not. All I remember about that is feeling proud of the place's popularity in the community, but almost embarrassed that my livelihood derived from hosting keggers.

Our wedding and my mother's death had blown my spiritual cover of agnosticism. These two women together gently shooed me back to St. Luke's. Max was baptized there, and it was still a good place to find and spend time with dad. Robert Elfvin, the rector, was a draw, a break from the irregular up and down rhythms of the liturgy which alternates between standing, sitting and kneeling

like calisthenics in slow motion. He roamed the
front of the sanctuary during his sermons, never referring to notes. He smiled often and laughed frequently and loudly. Father Elfvin was robust and
wide-eyed and so was his faith. He came across as
reassuring instead of preachy and we liked him;
most everybody did. People neither impressed nor
disappointed him much, but he really liked them
back. It was a comfortable arrangement, and I
trusted he was following an example from somewhere up the chain of command.

Sometime between mom's death and her funeral
I remember dad telling him, "Chief, you sure do
have a gift. You sure are in the right business."
Amen to that.

Alas, the more comfortable I became at church,
the more ill at ease I was away from there.

A drinking alcoholic with two treatment programs and two relapses behind him lives a very
itchy life. Things got even itchier when dad developed diabetes and started having circulatory com-
plications. A slow-growing prostate cancer was also
discovered and a series of radiation treatments begun that left him weakened and demoralized.

Early in 1993 he had to be hospitalized and a leg
– I think it was his right – was amputated above the
knee. On his birthday, March 31, the congregation
at St. Luke's was recorded singing Happy Birthday
to dad, a corporate return of his customary favor of
calling every member first thing in the morning on
their birthdays. When the recording was played for

him at the hospital he was cheered and touched. He started to get better. Early in the baseball season I watched with him on TV as a Cub pitcher carried a no-hitter into the ninth inning. We laughed it off when it was broken up – the story of our lives, ha-ha – and his morale continued to climb. It looked like the four of us siblings would have to devise a new way of life for him once he finished the physical therapy of learning how to get about as an amputee. We started debating whose home he might move to when he left the hospital.

One Sunday he was allowed to come home with Chris and me for the afternoon and have dinner with us. The outing began with high spirits all around, but degraded into a grim foretaste of what lay in store for us all.

At some point dad had to go to the bathroom. The half-bath on our ground floor was small and made it difficult to help him from his wheelchair onto the stool. It was the sort of indignity that should be alright between loved ones, a small thing for a grown child of a devoted parent to help with in return for a lifetime of support. But besides being embarrassing for dad, it was also physically painful so relatively soon after his amputation. Because of his age an eventual prosthesis wasn't a given. For a man who didn't want to be fussed over even when he was an invited guest of someone who loved him, the prospect of needing assistance every time he had to use a toilet was unthinkable.

I remember that Sunday daytrip to our house on

Harwood Drive as the last time I ever saw my father outside of a "horse pistol," the malapropism he'd always use when others were hospitalized to try and make them smile. His condition – his spirit really – declined after that, though it may not be said that he gave up. He made clear to us before slipping into an irrevocable unconsciousness that he was not ready to die. He insisted that he had unfinished business without detailing what it was. His last days and moments were in stark contrast to our mother's, at least as I perceived them. The biggest difference was that mom realized when it was time for her to go. In dad's case there was equipment that had to be turned off, a joint decision made to send him on his way. I'm sure that his reluctance to die was a sense of duty; not fear. I'm sure that we were his unfinished business. Heaven knew that he missed his wife and had been adrift without her. Our decision to let nature take its course was enabled by the mysterious, romantic notion that there would be a glorious rendezvous of souls in a paradise somewhere beyond death, the long-awaited vacation together that they never had.

The four of us encircled the deathbed as numbers on the monitors attached to our father dwindled toward zero, the irregular countdown to his launch into another dimension. We clasped hands and braced for an impact. As had been the case some three years prior when mom was dying, I felt a deep closeness to my brother and sisters, like an infusion of hot water radiating through a tepid bath.

And then he was gone. We were orphans. I cannot take for granted that the four of us will ever again have time together as blessed as shared attendance to our parents' dyings.

I wrote a eulogy for the funeral, but none of us felt capable of delivering it so Father Elfvin recited it instead. He did it justice but it would have been a better thing if one of the man's own children could have managed it the way their father did the readings for so many years in that very place.

At the cemetery a bugler played "Taps" while Christopher, by then a Marine, delivered the American flag that had draped the casket to Martha. A reception followed at our house on Harwood. It was good-spirited and reflected the truths that Ward Wellman was held in high esteem by all who knew him and the co-parent of four children who were rich in friendship if nothing else. Late that night after a long day of memories, smiles and beers I finally sobbed to my wife about the deaths of my parents.

A fitting occasion for the last of my many regrets as a son; real feelings rinsed clean of nourishment by alcohol – again.

* * *

Mary was pregnant when dad died and Luke Christopher Tasler was born in September when the family pendulum swung back toward life. And not long after dad's death in May, Chris became preg-

nant again. Her due date was pegged at my birthday, February 24, so we weren't quite prepared for
Ben when he arrived, poetically, on February 6, my
parents' wedding anniversary. 1994 would have
been their 51st.

Ben's original name was Jonathan Michael so
that was the name they put on his bunk in the Newborn Intensive Care Unit [NICU] after they discovered that his lungs weren't yet producing surfactant.
Patrick Bouvier Kennedy had been born with the
same condition, called Hyaline Membrane Disease
or Respiratory Distress Syndrome in August, 1963.
He died two days later, some three months before
his father was assassinated, because treatments em-
ploying synthetic surfactant or a bovine extract of
the substance hadn't yet been developed.

Just days before his dad's birthday Jonathan
Michael became Benjamin Michael and we brought
him home.

About this time I was in the process of buying
out Mary's share of our partnership in the pub.
Business was still good – very good. But things
were getting a little too closely held for comfort.
Mary had brought Dave aboard and I had no desire
to be his co-employer as well as his brother-in-
common-law. They left the pub to concentrate on
nesting beneath the old maple on Kingman Boulevard, having moved there after dad died. Eventually
they opened a restaurant together in a western suburb. They are partners in every sense of the word.

Spring came, bringing with it a new baseball

season. I had just turned forty. My cup was over-flowing. I was a merchant of merrymaking living with my handsome family in a neighborhood more or less as quaint as the one where I'd lived as a boy when I went out with some friends to see a ball-game on April 20, 1994.

Actually, ballgames had been reduced to a pretext for unbridled drinking long ago. I'd been thrown out of Royals Stadium in Kansas City after being cut off there and wheeled out of Wrigley Field in Chicago on an ambulance gurney [I tripped and fell carrying a tray of beers, opening a gash on my forehead like the coin slot on a vending machine]. This particular outing was to Sec Taylor Stadium in downtown Des Moines, but I was still a big league drinker.

I don't remember who the Iowa Cubs played that night or what the score of the game was. I do remember drinking a shot of Southern Comfort at the pub as a nightcap with one of my employees, a cute young girl named Kimberley. By then it was late and the ballgame had long since ended. It was early in the morning of April 21, my mother's birthday, when my friends took me home and poured me out of the car, leaving me for Chris to deal with as though our home were an emergency room.

While our toddler and infant slept obliviously upstairs my wife listened to her drunk, sobbing husband, sprawled on the dining room floor, pledge that I wouldn't drink again. That nightcap at the pub was the last drink I've had, so here's to you Kimberley, wherever you are.

But mostly, here's to Chris, who was never angry but always concerned. And here's to Mark, who Chris called while I writhed on the floor. He was nearly ten years sober when his phone rang late that night/early that morning. It was about time I toughened up.

My drinking had been the impetus for many a middle-of-the-night phone call, but something good actually came of this one. On some level I'd always figured that booze was another hiding place my brother had pushed me into just like he put me in that tree when I was a kindergartner. This time he was there to catch me when I fell out. What a shame it would have been if the only example of Mark's that I ignored was how to recover from alcoholism. I had let him overshadow my life for so long that tradition now dictated I let him save it.

* * *

When Fred Donald graduated from Roosevelt in 1967 you might say he was ahead of his times. You could also say that later they caught up with him. He was such a gifted student that he finished high school a year early as a National Merit Semi-Finalist. He was accepted to Grinnell College, a very selective school that seemed well-insulated from the larger world, rooted as it was in the good earth of central Iowa. When he packed for college there were no drugs to conceal; no habit that Fred lugged with him to school. He left home the son of two teachers looking to maybe walk in their footsteps, but a lot of parents' trails became hard to follow in the stormy sixties.

Grinnell, it turned out, was not so well-insulated. When Fred arrived there it was becoming a forum for student protests. He didn't fit and left after a year, transferring to the University of Colorado. His mother remembers him then as still essentially a straight arrow trying to dodge and hide from an emerging popular culture. He was out of his comfort zone in ways more consequential than keeping himself fed and in clean underwear.

When he first tried drugs in the late sixties he probably did so as casually as our parents' generation had tried cigarettes. Reefers were the new Lucky Strikes and Chesterfields on college campuses. People who puffed too much when a joint was being passed around were told not to, "Bogart," as though the smoke was being shared by Humphrey and Ingrid Bergman or Lauren Bacall.

One thing's tendency to lead to another took Fred's Rockie Mountain highs to the peaks he reached tripping on LSD, mescaline and other hallucinogens. By the time he came back home to the University of Iowa in the early 70's, he was ready to graduate to cocaine and the opiates. Drugs were as plentiful and varied as the wide assortment of penny candy we'd all stuffed our pockets with when our blue jean brigade stormed the Rexall and Roosevelt pharmacies years earlier. Now, instead of jawbreakers Reed was into speedballs. Instead of sugar, the active ingredients were crack and heroin. Instead of pennies and cavities, the costs were, well, incalculable.

The BA he earned in History was of little use to Fred as our generation tried to sidestep gaping cracks in American culture opened by the recurring social earthquakes of the 60's. He went to grad school at Iowa and added a Master's in Education in 1975, wanting still to become something like the people he'd come from. He tried to get a job in Des Moines teaching high school, but enrollments then were declining and all he managed were occasional assignments as a substitute.

In 1977 he joined with three partners and set out upon the cutting edge of the computer industry, designing and building database equipment. Fred was the globetrotting driveshaft of the fledgling company that launched prosperously and seemed on the cusp of fabulous success when its president and cofounder fell by the wayside in 1984. At that point Fred was a self-described junkie. He left the firm with a sizable severance and vague intentions of a spinoff venture that never happened. His getaway cash was quickly dissolved in drugs and he became instead an entrepreneur of a different sort. His product line went from communication systems to methamphetamine. Once accustomed to dealing with corporations and government agencies, his clients now included prostitutes and street people. His commissions, really, were the drugs that fed his own addiction.

Fred's first drug offense was an arrest in Des Moines during the summer of 1982. He was charged with conspiracy to distribute cocaine. About the time that Wellman's Pub opened in September of that year he was convicted pursuant to a plea of guilty. His sentence was a fine of $4,000.

By 1986 he'd migrated to San Francisco where he was arrested and later pled guilty to a charge of possession of a controlled substance. He was sentenced to three years in prison and three years of probation. The prison time was suspended in lieu of 200 hours of community service. Fred also declined the court's offer of referral to a drug abuse treatment program. Within six months he was arrested again and charged with possession of a narcotic controlled substance. Those charges were later dropped despite the fact that Fred was guilty.

In July of 1994, when I was just a few months sober, Fred was arrested in the Des Moines area again, this time for selling meth, a charge that led to a suspended sentence of ten years and a two-year probation. It was his third felony drug arrest and his second conviction. He had never been imprisoned. He had never been in treatment for drug abuse.

His descent from a breezy, sunlit childhood into the dark cavern of drug addiction and trafficking was as agonizing and tortuous for the Donald family as the blunt force of Stephen's death had been sudden and numbing for the Leonards. His whereabouts and way of life were as mysterious and foreign to

Lon and Ella as were Wayne's by then to Carl and Marsha Dean. His promise was as broken as were those of my brother and me.

1994 also marked Congress' passage of the most sweeping, comprehensive crime bill in American history. By then criminal justice had already been reduced to a lyric from, *Take Me Out to the Ballgame* with the adoption of "three strikes you're out" sentencing in some states, notably California. Similar provisions aimed at violent felons and drug kingpins were sewn into the federal dragnet that was thrown out in hopes of catching lots of big fish. Unfortunately it also caught some small fry.

In May of 1995 Fred was arrested in Des Moines and charged again with selling meth. On May 31 the U.S. Attorney's office formally filed a one-count Information in Federal District Court. Before that day was over Fred waived his right to Grand Jury proceedings and pled guilty, effectively taking a called third strike.

Christmas that year at the Donalds' was different. The tree stayed up longer than usual into the New Year because there were unopened gifts beneath it. Fred, still living somewhere in the Des Moines area awaiting sentencing, never came home for the holidays.

Any chance he had of avoiding a life sentence with no chance for parole disappeared when he refused to give the names of his customers to the government. Understand that Fred was not the head of a vast commercial network of drug distribution getting rich off the misery of strangers. He was a facilitator, much like the guy who arranged for our cocaine and fined us "bad boy points" when we were too noisy; whose balcony we played toss-the-salad from; who hosted our middle-of-the-night games of Trivial Pursuit. In short, Fred arranged for enough drugs for his friends to subsidize his own dependence, a habit that was costing into the thousands of dollars each month. It's a melancholy irony to note that Fred declined when those who would imprison him offered a chance to profit at others' expense.

On April 11, 1996, the presiding judge reluctantly imposed what he would later describe as the harshest punishment of his career on the bench when he sentenced Fred to spend the rest of his life in jail. He thought the sentence was inappropriate but he was nothing more than an umpire brought in to call a batter "out" after the strikes were already levied.

Twenty-seven years after tentatively sucking his lungs full of pot in naïve acquiescence to the emerging customs of his times, Fred Donald was shackled and shipped off to a federal prison in Greenville, Illinois. Over the course of those years, the ones when most lives come into their fullest blossom, Fred withered from a flowering young man to a chronic, recidivist junkie.

Without ever trying to treat it, the land of the free punished his incorrigibility by plucking him up and throwing him away.

* * *

Meanwhile I was freer than I'd been since junior high. Max was turning five and heading off to kindergarten, Ben was two and gnawing on pork chop bones and Chris was pregnant with our daughter. Business at the pub still thrived. My hands-on role was amended to lunchtime duty and Friday nights behind the bar where I held forth like a quasi-Sam Malone, the ex-jock and sober saloon keeper. I also roused the building each morning from its stupor, coming in early each day to tally the previous night's proceeds and put Humpty Dumpty together again. There were mornings when the zippered bank pouch inside the floor safe that stuck up from the floor in the dishroom couldn't hold the registers' cash. There's surely no more glorious tedium than methodically counting stacks of twenty dollar bills so thick that a thumb and forefinger cannot clamp them. On the best days we'd rack up sales that ran into five figures, a bottle of beer and a bowl of clam chowder at a time. I had the good fortune to meet personally and shake hands with almost every one of the million dollars plus that came through the place every year on its way to our accounts. I was clearing far in excess each year of anything our father ever dreamed of making even though the work, while hard and messy, was trivial.

One of the traditions that emerged in the wake of my hitch at the statehouse back in the mid-80's was an annual invasion of Wellman's Pub every spring on the day when the state general assembly adjourned. The legislative community would descend en masse in a lucrative, for me, celebration of either democracy or its suspension for the rest of the year, it was never clear which.

In December Emma was born less than a week before Christmas. Like Ben, she was a few weeks early and delivered with immature lungs. RDS is not uncommon in premature babies, but both Ben and Emma were beyond the point in gestation where it's typically seen. Still, it took both of them a little while to catch their breath upon arrival in the world. Emma too spent her first couple of weeks in the NICU unit at Iowa Methodist Hospital where her father had schlepped dinner trays to patients after school some twenty-five years prior.

She came home on New Year's Eve. On New Year's Day, 1997, we were five at home on Harwood Drive.

Emma is the eleventh and last grandchild of Ward and Mildred Wellman. She followed by a little more than a year her cousin Millie Jane, the namesake of our mother born to Mary and Dave in October of 1995. Over the course of nearly three decades from 1967-96 one generation had sown the next in our family.

The first of the new edition, Christopher, is the age of my wife. The boy whose birth may have saved his father from military service during wartime grew up and enlisted in the Marines before joining the Des Moines police force that his dad and

uncle pestered for so many years. Before those positions he was also the high school quarterback at
Hoover that neither of them ever was at Roosevelt.
He bears a striking resemblance to Mr. Incredible
for a real live person.

Christopher is a good man with three beautiful
kids, Anna, Joe and Ellie that make me jealous of
my brother the grandpa [and just as I'm finishing
this Mark's daughter Carlye bore him another
granddaughter, Piper]. Martha too is a grandparent.
Her daughter Grace, who also developed Crohn's
Disease while in high school, was thought to be an
unlikely mother due to her medical issues. She is
petite and stylish, two traits that disguise toughness
fiercer than Mark was ever able to instill in me, and
her two pretty little girls, Genevieve and Elizabeth,
must strike their mom and her mom as especially
divine.

* * *

1997 was blotted by the death of Phil Leonard
in July. He was only forty-one, but it is hard to say
that his life was short. He seemed desperate for a
niche right from that first day in the neighborhood
when he hurled his shoes at us in retaliation for our
barbs. He became even more of a loner when he
finally returned to school after being hit by that car
on Kingman in third grade, an event that was a harbinger of more difficulty that lay in store. His
brother Marcus tells me now that Phil shared my

fascination with NASA's manned space program, something I never knew when Stephen Leonard had all of us stargazing at the Waveland Observatory.

There was a thicket of oddity around Phil that made him unapproachable and hard to know. Sometimes even his grins and laughter seemed menacing and his speech was guttural; difficult to understand. I wish I'd known that we were both spacemen.

Marcus says that Phil died by suffocating on his own vomit. Death came no easier for him than life.

By his mid-40's Marcus Leonard, once the middle of three brothers was the only one left, the Ted Kennedy of his family. The assassins of Stephen and Phil were drugs and alcohol and they stalked Marcus too. He remembers his father delivering him to a treatment facility years ago during the long intermission that divided the deaths of his brothers.

"He cried." Marcus says. "But he should have been happy. He tended life like his gardens. He loved to plant and tend the seeds but he hated to pull the weeds." Perhaps he just wore out. Pediatricians pull so many.

Marcus hasn't been drunk since his father gave him that ride to sobriety. It was a tougher pill than the anti-polio sugar cubes we all swallowed when we were kids, and it didn't cure or vaccinate. But it was lifesaving.

When Phil died Marcus and his wife Ronda were living in California. While they were in Des Moines for the funeral they came to the pub one day for lunch. I sat with them for a few minutes on the patio and we tried to talk small and catch up with one another's lives. It was like trying to move a big, heavy object through a space too small and we couldn't do it. It was awkward and uncomfortable and I couldn't wait for them to be gone and Phil's funeral to be over. We could have talked about so many things that linked us like childhood and addiction and college and troublesome brothers, and everything might have fit. But instead we tried to chat about the ways our lives had become different, about business. It was the sort of vacuous dialogue that is heard when strangers are paired randomly on the first tee box at a golf course and I am sorry for my part in it.

It didn't occur to me that we might really need each other.

* * *

Wayne Dean at this stage was unaccounted for. Wayne had topped out as a dapper schoolboy, swatting sandlot homers by the hundreds in the summertime and catching swooning girls one after another the rest of the year. He was always a talker, quick both of wit and lip, a gift first honed on schoolgirls that would later be used to hustle highs when drugs became the objects of his affection.

I more or less had a crush on Wayne when he first joined my life. We were never so much pals as mentor and protégé. The one-year difference in our ages was significant in the low-society of elementary school, so even though we ran in the same pack daily during the summers we were otherwise separated by the natural order of things. By the time we reached high school we already regarded each other almost as old friends. Oh, our misadventures occasionally overlapped at bonfire keggers or parents-out-of-town, open house parties that got out of control, but Wayne and I were never drinking buddies. And he was swept away in the rapids of the drug culture while I was just tip-toeing into the shallows of pot-smoking at St. Olaf in the early 70's.

For a time after graduating from Roosevelt in 1971 Wayne and Lynnette Donald were close, sharing drugs if nothing else as part of the same social community that swirled around the Iowa City area. As far as I know I never encountered either of them during my own years there. Lynnette at some point righted her course and attached herself to good purposes. Wayne became a rootless drifter, the very living antithesis of his BMOC father, Carl.

Oddly, each might have served well as a poster boy for their respective generations.

* * *

There was a turning of centuries coming into view and the truth was that the last third of the 20th, that portion since the 60's, had been anti-climactic. A pace and mood had been set that couldn't be maintained, and the 70's through the 90's were like a long hitchhike home from Woodstock.

A reckoning at that stage of the fortunes of us from the old block would have revealed that we too had been at our liveliest during the 60's. But the attrition that ensued in our ranks beyond the neighborhood was staggering across a range from shot at but missed to whereabouts unknown to locked up for life to dead and buried – all this despite the good fortune that none of us had gone to war that raged halfway around the world as we became young men. We sustained casualties of a different sort.

While the greater nation was piecing itself back together and lapsing into the sort of tired malaise that often follows sustained effort our boulevard brigade and the individual lives that comprised it came apart.

As one millennium gave way to another the grim census of the sixteen of us born to the Wellmans, Deans, Leonards and Donalds included at least ten substance abusers, our addictions part of the grimy residue left behind when the high tides of the 1960's receded.

The consequences of those addictions were as far apart as we were.

Five

Outcomes...

I was forty the last time I had a drink. Many who carried on without me never saw fifty. Their demises remind me that my former lifestyle was really workmanlike suicide, a twenty-five year brush with death.

Sometime around 1980 I played in a golf outing hosted by a local bar. My teammates for the event were Jan Long, the former state champion swimmer with whom I shared my first beers, and Russ Dineen and Ted Moore, a pair of cousins who were my roommates at the time in a nice house we shared across the street from Merrill Junior High.

We won the event and celebrated in a manner and to an extent that was customary for us all. Ted was a couple of years older than me and must have been one of the last of our generation to contract polio as a young boy. He wore a leg brace and was hobbled, but he compensated for his physical limitations with a strong personality and loud mouth. He used to say that a sharp pencil was the best club in his bag as he took control of the scorecard at the beginning of a round, but he was also a good putter.

Years later at his funeral mass I realized when a eulogist made a fond, funny reference to that golf outing that I was already the sole survivor of our foursome. Alcohol and drugs killed the other three in middle age.

I wasn't the only escapee. Robbie Farris survived the hail of gunfire that night at the Pizza Hut in 1971, wiggled out of the Navy after high school and finally came to terms with himself when he went to seminary in his forties. The old buddy I might never have met if he hadn't first been tossed out of a parochial school was ordained into the Catholic priesthood in 1996 and I was among those in attendance who received sacraments from him.

Marcus Leonard, the middle and surviving brother seems also to be at peace. I suspect it is not happenstance that he has no children, but he is happily married and has achieved remarkable success as an executive for a communications firm in Las Vegas. That seems an unlikely outcome and venue for the sensitive, artistic guy that used to grin fearlessly at me on the roof of the Dean garage or in the cockpit of an MG pointing the wrong way in the

median of Interstate 80. He's a self-described athe-
ist, but I don't buy it; anyone who gets within living
distance of Marcus can feel that he's not alone in
there.

But of course it was Mark that talked me off of
the ledge. He's twenty-three years sober now and,
though our relationship has settled in at the level of
arm's length estrangement, he remains probably the
most influential person in my life, a role he never
deliberately sought.

When we were kids I was the one who dabbled
in golf, becoming gradually decent after my igno-
minious debut in competition at the City Junior
tournament. Mark never played the game until he
took it up with a passion when he quit drinking. At
first it humbled him, a good posture for a practicing
alcoholic that wants to become a recovering one.
But he kept at it. As the frequency of my play fell
and his rose, there was a period of overlap when we
played regularly together and at commensurate levels of skills and scores. Those were maybe the best,
most tranquil times we ever shared. Now I rarely
play and he plays often enough to have reduced his
handicap to three or so. He's still a salesman in the
paper business, though he no longer works for Carl
Dean, and good at the schmoozing that golf lends
itself to. I would play more if I could do it alone.

My brother is more honest than me in the sense
that he readily declares himself to people, take him
or leave him. Some are drawn closer, almost nerv-
ously, vicariously delighting in his no bullshit,

plain-speaking style. On the golf course he's not bashful in dealing with slow, discourteous players, for instance. If the group ahead is on the green of a par three re-stroking missed putts while Mark's group waits on the tee, he'll let them know there's oncoming traffic; he sort of honks at them to get out of the way. People not accustomed to such bluntness sometimes chuckle in its presence; me it makes uncomfortable after growing up wondering what Mark was going to do next.

Most of my life I admired my father, feared my brother and sought to impress them both. Unfortunately, as so often happens in family flow charts, my brother was my de facto immediate supervisor. When dad died Mark, long sober by then while I continued groping for the bottom as I had that day in the Iowa River while in college, wrote me a touching, heartfelt note that I briefly thought might be the basis for a new dynamic between us. It made clear his good feelings towards me so perhaps I can now reciprocate. I am not afraid of him anymore and, in the absence of our father, I have come to admire some of his aspects. In his fifth turn at a role first thrust upon him as a high school second baseman, Mark seems finally content as a husband and there is at last a tranquility about his life.

As the idea of gathering the separate stories from our block into one formed in me, it was remarkable to realize that Mark and I were among the luckiest alums just by virtue of being alive and sober and free. On some level and for a long time I'd thought of us as chronic delinquents, forever the neighborhood ne'er-do-wellmen. Now we are both low profile, law-abiding citizens, and you probably can't imagine how much that means unless you too know the streets where you live are safer just because you stopped drinking.

Besides me Mark has pulled many others to safety who were drowning in booze. He's an even better lifeguard now than he was decades ago at Ashworth pool.

On Mother's Day of 2008 I took some lilacs that Chris pruned from a bush in our backyard and went to place them at our mother's gravesite. Our parents are buried side by side in the same cemetery in West Des Moines as Ed, Stephen and Phil Leonard. It's called Resthaven and I suppose that suits it well enough. At its approximate center, just across the asphalted path that routes through the grounds there's a small pond. Children too young to recall grief or read the small sign that whispers a widely ignored suggestion the animals not be fed are occupied tossing bread crumbs to the ducks and geese that loiter there when it's not winter. Meanwhile grownups decorate the closed holes in their lives with lilacs and the like.

I withdrew the inverted vase that stores between the markers for Ward and Mildred Wellman and turned it upright to hold the lilacs whose fragrance on a spring breeze will always recall mom as though she's whisking past leaving a faint wake of perfume.

I placed my token and withdrew to the car parked just yards away smack between my parents' remains and the pond. I was sitting there remembering my folks while a breeze wiggled the tips of the oak tree that shades their spot. The car radio was on and tuned at a low volume to the Cubs' game. They were losing in the late innings.

Minutes later a car approached from in front of mine and parked a ways down the curb. Out of it climbed Mark and his son Matt. They too brought lilacs. We had no appointment there.

I told them I'd been sitting there listening to the ballgame and hoping that the circumstances might somehow spark a Cub rally even though it was Mother's Day, not Father's Day.

They were in the midst of a joint response when, even with the volume at cemetery level, the voice of Cub broadcaster Pat Hughes blared from the radio with news of a game-tying homer. In the background we could hear Hughes' sidekick, Ron Santo, alternately screaming, "Yes!" and laughing like the little boy I was when Santo starred for the Cubs from Chicago and my big brother starred for the Cubs from Raccoon Valley.

There were grins all around before we returned to our now mostly separate ways.

The Cubs eventually won that game to break a tie with St. Louis for first place. By Father's Day they were three and a half games in front of the Cardinals.

Since the orphanage of Martha, Mark, Mary and me was completed by the death of our father some fifteen years ago it may be said that we have drifted from one another in the vacuum where once were our parents. Like moons of a planet blasted from orbit by cataclysm we float about the same small galaxy of Des Moines tracing paths that occasionally cross, sometimes randomly and sometimes by design.

Mary and I have kids that play ball and go to school together. Luke and Ben were even teammates on a Raccoon Valley All-Star team that won the state tournament when they were eleven.

Mark and I have many mutual acquaintances and are still often mistaken for one another on the basis of physical resemblance. There are also confusions by people who don't even know there are two of us. I discovered on the arrest report stemming from one of my accidents that the officer on the scene had scribbled my name down as Mark, not Mike. Through no fault of my brother's, I have felt throughout my life that we are twins born to a mother who suffered through a labor that separated our times of birth by roughly five years and would be periodically renewed throughout our lives beyond her womb.

Martha and I may actually be more alike than any other combination of the four of us. Sometimes I wonder if that accounts for our general abstinence from one another. We are both long-winded, trying too hard to speak the way our mother prepared meals and our father ate them; earnestly and precisely. We both feel strongly about anything we are moved to care about at all. Once bound by shared parentage we now have to meet each other halfway across a wide and deep political chasm. The trick is to look back instead of down. Our ongoing reverence for deceased parents is often trumped by the living, present influences in our lives. Martha is married to a conservative, Catholic, paternalistic Viet Nam vet capitalist who knows the art of the deal and dresses his estimation of others in the camouflage of humor. I am married to a schoolmarm whose bleeding heart is usually pinned to her sleeve. She teaches kids to read, has a weakness for animals and is so naïve as to have married me with the expectation that we would live happily ever after.

The youngest of their three children preceded the oldest of our three by a decade. We're at the same dance; we just arrived at different times with different partners.

Martha is sixty-one now. All four of us are beyond fifty. The ties that bound us as children are as frayed as we all are, but still as fixable as an heirloom that loses sheen without losing value.

And what of the other three families featured here? I've managed the tacit endorsement and some level of contribution from at least one delegate of each, but just because the project was begun in a sentimental spirit doesn't mean it can be finished properly without risk of some resentment.

In the years since we were all neighbors the Leonards, Donalds and Deans have branched out more than the Wellmans, families expanding into new territories like burgeoning enterprises. Besides Marcus Leonard and his wife Ronda settling in Las Vegas, his youngest sister Marie is in California and so are Lynnette Donald and her family. Martha and her brood did most of the exploring for us, following Bob's career to the Chicago, Detroit and Washington D.C. areas when the kids were small before coming home. Mary has never lived away from Iowa for any significant period. Mark had a brief sojourn to California and I followed Jane to Seattle for those several months like a stray dog before returning to the only place where it was even remotely safe for me to drink.

Sprees to Chicago and Wrigley Field became increasingly perilous. Besides the one where I spilled beers and blood in the upper deck at Wrigley I returned from another not long before our son Max was born rather beaten up. Some disturbance I caused at a downtown Chicago restaurant got me a manhandling that I recall nothing about except that it left me thoroughly swollen and discolored and I probably had it coming to me, according to my two bachelor traveling companions, both of whom, incidentally, were also with me on the occasion of my last bender and have since died. Their vices drew so little attention to themselves that they were gradually, insidiously fatal. My own, ironically, became so flagrant and obnoxious as to beg for my rescue.

Marcus Leonard wasn't the only Kingman kid to enlist in the Peace Corps. Besides his hitch in

Kenya, Laura Donald did one in Brazil before settling back in Des Moines. Both she and her sister Lynnette, like their parents, have become career educators.

As for the Dean boys, Stu, Craig and Danny are all still in central Iowa; according to Stu, Wayne is still somewhere at the margins of life and the world.

The anti-climactic sale of the pub in the fall of 2006 was like the toppling of the first in a chain of dominos. Chris was just beginning her fourth year as a first grade teacher in the Des Moines public school system, her first under a new principal – Laura Donald! Their association led in turn to a party at Laura's home where I found myself for the first time in a long time talking with her mom. Stashed somewhere in my cluttered pre-occupation with self was a vague awareness that Fred Donald had gone to prison at some point on drug charges. His mother filled me in on details. She told me that there was a formal petition for a commutation of Fred's sentence before the government and that there had recently been a meeting at Roosevelt of some of his old classmates to generate letters of support; Mark had been there and since written one. I told her that I'd be glad to do the same, but really that conversation crystallized my sense that there had been an improbable degree of drug and alcohol attrition at work on our block over the years. I wrote the promised letter and then resolved to write this book.

If divestiture of the pub opened a window of time for writing it also slaughtered the goose that had been regularly laying those stacks of 20's for so many years. Chris and I knew that the combination of her teaching salary and proceeds from the sale would not long subsidize our big, old house. We put it on the market in the spring of 2008, quickly found a buyer despite a sluggish market and set about finding new lodgings. There were several reasons for looking smaller. Besides lower overhead we sought a place that was easier to tidy and we were also anticipating Max's departure for college a year hence.

Quite accidentally one day while taxiing kids to and fro we happened past a small home for sale on the very fringes of the Waterbury district. It is semi-secluded with a greenbelt, woods and a creek across from it. Built the same year I was born but much sturdier than I, the house has one other notable fea-ture: the lot where it sits facing Ronwood Drive abuts the back yard of Carl and Marsha Dean around the corner.

It is modest by Waterbury standards, a brick ranch at the bottom of a bowl that's rimmed by higher-grounded and more lavish homes, but its set-ting is park-like and serene. It appeared to be in most ways just what we were looking for and in short order we came to terms and arranged to move, notwithstanding my ambivalence about the renewed proximity to old neighbors. I was by then well along on the manuscript of this book and had been in some contact with Stu Dean in the course of it, but that was mostly while reconstructing good times. I wanted to know what I suspected the Deans would be reluctant to tell – even in confidence, let alone for publication – about what happened to them after the Kingman years.

Moving day was June 1st and I remembered on the morning of June 3rd as I annually do at some point on that date, that it was Wayne Dean's birthday, this one his 55th. I tried to call our new, old neighbors at the same phone number I recalled from forty years ago; they still have it. When Marsha Dean's recorded voice answered and bid me to leave a message, I did.

Marsha had passed by me one morning when I was mowing our new lawn just prior to moving in and stopped to welcome us to the neighborhood. In her seventies now, her eyes are still round and bright but they're not much involved when she forces a grin. I wondered what portion of her is reserved for here and now and whether a greater share is devoted to mourning a still absent prodigal son. A few days later we had a long, bittersweet talk on the phone.

The conversation rose and fell so fast that my stomach hurt. She chortled an assortment of choice memories: looking out the picture window early on summer mornings to see Stephen Leonard perched in her cherry tree helping himself while he waited for her boys to join him outdoors; the Leonard kids knocking on her door as a group to ask if she'd baked cookies that day; my mother remarking on how the baring of the trees each winter exposed our lost kites of summer like so many birds' nests.

She also recalled the night when I was granted asylum in her basement. A rowdy pack of us that didn't include any of the Dean boys had been drinking and carousing in the Waterbury woods and were flushed by the arrival of constables. A foot chase ensued and I finally shook my pursuers by rolling breathlessly underneath the bushes in someone's backyard. Upon realizing where I was I crept out of hiding and knocked on the back door like a ghost come out at midnight and Marsha took me in until things died down.

That recollection segued from good times to bad; she undressed her still open mother's wounds and let me have a quick peek at them. They are as deep as the others from around the old block that have bled across the years.

It is nearly September now and I still haven't even laid eyes on Carl. Talking to anyone about him the word workaholic is spoken. I've seen and spoken several times to Craig, who mows their lawn. He says he lives elsewhere with his wife and daughter but it's clear he too is again my neighbor. His car is there almost at all times. He is on disability as a result of an injury sustained some years ago while in the employ of his father. When he is not leaning against the handlebar of a lawnmower he hobbles about with a cane, usually with a cigarette in one hand, sometimes with a small dog tethered to the other by a short leash and always with a baseball cap perched barely atop his head as though it doesn't really matter that it's there. His complexion is mottled and he looks older than we are.

Our paths crossed often enough over the years for me to suspect that Craig's struggles now are consequences of the former ways and means of his life. I know the feelings. Perhaps Mark and I have just been randomly more fortunate than say, Wayne and Craig. Grace is mysterious beyond my understanding. It's as powerful, abundant and sporadic as sunshine and also like it in the sense that it can be sought or hidden from. Sometimes you have to take a deliberate step out of the shadows to feel it.

Marsha invokes maternal privilege in response to delicate inquiries about her sons and I understand. When I talk with Craig it is mostly idle chatter about the Cubs. He's on their bandwagon these days and now claims that his dad Carl has always been a Cub fan. If that is so it is just another precedent established by their father that the Dean boys ignored when we were kids.

Stu has driven by once. We shared a chuckle or two about the old days and wondered together about what, if anything is meant by this sudden re-juxtaposition of our families. In the air between us was an odd mix of nostalgia and wariness, as though the memories of the good times can't be tickled without also irritating the rash of years that some would just as soon forget.

Both Stu and Craig have daughters, young women who are surely great joys to their paternal grandparents, particularly their Grandma Dean who delights in their feminine kinship. They both play competitive tennis, one at a small college and one still at the high school level, their exploits modest residues of Grandpa Dean's athletic prowess, as were Stu's city racquetball championships some years back.

When we first discovered our new home's availability and began seriously to consider its purchase we were exploring the grounds there. In back is a long, narrow concrete slab that is abruptly ended by a section of chain link fence on one side and a grassy side yard on another. On our first visit the side yard blended unfenced into the Dean property which slopes away from their house towards ours and is terraced by two landscaped stone crescents. By the time we moved in a new section of chain link had been inserted that made clear where their property and ours divided. It is better to interpret the fencing in the poetic spirit of Robert Frost's assertion that, "good fences make good neighbors," but the line drawn in the grass effectively separates then and now as well as theirs and ours.

Occasionally I see young kids from this new neighborhood wander into the Dean yard. One day a threesome of small boys raced in on bikes, dismounted on the run and leaped loudly and daringly down from one ledge to the next while our two setters, Mitt and Maple, barked jealously at them from our side of the border. I felt myself grinning at the witness of their play and my whole self lurched into reverse in the presence of these ghostly squirts.

From my vantage point I could not tell if anyone was watching from the Dean house which features a big picture window on the backyard, just like the one they had on Kingman.

I have also seen swashbucklers fencing with swords fashioned from branches of the saplings that flank the creek bed just beyond the greenbelt across our new street. Such sightings cheer me, as did the neighborhood lemonade stand that opened for business occasionally during the summer. I stopped there for a drink at every opportunity. Two bits for a gulp of the good times seemed a bargain.

Besides the letter I wrote in support of the petition for commutation of Fred Donald's life sentence I have also managed an occasional correspondence with Fred himself. I didn't think it was possible for there to be awkward silence in letters, but it is. He has told me that whenever he receives mail he feels obliged to respond, but his reciprocity comes with a stipulation as to the brevity and monotony of content that characterize his letters. They are written by hand in a script that is neat and legible but they start well down the page so when he signs his name near the bottom his half-page receipts for the typed visits I pay him seem longer than they really are. He sends them to me the way children scrawl out obligatory thank you notes to distant relatives who send them gifts they haven't much use for. They tend to be appreciative that he's remembered but resigned about his prospects for release. His mother told me recently that in addition to the walls and fences enclosing the prison campus, Fred has built another between himself and hope.

He did confide to me in one of his notes that among the things he misses most is playing golf, an expansive game he was good at as a youth and one that affords the freedom to follow a ball practically anywhere. There may be no sport that better frames civilized man than golf; an individual ranging through nature, governed by some great spirit of fair play - even when no one's watching - while following the course laid out before him. Baseball, basketball and football you can play in jail. Golf is a free man's game. The next round I played felt like prosthesis for Fred's freedom.

I asked him once if I might come and visit him in person. I was fairly sure what his reply would be so I was neither surprised nor offended when he declined. Given the difficulty we have conversing by mail Fred was probably wise to avoid a face-to-face, but I felt obliged by a desire to be thorough to suggest that I make the trip. Ella Donald describes it as a very pleasant drive, by the way, scenic and easygoing before ending unceremoniously at a federal penitentiary. She could as well be musing about the arc of her son's life.

Typically when I write to Fred filling one page gets to be like meeting the minimum requirement for a term paper in school. When I'm talking to a telephone answering machine I'm often so wordy that a recording interrupts to tell me I've got fifteen seconds to shut up. But it's different when you're groping for things to say to someone who's been consigned to jail for the rest of his life despite never doing violence to anyone. Our dialogue is like a game of ping-pong between two players who aren't very good.

My last letter was posted with a stamp depicting the cracked Liberty Bell; how cruelly and unusually apropos. There's fine print inscribed upon the bell that's taken from the 25th chapter of Leviticus. It reads in part, "ye shall return every man unto his family."

While Fred languishes in prison his father now is locked in the dungeon of Alzheimer's. In lieu of Fred's release, what a pathetic mercy it will be if Lon forgets his son and what's happened to him. The Donald family may be nearly past the point of return to one another. I wonder how many nights Lon and Ella lie in bed in wide-eyed disbelief that their once-promising child would be branded as irredeemable in a nation that flaunts freedom and providence the way high rollers do a wad of cash.

Hell's bells, hear them ring.

The Donalds still live in the old neighborhood. Three houses around the bend Carrie Leonard and her family now live in the house where she grew up. Her mother moved to a condo approximately where Raccoon Valley Little League used to be after Dr. Leonard died in 2001. He was ever a credit to his profession, and she a credit to him; something I rediscovered last spring when she made me comfortable in her living room and offered me chocolates and kind words about my folks. She is still as gracious in discussion of painful times as she has been since they were branded on her memory.

Around the corner on Kingman Blvd. my sister Mary and her family make their way beneath the big, old maple tree that still looms there. It strikes me now as the only thing in those parts that hasn't changed. Most places from the past appear miniaturized upon revisitation; schools in particular seem shrunken when re-entered for the first time in many years. But the maple tree on Kingman is yet as high and wide as ever. I've never been far enough away for enough time to let it grow larger than life in my mind's eye; it remains authentically vast.

In their backyard Dave has contrived a pitcher's mound behind the garage that was built years ago after the barn fire. It's there to facilitate the training of Luke as a ballplayer. My nephew has a great sense and instinct for the nuance of how games are won as opposed to merely played. I believe that was born, not coached into him, but it's good to hone natural tools and Dave has certainly done that. He and Mary have also been good caretakers of the building and grounds where our family was at its best under the following conditions: six people, one bathtub, zero showers, two rotary telephones, one car, one television, three channels, one toilet and two small air conditioners.

There are times when Ben Wellman and Luke Tasler and a cast of extras play whiffleball on more or less the same field where Robbie Farris and I did

battle forty years ago and I got marooned on the
roof. The old gravel driveway is smooth and blacktopped now and that has finally led in turn to a basketball hoop. I guess that offsets the loss of the old
apple tree where I killed an innocent bird and
picked fresh, green cobbywobbles against the advice of my all-knowing mother.

The island is still where it used to be but has
overgrown with trees. A new generation growing up
nearby makes no use of it. Kids are driven past on
their way to and from schools and the myriad activities they have to register and pay for that have rendered sandlots like the island obsolete. Our daughter
Emma has two friends living in houses that flank
the Leonard place so I regularly run errands back
and forth through time. Ordinarily I maintain the
camcorder is a regrettable device that has turned
most parents into documentary filmmakers [yes, we
have one], but I confess that I would be riveted by
footage of Wayne and me belting rubber balls from
Rexall off the island in a sandlot slugfest. As it is I
get by on snapshot memories and black and white
team photos from Raccoon Valley that very occasionally find their way to the tops of boxes being
sifted through in search of something more urgent;
sort of like running into an old friend on the way to
work.

The Roosevelt Shopping Center goes on. Now
it's known as The Shops at Roosevelt. Only the
barber shop and Hillyer's Cleaners persist from the
old days and even they have changed hands over the

years. The old mix that included a pharmacy, a grocery, a shoe store and a florist has given way to an
assortment of boutiques and galleries that seem un-
necessary and effete by comparison. Last year the
end of an era was written indelibly in the ink of the
tattoo parlor, of all things, that set up shop in the old
Reichardt's storefront. Nothing could be further
from the buttoned-down, pinstriped, blue-blazered
truth of Bill Reichardt.

Matulef's, the mom & pop grocery where we
shopped for our first baseball cards and later our
first bootlegged six-packs, has given way to a bikini
shop. The pharmacy and its soda fountain, once dis-
pensaries of elixirs ranging from Pepto Bismol to
Green Rivers, is currently an aquatics shoppe. It
would have been a meat market for Harvey
Michaels. I can imagine him walking in, buying
some fish and promptly eating them alive in front of
the sales clerk, to the delight of the gallery that
passed the hat to whet his appetite.

At least the Playhouse has survived just to the
south of the shopping center. Originally a "B"movie
house when it opened in the 1930's, it's been hum-
ming the lullabies of Broadway on Des Moines'
42nd Street since 1953.

As I write this a billboard sits atop the building
where Matulef's used to be referring people to the
following website: "mymarriageisdead.com". I
guess that's what you call a sign of the times.

A few blocks north the Uptown Shopping Center has undergone similar upheaval since our hal-

cyon days. The branch library where we checked
out sports biographies and the Rexall where we
checked out Playboy and stuffed our cheeks and
pockets with penny candy are long gone. Home
Carpet, where we sprayed the clientele with navy
beans while hidden in the massive rug rolls like
hunters in a blind, is now a series of establishments
that includes a health food store. Safeway's latest
incarnation is a glorified convenience store called
Drugtown. It's a subsidiary of Hy-Vee, a local grocery chain. After the sun goes down it attracts an
eclectic mix of students from Drake and seedy,
thirsty residents from downtrodden neighborhoods
nearby to the east because it features a liquor store.
It's the sort of place where accidental parents can
dash in to grab a box of diapers for the baby and a
bottle of formula for themselves while they're at it.

Across the street the Capri movie house where
Ben Hur and Lawrence of Arabia stayed while they
were in town is now one link in a chain of video
stores. Fortunately the Varsity goes on as an art
house and is still my favorite place in town to see a
movie. You can even get homemade caramel corn
there for a buck-and-a-half!

Both of the neighborhood marketplaces have a
Git 'n Go where people whiz in to fuel their cars
with gasoline and themselves with outlandishly
sized super tankards of coffee or caffeinated soda.
We used to ride bikes over to Victor's, a *service
station* that formerly occupied the Roosevelt Git 'n
Go lot, where we guzzled ten ounce bottles of pop

that cost ten cents. While we stood inside chugging and burping Mr. Victor was outside pumping gas that was cheaper than soda pop; windshield wiped at no extra charge.

Ashworth pool is one experience common to the childhoods of me and our kids. It's little more than a gaping bathtub now as measured against other area oases that feature labyrinthine slides and full menus of junk food, but it retains the timeless and elemental satisfaction that only cool water can offer on hot summer days. I drive carloads of kids there and always insist that the windows go up and the air conditioning off when we turn from Grand Ave. to the homestretch toward the pool. That way every-body is roasting when they burst from the car and the first plunge of the day is all the more exhilarat-ing. Sometimes when the Cubs are playing a day game I stay and swim too. I like to bake on the pool deck and listen to the ballgame on the radio in be-tween cooling dips into the past. Not so refreshing are my realizations on each visit that we arrive and exit via the road where Stephen Leonard was killed.

Waveland too has persisted more or less as it's ever been, though golf is the only one of its many former applications that I still use it for. Even there, several years ago the centuries-old burr oak tree be-side the ninth green that inspired the course's logo succumbed after being damaged in a storm, an echo to the felling of so much and so many from our younger days.

* * *

Ours were the last deregulated childhoods in America, wedged between the hardship and deprivation of our parents' and the material excess of our children's. Behind the scenes of a national stage packed with the non-stop action of the newsreel 1960's the biggest generation in American history wandered away.

As fond as my memories of the days of root beer and mulberries and as deep-seated as my longing to write, it took finally the stark contrast between then and now to begin this and a series of encouraging nudges to see it through.

The reappearance of Laura Donald as Chris' principal and neighboring up again with the Deans were obvious signs to someone on the lookout for such things. More subtle but just as emphatic have been the wave of Tiger Swallowtail sightings during this season of renewed concentration on Stephen Leonard. More of them have grabbed my notice than we ever spied and netted while romping the yards on butterfly safari. Maybe they've always been commonplace but Stephen made us all think they were rare. Every one I've ever seen has conjured him.

One day when Chris was at work in the garden of our new home I carried a bag of mulch to her and nearly stepped on what turned out to be a cecropia moth. It unfurled itself magnificently on Chris' index finger and remained there for several minutes until she placed it on a shrub. We surmised that it must have been newly emerged and seemed in no hurry to leave while its wings dried and tentatively flexed for the first time. The cecropia is the largest moth found in North America with a wingspan as long as half a foot. It's seldom seen because it's nocturnal. Its larvae are often found on maple trees which makes the fact that this is the only one I've ever met unlikely.

Cecropias don't live very long and are the adult stage of a species with so many predators that lots never get to spread their wings.

True, my belief that such events are a series of signs is really just a choice I've made. So it is with much of what each of us holds to, given the relative dearth of absolute truth that's of any lasting use or import.

Some sleep peacefully dreaming that the Bible imparts all the truth that needs knowing, a prospect that keeps me awake and gives rise to as many questions as answers. These stories are my question in response to the citation from Psalm 1 that begins this book. I dared hope that by its end I'd have an answer, but I am nearly there and I do not. Maybe that is alright. Maybe there have been other purposes served. I sought to honor, even absolve if you like, the parents. I have in my days broken faith with ninety per cent of the ten commandments and lived often as though my guru were H.L. Mencken, who once observed, "say what you will about the ten commandments, you must always come back to the happy fact that there are only ten of them." But it is possible and important to honor parents like the sixteen of us at Kingman all had beyond their lives and throughout our own.

A classic symptom of alcoholism is remorse arising from drunken behavior and much of mine was because I felt I'd dishonored the people who loved me first and longest. I thought the world had cheated the ones I most admired in assorted ways and that I was in on it. When I started my own family and resumed a long dormant affiliation with St. Luke's I was returning to a place where my parents, particularly my father, were well thought of, and I liked that. Eventually I took turns there on the vestry and as a lay reader as though stepping into a family business. But like the son of craftsmen who discovers he's all thumbs I've found faith as my parents demonstrated it hard to come by. I have managed only enough to want for more.

Not the sort that expresses itself in sanctimonious preachings from the pulpit of talk radio, but the sort that tells me a God who requires us only, "to act justly, and to love mercy and to walk humbly…" [Micah 6:8] would not countenance life imprisonment with no chance of parole for a non-violent man who has facilitated the release of more heinous felons during his twelve-plus years in jail.

Not the sort that bludgeons others with judgment, but the sort that celebrates parables about the homecomings of prodigal sons.

Not the sort that eulogizes a young man with

simple reap and sow theology as though his life amounted to nothing more than a cautionary tale for his generation, but the sort that enables parents to get back up after the death of their eldest child and raise his younger siblings.

Not the sort that would forswear a pair of wayward, profligate brothers, but the sort that prays patiently, relentlessly and expectantly for their deliverance and restoration.

I have my moments.

It dawns on me that the world is teeming with people who shun the church and organized religion based on their exposures to them as children; sort of like cutting off their spirits to spite their souls. I, on the other hand, still consider the examples I lived with as a boy to be good models.

But much of the time I feel lost and low on gas at this crossroad in my life. There are days when I can picture Chris and the kids coming home to find me on the bathroom floor after a mishap while getting from the shower into my shorts. I hop about trying to stab a leg through thinking about all I've survived only to have it end like this. I have become paunchy and gray and tufts sprout from previously hairless parts of me like weeds poking through cracks in a sidewalk. My eyes are still blue but otherwise blurred and box scores are only decipherable through reading glasses. The slightest uprising against the inertia that usually shackles me results in starched and squeaky muscles, joints and bones. Any sustained rebellion by good intentions of better health is thus discouraged and reconsidered later over a smoke after a meat loaf dinner.

The appetite that once fueled growth into physical adulthood has turned on me and now ushers toward the morgue.

I end most days by collapsing into bed with the same sense of exhausted, grateful relief that a ballplayer feels upon crossing the plate safely after another sprinted rounding of the bases.

* * *

A long last call at Wellman's Pub began about the time the walls came tumbling down in New York. The first three quarters of 2001 were record-breaking. From that point on sales started a slow, steady descent. Stupidly, I installed a computerized POS [point-of-sale] system that I reasoned would streamline customer service and increase employee accountability, offsetting my loosened grip on daily operations. The system was expensive and poorly supported. It caused more problems than it solved and became in my mind a mistake in judgment that I never forgave myself. By the time I finally sold the pub I reasoned that I'd been squeezed out of a business I had no business in so I could do this.

I need to do something that my older brother didn't do first before one of us dies, and I am relieved of the paradox of a livelihood derived principally from the sale of something that almost destroyed me.

I never came to feel the place was wholly mine. The profits and the responsibilities were but the idea never had been, so on some level I always felt like I was still tagging along after my big brother.

Even so, sometimes I yearn to start the day by counting a plump pouch of cash and toting it to the bank. I enjoyed the hot bowls of homemade soups and friendly chats with satisfied customers around the bar at lunchtime. And it was always a pleasure during the baseball season to update the Cubs' "magic number" for clinching the pennant on the big slate blackboard that dominated the pub's entryway. Also featured there were the word of the day or the quote of the day. I learned that "GARDYLOO!" was what folks used to holler as they dumped their household slop buckets out the window onto the street and I came across a lot of musings from H.L. Mencken besides the one cited earlier about the relatively few rules that God etched in stone. Another that stuck and comes to me during election years like this one is, "democracy is based on the notion that the people know what they want and deserve to get it – good and hard!"

Mencken would have fit right in with the squad of regulars that hummed the smart but cynical background vocals and set the rhythms of what, on its good days, was an old fashioned neighborhood think tank.

By the end of it I barely knew most of the twenty or so people that I employed. But over the life of the place there were a special few who righted their lives and went on to better things after long and loyal service. I hope now to follow their example.

Plentiful cash, scratch soups, loyal staff and faithful patrons: to those extents I miss the place now and then.

* * *

2008 is a year still fraught with historic possibilities. A black man edged out a woman for a major party's presidential nomination. If that can happen it doesn't look like the pendulum will swing back as far as the early 60's, nor should it in all ways. But if the ice cream man and the sandlot aren't coming back, maybe something like national leadership can. Maybe we'll figure out what we need instead of what we want, and get it – good and hard!

Things went crazy when all the leaders got shot down. The nation went to the moon and in some ways never came back. Even the soldiers at war were doing drugs. The American scene was scary cool which made great theater if you were growing up then but not so much if you were raising kids. Epochal music rose to the occasions and there was prolonged gape-mouthed weeping on a national scale.

Now we complain on our mobiles about the cluttered calendars we've arranged for ourselves while waving and grinning at one another from opposite sides of the soccer complex that displaced the drive-in movie theater that was way better for families than the soccer complex is.

Our son Max just began his senior year at Roosevelt. Ben is a freshman there and Emma has started middle school at Merrill. Meanwhile their father is lately preoccupied with kids he grew up with instead of his own. They let me get away with it. They must be okay with me hanging around the house all the time instead of an office or a job somewhere, although Ben did apparently assume that inheritance of the pub was his birthright. I hope it hasn't been too awkward for them explaining my apparent idleness; it's been tough enough for me since all most of us know to ask about one another is, "what do you *do*?"

The kids don't fully know that they've been denied much of what was best from my childhood. Contrary to the customary paternal ambition of providing one's children with more than oneself enjoyed, I'd settle for our kids having no less, but I'm afraid it's too late for that. My compensation will be if they no more than read of the aftermath. I am left to pray that it not be repeated.

I'm as blessed – I must say - a father as I was a son, on scales out of all proportion to what I shall ever have earned. Our children are my proverbial three wishes come true.

I guess that makes their mother the magic lamp I found and rubbed. She is also the only woman besides my mother who has ever made my real life seem indefinitely enough.

* * *

It is not for anyone to say that times gone by were broadly better or worse than present ones at any point any more than it can be said that a finished portrait exceeds one being painted because it is more discernible or a swallowed meal is more savory than one that's only been sniffed. My hunch that kids were better served in the free-wheeling, face-to-face, unsupervised society of one another than they are in the captivity of cell phones and fully uniformed, supervised, statisticized program after program that parents flock to with camcorders like their kids are tourist attractions ain't necessarily so. And if, in one small sample group, ten out of sixteen raised in the former conditions die prematurely or become dysfunctional adults, those outcomes might be compelling evidence contrary to the hunch.

Of course, such data do not account for variables like spiked gene pools, chains strung darkly across entrances to city parks, defendants sent to prison by the same rule that sends batters back to the dugout or armed, off-duty, out-of-uniform cops hired to keep the peace at Pizza Huts [interesting sidebar: earlier this year one of the local PH's fired a delivery driver for carrying a gun and using it when a customer similarly armed tried to rob him].

For better or worse my generation, the biggest

and maybe the freest in American history, has turned parenting into a management style. Kids don't play sports anymore, they work at them. They're driven everywhere they go and most of the bike riders these days are grownups in silly outfits. Family dinners are convened in minivans during gridlock at fast food eateries that don't lend themselves to the saying of grace because every passenger is plugged into a different device. Oh, for a quick prayer followed by some raw, tough love and something tenderly stirred poured over toast or mashed potatoes! The family dinner table used to be the best place for the free exchange of ideas and opinions. Now we have the talk show. My father would have said that format was full of malarkey. Then he would have exclaimed, "Ye Gods!" and/or, "Judas Priest!" in dismay and turned the program[s] off.

When it started to become commonplace for young men to wear their ball caps backward like only baseball catchers used to do [note: catcher's gear is also known as, "the tools of ignorance"] the trend became a pet peeve of mine. Grudgingly, I have come to regard it as the perfect badge of these times.

* * *

Tomorrow morning bright and early Max and Ben and I will drive into the sunrise bound for Chicago. As we set out the Cubs remain in first place.

When we arrive in Wrigleyville we'll patrol behind the ballpark during pre-game batting practice hoping to run down a ball swatted clear out to the street. Besides the fact that balls still get lost in the bushes inside, I love that Wrigley Field is a place where a ball can literally be, "outta here!"

Shagging BP homers with my sons instead of running the bases from bar to bar with drinking buddies has been nothing less than trading blacked out road trips for unforgettable ones. I'm lucky to be living memorably again, just as I did in the first place.

The redemption of my life and my brother's makes real a hope that something commensurate may come to pass in the lives of Fred, whose continued incarceration is unjust, and Wayne, whose self-imposed exile is unnatural. As for the untimely and irreversible deaths of Stephen and Phil Leonard, all I can offer is that each of them is stored forever in the better part of me and many others.

Our neighborhood and the people in it comprised a little society that was the only place and time where I've ever belonged outside the even smaller one where I live now that consists primarily of my wife and kids. I have passed in stages from a young boy full of promise to an aging one with no immediate prospects.

I'd like to know God better. Doing this is a means toward that end since I have largely ignored for too long my holy suspicion that this sort of thing was always the plan. He's been my collaborator throughout, despite that many of Christ's self-described followers drive business away like surly clerks at a chain store invoking policy in lieu of service.

I have found deliberate prayer to be more worthwhile than the ceremonial exchange that's part of the weekly service agenda throughout Christendom, as though God's peace, like a common cold, can be got by a limp, clammy handshake. Just like us, the lord of the universe is better known one-on-one than via hearsay which makes it hard sometimes to deepen my faith in a communal context. Fellowship tastes good to me in a potluck casserole but I don't like the way it sounds in patriotic hymns made part of a worship service. Mixing faith with secular politics demeans it and I would rather search for God above the temporal fray than in the depths of our civic muck. He is a governor of souls, not nations.

If Mencken sometimes sits on my one shoulder then C.S. Lewis perches on the other, a baptized and brilliant young pagan who reached the point where he could not think his way around God any longer; a churchgoer who came at first only for the refreshment of communion and stayed to share the glorious silence of simple people huddled and humbled in prayer.

Which is the greater bewilderment: that one great mind may deem God a fiction and another the absolute truth, or that my muddled and mediocre one is capable of both?

Too many evangelists remind me of Tiffany Davis. She was the girl in third grade that always finished her work first and took it upon herself to report names of those who misbehaved while Miss Moe was out of the room. Nobody was drawn to Tiffany except her counterparts in the other classrooms and she was fine with that. What really frustrated her was that people she singled out for damnation were never punished to her satisfaction. None of us was any better or worse in the eyes of Miss Moe because of Tiffany's tattles. In fact, I think Miss Moe rather liked me.

My place has always been with the tattled-upon.

Ecclesiastic ambition does not lend itself to job applications or resumes and the residuals from the pub are waning as our economy teeters and I totter. Perhaps my lone practical skill is that I am a good speller, but I'm adrift in a land where people are fed at the, "drive-*thru*." So you see why I am again as fearful about what's in store as I remember being when I suffered from adolescent insomnia on the "sleeping porch," the upstairs solarium that we used as a bedroom on Kingman. How was I supposed to learn how to kiss or drive a car and would my armpits ever run dry?

But on breezy nights in the spring when the moon was round and the windows were open the rustling leaves on the big cottonwood in the Wolfs' yard on 43rd Street looked like pom poms and sounded like distant cheers. My anxieties gave way to athletic fantasies that wore me out after many touchdowns, home runs and last second free throws, and I would fall at last asleep on the lumpy mattress made by the shoulders of fawning crowds. Such were my prayers.

Now something real must happen. It's heartening to note that I sleep pretty well even if that's owing more to general depreciation than it is to peace of mind. I am cornered – a cynical yet sentimental pilgrim with no chits to call in, no strings to pull and no connections to leverage. After twenty-five years in a very social, public enterprise, there's no network to tap now that I'm at loose ends; no well-placed pals reaching out to affiliate. I have isolated myself at a price just now coming due and I'm not sure how it's to be borne. Though unsung I am well-loved and I trust that greater truth shall somehow prevail to the advantage of those whose futures are innocently mingled with mine.

Security for me used to fit in a grocery cart or a drawer of socks and boxers, but it doesn't anymore.

It occurred to me during the course of this project that families are sometimes like the smoke rings dad used to blow for our amusement; well-defined at first, but ultimately ephemeral and bound to drift and disintegrate. I think that was my bias when this was begun about the four bunched together there around Kingman Boulevard - that there had been good times followed by tragedies, disgraces and embarrassments which could not be undone. But I have been struck and moved by the resilience that has sustained the Kingman clan and seen each of its subsidiaries extend into new generations. It's sometimes astonishing what can be endured. Families are not just closets for skeletons, they're alive, and the only thing that makes them special is the regard their members have for one another. Everything else is garnish and beside the point.

I have no particular desire at this stage to reunite again with high school classmates, though I might like once to do that sober, just to say "ta-da!" That phase of my life was a derailment that I haven't figured out how to celebrate.

But to rejoin the first people I ever knew and run again through the savannas of *Those Were the Days*; that I would enjoy! I always have.

Thank God I lived to tell…

Author's Notes
and
Acknowledgments

This has sometimes been like mixing loud colors into pastel shades. My sources ranged from personal memories [many of them singed at the edges with their gist preserved like documents that survived a fire] to those of family and old neighbors to police records to microfilmed newspapers to records archived at the United States Military Academy. I have talked face-to-face, via e-mail, the U.S. Postal Service, and by telephone with many of those mentioned here. Each of the perspectives I looked back from told an isolated part of a composite story but what I've pieced together is not whole; at best it is faithful – faithful in fact to what's on the record and faithful in spirit to people whom I realized going in used to mean a lot to me and, I reaffirmed, always will.

There were powerful sensations when, for example, I perused arrest reports and cadet service records that lay side by side on my desk and considered that the delinquent was the son of the plebe; that they were me and my father; that the same hand that signed him into West Point signed me out of jail and always signed correspondence aimed my way, "Your Lucky Dad…"

When we were in the midst of moving last spring I was boxing up books at the old house. One of them was, *My Daddy Was a Pistol and I'm a Son of a Gun*, by Lewis Grizzard. Based on the title alone I gave it to my dad on Father's Day a long time ago. It must have reverted to me in the divvying that followed his death. Inside I'd written: "Some day I'm going to write something about you. I'm not sure what or when – only that I will."

And so I finally have. I don't know if he ever read that book. I wish he and my mother were around to look at this one.

It has been a good thing to ponder at some length that life is both mundane and sad in ways that can be nothing short of thrilling.

You should know that the names used here are sometimes real – as in the case of my immediate and extended family- and sometimes contrived out of sensitivity to wishes expressed by people who recognized my right to do this but didn't want it done at the cost of their family privacy. There are no secrets revealed here but it is understandable that some would not be anxious for a broader circulation of certain events and circumstances.

To the best of my knowledge nothing's been told to me or to you that's materially false. That's not to say that everything you've read is true, only that I'm not lying. I hope you'll agree there's a legitimate difference in that distinction.

I have been purposely reticent about the means of my ongoing recovery from alcoholism other than noting that my brother charted its course. There are traditions at work in that area which dictate circumspection. A read between the lines might yield a logical inference. I'll just say that I did not, could not and do not manage it alone, something I am obliged to share in greater detail with anyone on a need to know basis, but which I am bound not to exploit at the level of publication.

My deep appreciation is owed widely and I hope that many deserving of it will recognize its expression somewhere in pages prior to this one. Besides those so included, I must make a deliberate point of thanking Mark Gangeness for giving me, among other things, his blessing, and Jennifer Miller for calling me, among other things, an author. I trust neither of them would now recant.

My last thought is that none of the Kingman kids fell any further from the trees than I did from the maple in our front yard when I was a kindergartner. The ground beneath us just tilted.

* * *

"And now these three remain: faith, hope and love. But the greatest of these is love."
[1Corinthians 13:13]

Printed in the United States
134487LV00001B/64/P

9 781432 737399